The ROYALS

Crave Me

GENEVA LEE

The ROYALS

Crave Me

GENEVA LEE

evenafter
ROMANCE

CRAVE ME

Ever After Romance

www.EverAfterRomance.com

www.GenevaLee.com

First published, 2015. Second edition.

Print ISBN: 9781635765335

Cover Design © Date Book Designs. Image © iktash/Bigstockphoto.com

To my husband—birds of a feather.

PROLOGUE

Westminster Bridge stretched into oblivion, lost in the fog sitting like smoke over the Thames. Tourists straggled across, taking photos beside clinging lovers as runners jogged. One by one the haze swallowed each of them.

They disappeared from my sight, never to appear again —like people disappear from your life. There and gone.

I pressed my hands to the balcony railing to steady myself. A city of a million souls, and I had never felt more isolated. The hollow ache in my stomach spread through me with each breath I took, reminding me I was empty. I was alone.

An hour ago I hadn't been. An hour ago I had a plan and a future—and him. But now that life was gone.

"There you are." Clara stepped onto the balcony and moved beside me. She rested a hand gently over mine.

"I haven't gone anywhere," I said flatly. My whole future

had, but I was still here. "Jilted fiancée sounds less glamorous than bride-to-be, don't you think?"

"Nobody is labeling you, and if they do they'll only call you the woman who clocked Pepper Lockwood, which in my book makes you fabulous," she said firmly.

It had felt pretty good to finally hit that tart. The only thing that would have been better was if I'd been able to hit her and Philip. "I should have seen it coming. Philip's been acting oddly for weeks."

"No one saw that coming," Clara assured me. "And this is in no way your fault. Philip cheated on you. He ended things."

The diamond ring on my hand grew heavy, as if it were an anchor, tying me to a past that I needed to be freed from. I slipped it off my hand and held it to Clara. "At least that will fetch a pretty sum. Enough to live on for a bit."

"Don't make snap decisions." She took the ring, clenching it in her fist, but her forehead wrinkled in concern. She didn't try to talk me out of selling it though. We both knew I would need the money while I looked for a job.

A job.

I told myself I had an excellent education—that I would have no trouble finding work. But I wasn't sure how a year of planning for a wedding that wasn't going to happen would look on a resume.

"We'll worry about that tomorrow," Clara said in a comforting tone. She tugged me away from the railing as the terrace door slid open to reveal a handsome, curly-haired man. "I have procured all the liquor in the world," Edward announced. The younger prince had proven himself a true friend and tonight, it seemed, would be no exception to that fact. "Literally. There is none left in the world. It's all ours."

He reached over and placed an ice pack on my knuckles then held up a bottle. "For your right hook. And vodka for the rest of you."

I took one last look at the city below and turned to my friends. "What are we waiting for? Let's get pissed."

CHAPTER ONE

 $\mathcal{L}$ ondon did not care that I had somewhere to be. That much was evident from the crowds herding themselves obliviously through Kensington. The few trees scattered along the busy thoroughfare had turned traitor, shifting from green into glorious shades of gold and rust, and it seemed every tourist in the city needed a picture of them. I pushed past a large group that had stopped for a photo op in front of Top Shop. Muttering an obligatory apology for ruining their shot, I dashed down a less crowded side street. I caught sight of a red-lacquered door that read Smith Price, Esq. on the other side of the street just as the alarm on my phone rang out to remind me I had an interview in five minutes. Jogging across as quickly as my impractical shoes would allow, I paused at the door and took a deep breath.

I ran a hand over my hair, pleased to discover it was still laying straight after the mad dash I'd made from my flat. I'd recently opted out of the long, wavy locks that I'd been growing out for my wedding. New life. New look. The shoulder-length bob I'd chosen—complete with a thick fringe that fell over my forehead—was easier to style and apparently immune to the frantic chaos of London streets. Briefly I considered checking to make sure my red lipstick didn't need freshening but thought better of it. There wasn't the time. I was due in his office in one minute. I smoothed my black pencil skirt down, prayed I hadn't snagged my stockings, and checked the top button of my fitted ivory blouse. I looked the part. Now all I had to do was land it. A steady job would be the final piece in getting my life back on track, and it might finally provide me with the extra money I needed for my own start-up company.

Inside, everything changed. I'd stepped from one of London's most sleek and modern streets into the past. The place dripped with rich mahogany and leather. Large bookshelves lined the walls of the small waiting room and behind an oak desk sat a very prim woman, guarding an office door. She pursed her lips and stared me down. Maybe I hadn't dressed the part after all. I guessed her to be in her mid to late forties, but then again, the giant stick up her ass might have made her look older. I smiled sweetly and strode toward her.

"I have an appointment with Mr. Price."

The disapproval on her face didn't budge, even as she nodded. "Right on time, Miss...?"

"Stuart," I offered, suspecting she already knew that. A

woman had confirmed my interview time, and she was the only one here. It wasn't worth it to point this out, however, given that I'd spent the last six months bouncing between interviews and temporary jobs. Instead I swallowed my pride and waited. I'd gotten rather good at that since I'd caught my fiancé cheating on me. Perhaps I should consider listing the skill on my resume.

"Mr. Price is expecting you," she said as she stood and gestured for me to follow her through the door she guarded.

I stepped into his office and stopped dead in my tracks. I'd googled Smith Price yesterday, but it had never occurred to me to look up pictures of him. Considering the long list of accomplishments and the caliber of clients associated with his firm, I'd expected someone older. Much older. But the man sitting at the desk in front of me, looking like God's gift to three-piece suits, couldn't have been more than thirty years old. His dark hair had been combed carefully but couldn't quite hide a slight wave that cried out to be pulled. Dark lashes framed eyes that were stunningly bright green, even from this distance. But it was his jawline, smooth and strong, and his broad shoulders that oozed a primal masculinity. He was leaning back in a leather chair, his hand resting thoughtfully on a shapely set of lips. Something stirred inside of me, beating against the wall I'd built to protect myself from men, especially men like this. I squared my shoulders and forced a professional, and disinterested, smile onto my face.

Price didn't stand as his secretary led me into the room.

He simply watched, his eyes traveling slowly up my body. The intensity of the gaze burned across my skin, sending a flush of heat over my cheeks. For one brief moment, I thought my knees were going to buckle, and it took all the composure I could muster to stay upright in my Louboutins. Thank God I'd gone with the more responsible heel, or I would have found myself arse over tits on his office floor. His eyes stopped on my mouth, and I suddenly regretted wearing such a suggestive shade of red. But I hadn't expected Smith Price to look like—well, a sex god. His own lips twitched, as if he guessed what I was thinking, but then his face returned to a stony mask. Completely unreadable. Completely disarming.

And worst of all, completely sexy.

This is not good! the high-pitched voice in my head shrieked in warning. You need this job and you'll never get it if you can't show you have a few brain cells. Speak up! I opened my mouth and took a deep breath. If he wasn't going to introduce himself, I needed to do the honors. But more than anything, I needed to refrain from sounding desperate. No vulnerability. I'd spent one whole minute in Price's presence, but I already knew what would happen if I showed any weakness. I'd be in his bed and out of a job.

"Mr. Price, it's a pleasure to meet you," I said in a smooth voice—too smooth and way too sexy.

Keep your knickers on your arse and off the floor, I commanded myself silently.

His fingers shifted to rest on his chin, revealing those chiseled lips that I couldn't tear my eyes from. This interview was going nowhere if we couldn't stop staring at each other's mouths.

"Smith." The simple correction was enough to break the spell, and my eyes flashed up, finally meeting his. The look was long and hard. The kind of look you share with someone you've known a long time—someone you've known intimately. His eyes weren't guarded like the rest of him, and I knew without a doubt that this was purposeful. He wanted me to see what he was thinking. I could drown in the green pools of his irises—lost to the turmoil reflected there. It mirrored my own. My belly constricted as desire wound itself tightly in my core. One pluck and it would unravel. I would unravel.

"Sit, Miss Stuart," he ordered, turning his attention to his desk. I seized the opportunity to look away and regain a bit of control as I slid into the chair opposite his. When our eyes met again, a curtain had descended, concealing his thoughts. "I suppose you have questions about the position."

I didn't actually. I'd expected to walk in here and be grilled. Fumbling to find my voice, I finally managed to force out the first one that came to mind. "What exactly are the expectations...for the position?"

It seemed silly to tack on the last bit, but Smith struck me as the type of man that needed clear boundaries and definitions.

"My private assistant."

He didn't elaborate further. Apparently, he was going to make me work for each shred of information.

"Here?" I asked, gesturing to the office around us. "Will I be assisting with cases?"

I wasn't certain I could actually help him with legal work, but I sure as hell could fake it until I figured out what I was doing.

"Do you have a legal background I'm unaware of?" His tone was low and cold.

I fought the urge to shrink back in my seat. Instead I squared my shoulders. At least if he was going to be an ass, it would cure me of my initial attraction to him. His head tilted, waiting for my answer. He stroked the slight five o'clock shadow peppering the strong curve of his jaw. What would it be like to have that hand on me? How would it feel when his stubble scratched along my thigh?

Maybe I wasn't cured after all.

"I don't," I said, adopting a similarly cool attitude. "That's just as well, because my private assistant does not assist with casework." He smirked as he spoke. He actually fucking smirked.

What kind of grown man smirked during a job interview?

The kind that knows exactly what you really want from him.

I ignored the voice, losing patience with myself as much as I was with him. "Then what do you want me to do?"

The smirk shifted into a crooked grin that vanished in seconds. "You will assist me in my private affairs. Obviously my secretary handles my schedules and court appearances. You will oversee my personal life as well as my personal relationships with clients. I'm a busy man, Miss Stuart—"

"Belle," I interrupted him, relishing the chance to correct him.

"Miss Stuart," he repeated. "I'm a busy man. I don't remember birthdays. I do not shop for wedding presents. And I never dine alone."

"I'm supposed to have dinner with you?" I choked out. This was starting to sound a lot like marriage without the benefit of his bank account—or orgasms.

"Not at all times," he continued. "I often have dinner plans. On nights that I do not—or on the occasion that my plans require an escort—you will be present."

"I had no idea this was going to be a lifestyle." The glib remark was out of my mouth before I'd thought it through.

Smith's jaw tensed but he didn't speak, which only made the air in the room feel heavier. This job was pressure. The question was whether or not doing the job would be more pressure than finding another opportunity. Despite my pedigree and education, I'd yet to receive a call back after an interview. But I couldn't let the feeling of inferiority those snubs elicited force me into making a mistake.

"May I ask you a question?" The time for being blunt was now—before I got in over my head.

"You already have," he pointed out, "and I didn't bite."

His answer sent my eyes to his lips, and my mind to fantasizing about what it would be like if he did bite. I had a sinking suspicion I wouldn't mind it if Smith Price bit me.

Now would be a really good time to run.

But I didn't want to. I felt locked to the chair, locked to this room and this man. I told myself it was the possibilities that the job offered, even though I knew it was more than that. He had already wormed his way under my skin. I could feel him there—an itch that I desperately wanted to scratch. Staying meant I'd have to fight that urge, but leaving felt impossible.

"Assuming you select me for the position"—I paused, wondering if he was going to call me out on my conjecture — "why would you choose me?"

"There are a number of reasons why you'd make an excellent candidate." He settled back in his chair, raising his arms to rest casually behind his head as he regarded me. "Your education, for starters."

I nodded, even though an Oxford education seemed wasted on running errands and being a dinner date.

"From the look in your eyes, you disagree."

"No, I—"

"Allow me to finish." The words he chose were considerate, but his tone was full of expectation. He expected my silence. He expected to speak uninterrupted. And I suspected that he expected me to agree with whatever he was about to say. "Your education will benefit me. I prefer a companion with which I can hold a conversation. I also prefer a well-bred escort for business affairs. Not all of my business associates share the same predilections."

I raised an eyebrow. "Predilections is a strong word."

"Not all whores stand on the street corners, Miss Stuart.

Most of them simply find a man willing to purchase their favor in exchange for their pussies. While I'm certain it's comforting to have something to stick your cock in at home, such relationships are a liability that often end in embarrassment or blackmail," he finished.

He had a point, even if he'd ratcheted himself up on my knobhead meter. "But as you said, I'm educated. I'd be much more likely to understand what is and isn't blackmail worthy." "You will have signed a nondisclosure agreement," he informed me, shifting in his seat so that his face fell into shadow. "And I promise you will find yourself very much

bound to it—as well as bound to me."

The lump in my throat slid ominously as I swallowed this. Bound. Did I want to be bound to him? Legally, at least. It was difficult to consider, given the thoughts his choice of words had conjured. I wasn't going to need a drink after this. I was going to need the whole bloody bottle.

"There are other reasons," he continued. "It wasn't until I ran a background check on you that I discovered you were best friends with our new Queen. I found it quite impressive that you managed to stay out of the press. You must have some knack for flying under the radar."

"Or I'm really boring," I countered.

"I doubt that," he said in a low voice that sent a tingle rippling up my spine. "My business requires privacy. I need a person who comprehends that. You are intimately familiar with that obligation."

"I was friends with Clara long before she met Alexander." "It's a compliment." Smith waited for me to challenge this interpretation. When I didn't, he continued, "And of course, you look the part."

"I look the part?" I repeated. Surely he didn't mean what it sounded like he meant.

"You are a beautiful woman. There's no need to pretend otherwise."

I tried to keep my cool and failed miserably. "That's dangerously close to harassment."

Smith Price was an enigma. Or maybe he wasn't. All he wanted was a pretty girl who wasn't dumb to attend to his every whim. When I actually thought about it, it was what all men really wanted. Only he was willing to pay for it— without the expectation of sex in return. The realizations should have neither shocked nor disappointed me, and somehow it still did on both counts.

"Companies employ attractive individuals every day. It's hardly illegal when it's requisite to the position." Smith shrugged and leaned forward to rest his palms on his desk. His hands didn't move. His fingers didn't tap impatiently. He was completely in control of himself and this situation. That's what scared me.

It was also what excited me.

"As long as there is clear differentiation between my job and being your girlfriend." The implication was clear. Perhaps the way he'd been studying me since I walked into the room was simply him measuring me up, but it felt a lot more like he was fucking me with his eyes. I was used to that—used to men mentally screwing me. I just wasn't interested in actually getting screwed. I didn't need to be tempted to change my mind, and judging from the way my body responded to his penetrating gaze, I needed to make that crystal clear.

"I assure you I have no interest in romance. Another man might utilize his position of authority over you, bribe you with presents, or make unsavory proposals. Our relationship will be strictly professional." His voice trailed away as if he was leaving something out—a clause or an afterthought—but he didn't finish the thought. "Do you have more questions for me?"

I should, but I didn't. It was getting harder to think in his presence. All I could do was shake my head.

"Then I think we're finished here." It was an abrupt end to the interview, but one I had seen coming.

It was for the best. Of that much I was certain. But despite all the red flags and warning signs, I couldn't get past the lost opportunity. This job had paid. Well. I was doing okay financially, given the life-changing events of the last few months, but that largely had to do with my Aunt Jane refusing to take rent money and best friends who constantly picked up the tab.

I mustered up the shred of dignity I had left and forced a smile. "I'll look forward to hearing from you."

"You won't have to," he said dismissively, and my heart sank into the pit of my stomach. "I'll expect you here tomorrow at one to discuss my current agenda and needs."

I tried to look past the suggestiveness of those words and focus on the fact that I'd actually landed the job. "I'll be here." "Be prompt, Miss Stuart. I'm not a man who likes to wait."

A sharp sting sang through my lower lip, and I realized I was biting it. Smith's eyes lingered on my mouth. He'd noticed before I had, and despite what he'd said about our relationship, the hunger burning in his gaze was anything but professional.

I needed to get out of here and clear my head. It was the only way I could decide if I would be in this office tomorrow at noon or sending a cowardly email. I popped out of my chair, relieved to be the one lording over the room in my four- inch heels. I paused, hovering in front of his desk. "Let's be clear on one thing. I'll attend these functions. I'll work from your home. But I'm not sleeping with you."

"Noted," he said, but his answer was anything but reassuring. I couldn't be certain if he viewed me as a challenge or a done deal. Either way, I knew one thing: keeping my legs shut in the presence of Smith Price was going to prove difficult. Maybe impossible.

But it was one challenge I was happy to accept.

CHAPTER TWO

*C*oco's was overrun by the time I made my way from Kensington to Notting Hill. The once quaint bistro had become a haven for curious tourists and paparazzi hoping to snap a picture of the Royal baby bump ever since the tabloids had run a story about the weekly dinner date I kept with Edward and Clara at the establishment. Pushing my way through the crowd, I caught sight of Clyde, Coco's manager. He dabbed a napkin across his forehead as he scanned the crowd. I couldn't help but notice that the lines on his forehead had deepened as his hairline had receded since he'd taken up crowd control. I'd grown fond of him, making a point to come in the front door to be sure I saw him each week.

"Clyde!" I called, waving my arm over my head. It was undignified, but so was being smashed between smelly wannabe photographers.

Clyde released a long breath and sprung into action,

motioning for servers to help make a path for me. As soon as I was at his side, he whisked me through the kitchen and up the backstairs to a private dining room.

"The crowd is worse than ever." I shouldered my purse as I slowed my pace to match the weary restaurateur.

"They seem to be swellin' along with Clara's belly," he said in his thick Irish brogue. "I don't know how many more souls we can fit into this establishment. It's fixin' to burst."

"So is Clara," I said in a teasing whisper. "Once the baby comes, we'll be out of your hair." I suddenly wished I could take the comment about his hair back, but Clyde only nodded sadly.

"It's not been any trouble to have you here." He held open the door for me.

"We both know that's not true." I stepped inside and paused before planting a small kiss on his cheek. This might very well be the last time we saw him for a while. "Thank you for everything."

"It's been no trouble," he repeated gruffly before excusing himself.

"Flustering Clyde?" Edward tsked as he stood to give me a hug. "A kiss from a pretty girl? I'm not sure his heart can take any more stress. "

"I was simply thanking him." I swatted at his shoulder, but Edward only laughed and pulled out a chair for me. "She's not here yet?"

Edward took a long sip of his wine, sighing as he set the

glass back down. "Alexander has gone into full-scale alpha mode."

"When isn't he in alpha mode?" I asked dryly as I poured my own glass from the open bottle.

"She's due in two weeks. He has a right to be protective." The response was dismissive. Edward, like most of us, had a tendency to forgive his older brother's need for control.

I might have argued with his logic if Clara hadn't been a magnet for trouble in the last year and a half. As it was, it made me feel better that Alexander kept such close tabs on her—most of the time. The rest of the time I wished I saw her more often. I doubted it had less to do with Alexander's protectiveness and more to do with the near obsession the two displayed toward one another.

"I guess we should all be so lucky." I shrugged my shoulders and settled back in my chair.

"I suppose." Edward's mouth twisted into a wry grin. "David isn't exactly the type."

I winked at him. "Maybe that's your job."

"What's his job?" a tired voice asked from behind me. A moment later, Clara was at the table, lowering herself slowly into the remaining chair with one hand cradling her ever-growing bump protectively. She might have sounded exhausted, but her fair skin glowed and her chestnut hair had even more bounce than normal. I might have hated her if I didn't love her so much.

"We're trying to decide who's the Alexander in my relationship."

Clara grimaced. "Hopefully neither of you."

"Trouble in paradise?" Edward's forehead crinkled in concern.

"He's just being a tad overbearing. You're lucky I convinced him to let me come at all tonight. Norris and half of the British Armed Forces are downstairs. What's the point of having a back entrance if you show up with a small army?" She patted her stomach and smiled grudgingly. "I imagine it will be even worse when she makes her appearance."

"We'll come to you," I promised her. "And it's not so terrible to have someone looking out for you."

Clara locked eyes with me and nodded, immediately sending a wave of guilt rushing through me. I hadn't meant it to sound like sour grapes but it had. The fact that she was happily married wasn't anything to feel badly about. I'd told her that a hundred times, but it never quite sunk in.

"So I have news." I unrolled my silverware as I quickly switched topics.

"Tell me you got laid!" Edward threw his hands up in a pleading gesture to the heavens.

"Very funny," I said, tossing the napkin at his head. "I have sworn off men, remember?"

"Then tell me you got a vibrator, love," he retorted.

"She had one long before she broke up with Philip," Clara said dryly.

I wagged a finger at her. "That is true. But sadly, this news doesn't end in an O. I merely got a job."

"That's fantastic." Edward's face split, as if this

announcement was half as exciting as finding out I'd shagged someone.

"What happened to your idea for that clothing company?" Clara asked.

"Oh, I'll never get around to that," I lied. I'd only mentioned the idea once to my best friend, but Clara never forgot anything. There was no point in involving either of them in something that was likely a pipe dream. Especially because I knew they would both be all too eager to finance the venture, which was the last thing I wanted. "Office work is the boring stuff us mere mortals are made of."

"Uh-uh!" Clara mimicked my earlier finger wag. "You were aristocracy long before I was."

"Ah well, that hasn't really worked out too well for my family," I reminded her. I didn't add that my mother's perpetually failing estate was one of the many reasons that I needed said job. "A girl must eat."

"And eat we shall," Edward said as a waiter appeared with our standing order.

I reached for the serving spoon, and he batted away my hand.

"No, us immortals shall eat while you entertain us with tales of your lowly peasant existence. What is this job you speak of?"

Clara meanwhile grabbed the spoon and started ladling pasta onto my plate. "Eat, but do tell."

"I'm going to be a personal assistant." I twirled my fork in the pasta, my stomach rumbling as I watched the decadent Alfredo sauce coat the linguini.

"To a celebrity?" Edward asked.

"To a lawyer," I said before slowly slurping down the noodles.

"Distinctly less glamourous."

"You haven't seen the lawyer." It was out of my mouth before I'd really considered the ammunition I was giving them.

"Oh really?" Clara's voice peaked in excitement.

"She's going to sleep with him," Edward noted, as if it was already a proven fact.

"Don't get any ideas," I warned them. "He seems like a first-class knobhead."

Clara and Edward shared a knowing look.

"She's definitely going to sleep with him," Edward predicted. "She's already thinking about his knob."

THE LIGHTS WERE low in my flat when I stepped inside. Music drifted across the open space in a slow sensual melody that crackled slightly. I peeked around the corner, not wanting to disturb my aunt, and watched as she swayed softly, her loose kaftan swirling in a muted rainbow around her elegant form. I'd always idolized my aunt with her wild platinum hair and even wilder clothes. The fact that she was as spirited as she looked was an added bonus.

"Tell me about your day," she called without ever turning around.

"I can wait." I slid my purse onto the kitchen counter and lingered there, resisting the urge to drum my finger-nails against the granite.

"Nonsense." Jane swooped to retrieve a bottle of wine from the cabinet. "Grab the glasses."

A sense of peace settled over me as I plucked two long-stemmed globes from the shelf and placed them on the counter. Most twenty-somethings would have minded living with a family member, but I had no such qualms. Jane was a hurricane of a woman, constantly shifting and moving from place to place—and man to man. I hadn't been ready to live on my own when Clara got married, especially not after ending my own engagement. Making the choice to move in with Jane had been simple, and given how hard it had been to find a stable job over the last few months, I'd become increasingly glad she had asked me to live with her.

"How was the interview?" she asked, passing me a full wine glass.

"Interesting." I tapped my finger on the delicate stem, watching as the thin crimson liquid swished along the sides of the globe, coating it for a moment before retreating back to the bottom.

Jane raised a penciled eyebrow. "How so?"

"Well, I got the job." I paused as I searched for the right words.

"But it scares you," Jane guessed.

"My boss scares me," I admitted.

"Is he an asshole? Or does he just have a stick up his ass like most lawyers?"

"I can't tell. He's direct." I continued to choose my words carefully. Not because I wanted to keep anything from Jane, but because I was trying to understand the emotions tumbling through me. Just thinking about the interview had produced tiny flutters of anxiety in my belly.

"And powerful?"

I nodded. He was definitely that. I knew very little about Smith Price, but that much I could sense. Power. Authority. He radiated those qualities. They emanated off him like rays from the sun, and I suspected that if I didn't have the good sense to protect myself, I was going to wind up burned.

"And handsome," Jane finished for me.

"Yes," I whispered as my stomach did a little flip. "I'm afraid that working for him is going to get me into trouble."

Jane reached over and took my hand, shaking her head as a bell-like laugh peeled from her. "You could use a little trouble."

"I've had enough trouble for a lifetime." It was the last thing I was looking for after Philip. But Jane always had a tendency to flit from love affair to love affair. It made her happy, but it wasn't what I was looking for in life. "I want to focus on me and work on my business plan, not get distracted by a man."

"The thing about distractions is that they're necessary. You can't work constantly. That's no life. Every woman needs a healthy dose of romance. You don't have to choose between a career and love," she said softly.

"Maybe I don't know what's healthy," I pointed out, my eyes darting to study the table. "I was going to marry a man who was in love with someone else."

"Belle." Jane's voice took on a gentle tone as she said my name. "You were infatuated by the idea of love. The wedding. The lifestyle. You wanted stability, and God knows, after your childhood, no one could blame you for that."

"Now I want my own stability." I lifted my head and met her gaze.

"Then make that happen, but don't stop living. Not taking chances isn't stability, it's a slow way to die."

"So I should take the job?" I asked.

"Do you need the job?"

"That depends," I said, grinning despite myself, "how long can I keep paying rent in cheap wine?"

"Take the job and pay me in good wine." Jane winked. "I don't want rent from you, but I do want you to start this business. So unless you've had a change of heart about investors..."

I waved a hand. "I need to get it started by myself."

I had no idea if there was room for my company in the marketplace. So much had changed since I'd been at university, there was no way I was taking Jane's nor anyone else's money until I was standing on my own two feet.

"You know I won't pressure you, but the offer is always open."

"I know." I took a long sip of my wine before abandoning my glass. "I should get some sleep. It seems I have work tomorrow."

"Belle, have you told your mother...about the job?"

I tensed, my body responding automatically to the mere idea of calling her. "Not yet."

"Don't," Jane advised.

"She'll find out."

"Then that will be soon enough." Jane stood and wrapped her arms around my shoulders. "If you want to focus on you, that might be a good place to start."

"You might be right about that." But even though I knew she was, a heaviness had already descended on my chest. I shook my head, trying to clear the wave of guilt.

Jane gave me a small smile and pressed me close, hugging me until the guilt disappeared entirely. "I'm proud of you."

"Will you still be proud of me if I break down and throw myself at my boss?" I asked wryly.

"Darling, nothing would make me prouder."

CHAPTER THREE

*I*t was five minutes past one—an inauspicious start to my new assistant's career. My fingertips drummed across the windowsill. I didn't appreciate waiting. I hadn't waited for any woman in the last three years. If Belle Stuart hadn't intrigued me so damn much, I'd have already left instructions with my receptionist to show her right back out the door when she deigned to show up. Doris, the old battle-axe that I'd employed for the last five years, would have no problem giving her the boot.

It was a mistake not to send her packing. I had finally settled on this fact when a soft knock that definitely didn't belong to Doris announced she was here.

I straightened up, clasping my hands behind my back, and waited a moment before I answered. "Enter."

The door opened, but I kept my back to her, training my eyes on the street outside. It was important that she learned early on that she didn't command my attention, rather that I would choose when to give it to her. That didn't mean I was immune to her presence though. Her soft breathing carried across the silent room, and my fingers tightened over my wrist.

A mistake.

Given my position by the window and given that my arms were crossed behind my back, the movement was in her line of sight. It didn't matter if she'd actually seen it. I'd make another mistake in the presence of Belle Stuart. My first might have been hiring her in the first place. I couldn't allow myself to be affected by her. She must only be permitted to see what I allowed. No more slip-ups. The fact that I was aware of the problem would presumably make it easier to contend with it in the future.

"Mr. Price." Her words were timid. Unlike the woman I'd interviewed the previous day. Perhaps she would prove a study in contrasts. Strong but vulnerable. Cold and still inviting. A lady in clothes and something dangerously wild out of them.

Time would tell.

Of course, it might be embarrassment over her tardiness.

I turned to her before I made another mistake. My hand curled into a fist, stifling the twitch that tingled across my palm. Maintaining control was going to prove a challenge around her, especially if she chose to blatantly ignore my instructions. For now, a simple correction was in order, but I had no doubt that eventually I'd have the pleasure of giving her a much more serious reprimand. "Smith."

"Smith." I enjoyed how it sounded as she tried it out. My name on her lips was familiar—intimate. Belle crossed one leg behind the other and rubbed it nervously along her calf. Shoes with red soles again. Some type of luxury brand. Normally I might ask my assistant to send a pair to the beautiful woman standing before me. A present that would grease the path to what I was really interested in. The right present cut through all the unnecessary shit—dinner, conversations, romance—and got straight to the point: my cock buried in warm pussy. The other things were necessary, at least the dinner and conversation, if I wanted more. In my experience, the right amount of attention and then a woman would do whatever I wanted.

I hadn't decided what I wanted from Belle Stuart yet.

"I'm not a man who likes to wait," I advised her. "You would do well to remember that."

"Of course." She inclined her head, but I caught her eyes flash.

Belle Stuart didn't like to be chastised. That was unfortunate given how much I enjoyed reprimands.

Extending my arm, I motioned to the leather cigar couch. "Join me. There's paperwork to discuss."

I found the folder that contained the various documents and contracts I required her to sign without taking my eyes from her. She lowered herself onto the couch, her hands smoothing down her backside as she sat. Her grey skirt was slightly too tight or had been altered to hug her ass in a way that made me want to find the tailor and give him a bonus. She crossed her legs as I took a seat next to her, her hands folded in her lap.

Mixed signals.

Dropping the papers on the oak coffee table, I leaned back, dropping one arm over the back of the couch. Her posture stiffened. I wasn't touching her. Not quite. But she had reacted all the same.

Interesting.

"Given that you will be accompanying me to a variety of business meetings, you'll be required to sign a nondisclosure agreement as well as an arbitration agreement."

"Arbitration?" Her eyebrow notched up.

"Basically it means you won't sue me without trying to work things out first." It was common new hire paperwork, but all of it was airtight. It protected me and my business.

"I think I'd just blackmail you instead." Her cherry red lips curved into a smile, and I realized she was joking.

"I wouldn't recommend that," I told her in a low voice.

The amusement vanished from her eyes, and she leaned down to gather the contracts, treating me to a glimpse down her blouse. Her tits were on the small side, B-cups maybe. Big enough for a mouthful.

I drew a pen out of my suit pocket and dropped it on the table. I could have handed it to her, but now she would be forced to lean over again.

"You mentioned dinners," she said as she scanned the pages. "Will they all be business-oriented or will some be for pleasure?" Her cheeks went pink and she gasped. "I mean, will we be dining with your friends or only your clients?"

"Some men believe in keeping business and pleasure separate."

"And you?" she asked breathlessly, her eyes lifting to mine.

"I've always enjoyed mixing them."

She broke the stare first, trying to cover her restless fidgeting by flipping to the next contract. "So you will need me frequently in the evenings?"

"And on weekends," I added. "Is that an issue?"

"A girl has to have a life." She shrugged, but I noticed color still stained her face.

"This position is more of a lifestyle. I think you'll find if you flip to the last page that the salary and benefits are more than adequate recompense for your time." I waited as she searched for the offer I'd purposefully placed at the end of the paperwork.

A desperate girl would have already asked what I was paying her.

A stupid girl would have signed the contracts before I told her.

Belle was neither desperate nor stupid, but she wasn't exactly trusting. That was why I had hired her in the first place, despite the dangerous attraction I'd felt toward her from the moment we met.

She studied the page silently, not speaking until her eyes had reached the end. "This is too much."

"Most people would already be signing the contracts

and waiting for their first cheque," I said dryly. The salary I was offering her was part of a message: I expect loyalty. Six figures, a private driver, an expense account—that was the price I was willing to pay.

"I'm not a whore, Mr. Price. I can't be bought. This isn't the kind of money you pay an assistant."

"Perhaps not." It was my turn to shrug. "That's the second time you've referenced your unwillingness to sleep with me as part of the job. Let me assure you, Belle, I have no interest in fucking my employees. I don't need to pay a woman to spread her legs."

Her eyes found the floor. I leaned forward, dropping my elbows to my knees to find her downcast face.

"Are we clear?"

"Yes." Her jaw tensed as she nodded. "Now let me be clearer, I don't spread my legs, Smith."

I couldn't keep myself from grinning. Some men disliked a sharp tongue. I enjoyed the sting.

"I would be disappointed if you did," I said simply, surprising myself. "Regardless, it's a nonissue."

It was far from a nonissue. She wasn't trying to warn me away, she was attempting to convince herself. The flush on her cheeks had crept down her neck and blossomed over the swell of her breasts. She bit her lip, as if she was also picturing my mine sweeping over her collarbone and brushing up the curve of her neck until my own teeth sank into her plump lower lip.

Belle cleared her throat, effectively bringing us both back to reality. I lounged into the corner of the couch, shifting my leg so that it bumped against her knee. She shuffled the papers and sucked in a breath, but she didn't move. Our legs stayed pressed close, separated by the silk of her stockings and my wool slacks, but I could feel the heat radiating off of her.

The trouble was that Belle Stuart didn't want to sleep with me. She wanted to be taken. She wanted to be fucked hard. Her whole body screamed for it, but until her head caught up with the rest of her, I'd be happy to continue this little game of foreplay. And there was the fact that she'd been hired to assist me. Sex would complicate that. It would also break my only rule when it came to women: no strings. I preferred quick, clean one-night stands or a carefully screened escort. This woman was currently signing a contract that legally bound us together. It was almost as bad as marriage. Better to keep my distance.

I stood and noticed the room immediately felt cooler, but I loosened my tie anyway. There was no need to be completely formal around her. It would set a strange precedent. My last assistant had brought me my coffee in bed each morning. I chuckled as I considered the uppity Ms. Stuart having to bring me breakfast. She was going to appreciate that I slept nude, and I was going to enjoy her trying to hide her excitement.

"Is something funny?" she asked, her body turning to follow my movement as I crossed the office.

"A lark." I waved my hand dismissively. "Nothing important."

"I love a good joke." She called my bluff, tilting her head to watch me.

I opened my desk drawer and drew out a small white box. "I'm still deciding on the punch line."

"You're easily amused then."

"Hardly." I returned to her and held out the box. "It's merely that the subject fascinates me."

"Perhaps we share a common interest." Her hand skimmed over mine as she took it from me. Cool and soft —the velvet touch of a woman.

My cock stirred, drawing my mind to thoughts of that delicate hand wrapping around it. "I feel certain we do."

"But you still won't share." Each word was pointed— laced with a meaning that I understood instinctively. Whatever was passing between us was primal. An undeniable force of nature pulled us toward one another. I needed to shove my dick in her and fuck her until she was full of me. And she needed to be taken, held down—possessed.

Instead I waited as she lifted open the lid to reveal a new phone.

"I have a phone," she said, even as her fingers traced the champagne gold frame.

I'd chosen correctly. Even if she was going to pretend to be obstinate, it was obvious she liked it. Something had told me Belle liked the small touches—the hint of luxury. She was a woman with taste.

"This phone is for me. Only I will have the number, and you will keep it with you at all times."

"What's next? Are you going to take me home and chain

me to your wall?" she asked in a flat voice, shoving it toward me.

Belle's slender neck collared and chained. It was going to prove difficult to hide my erection if she kept planting ideas like that in my head. I took a small step behind the couch, forcing her to swivel around. The tufted back wasn't nearly high enough to hide my rock hard dick.

She kept her hand thrust in the air, but I shook my head. "May I ask you a question?"

"Obviously."

Jesus, she was even sexy when she pouted.

"Why take this job if you so obviously loathe me?"

Her pretty little mouth fell open. "I don't...I'm not sure why...I don't even know you."

"And yet you've made plenty of assumptions," I pointed out. "You assume I want to sleep with you. You assume I think you're a prostitute."

"I didn't say that—"

"Actually you did."

"Correct me if I'm wrong, but you want a beautiful woman hanging off your arm." Her arms folded over her chest.

"It's nice to see a woman with confidence. Men grow tired of pretty girls acting ignorant of their looks. I don't dispute that's the case, but I also hired you because you're Oxford educated, are well-bred, and more than capable of meeting my demanding schedule. Or am I wrong about those things?" I asked, savouring the opportunity to call her out.

"I am all of those things." She stood and snatched the phone from me. "And much more. I simply don't want to be an expensive accessory."

"I assure you that I'll work you hard." I didn't bother to keep the insinuation out of my voice. "Harder than you've ever experienced before."

"I look forward to the challenge," she breathed.

Christ, did she have any sense of self-preservation? She'd spent the last half hour dangling herself like meat over the lion's den and poking the beast when it came near. She was lucky not to have been eaten alive. It was all I could do not to pounce.

"A driver will pick you up in the morning." I wanted to step closer to her—to see what she would do when she was riled up—but the sofa provided a solid barrier. I'd never been so grateful to a piece of furniture before.

"About that. I can take the Tube or catch a cab. I'm not certain a driver is necessary."

"I decide what's necessary." I ignored her protest. She'd learn soon enough that I wasn't one to make requests.

Her eyes narrowed, but her mouth clamped shut. It was a shame actually. I quite liked when it was open.

"Anything else?" she snapped, rounding the couch. She jerked her purse over her shoulder and stared me down.

"Yes. Keep your phone on."

Flashing me a fake smile, she pivoted and marched out of the room.

A breath I didn't know I'd been holding released, and I lumbered back to my desk. Sinking into my chair, I stared at the door she'd just walked through. Her perfume still hung in the air. Hiring her was a mistake. I knew that now. This was proving to be less a game than a test. One I was certain I was failing. I'd seen her file. I knew exactly why she was erecting a barrier between us. I'd always been able to do the same. She wasn't the first attractive woman I'd hired for this position. All of them had eventually offered themselves to me, and I'd refused each of them.

But I had no doubt that if Belle had wagged her finger, I'd have had her pinned to the wall five seconds later. Keeping this professional might prove impossible so long as my thoughts continued to center around breaking her. I wanted to dismantle her walls until I freed the wild creature she had locked away. I wouldn't be satisfied until I claimed her.

Which was why I never could.

I slid open my desk drawer and drew out a picture frame. Running a flannel cloth over the glass, I stared into the eyes looking back at me. They were so alive, so bright.

"Why haven't I fired her?" I asked the photo, but no one responded.

No one ever did.

CHAPTER FOUR

*S*he moaned as I pushed her legs open, her teeth biting into her full bottom lip. Nice and slow— that's what she deserved. But as I sank inside her, burying myself deeper, my pace quickened until I was slamming into her. God, she felt fucking amazing. I wanted to tell her that, but there was no way she'd hear me over her screams. This was where I belonged. I knew that now.

Slipping my arm around her waist, I flipped her over, eager to get a view from behind. Instead, I jolted awake, drenched in sweat and facedown in my sheets. Alone. It was only a dream. The realization was as unwelcome as my empty bed. My hands fisted into the feather pillow over my head, ready to rip it apart in frustration. Immediately a sharp sting prickled through my palm. I fumbled for the remote I kept on my bedside table and hit the button to draw the curtains. Light seeped in as the blackout drapes that kept the room in absolute darkness automatically opened. The hollow shaft of a feather had poked through the pillow casing. I plucked it out and stared for a moment at its downy tuft. Softness with a hint of pain. There was a certain poetry to it. I blew it into the air. Then found my mobile on the nightstand.

SMITH: Coffee. Black. Garrison will pick you up in five minutes in front of your flat.

We hadn't discussed important items like my morning coffee yesterday, or what time I expected her at my house each morning. Personally, I'd been too distracted by wanting to fuck her. Now I didn't have coffee, and I still wanted to fuck her. I groaned as I rolled over, liberating the rock hard erection I'd awoken to. Maybe it was better that she hadn't been here to wake me up this morning. Then again, it was a shame not to put this to good use.

BELLE: Do you have any idea what time it is?

SMITH: Time for coffee.

My free hand stroked my shaft as I responded. There was no way I was getting off this easily. The only cure for morning wood was a warm pussy. Although I imagined her tight ass would do just as well.

BELLE: Tell this Garrison I'll be ready in twenty minutes.

SMITH: You have five.

BELLE: Go back to sleep and wake up on the right side of the bed.

I could hear the annoyance in her message. She definitely had the wrong stick up her ass. I had another one in mind. My cock twitched in agreement.

SMITH: Wake up and do your job.

BELLE: You can keep yourself occupied for half an hour.

I considered snapping a pic of my dick in hand to show her exactly how I would be occupying that half hour. It might actually get her here faster. Then again she might never show up at all. It was difficult to read her still. Generally that wasn't a problem I had around people, particularly women. It's what made me a good lawyer. I knew she wanted to fuck me. It was written all over her body. Of course, it shouldn't surprise me that she was going through a man-hating phase given the information the background check had revealed. It wasn't like I was going to be the man who would heal her, but that didn't mean I wouldn't help her rebound if I had the chance.

Thinking like that was going to get me into trouble.

In fact, I didn't need to be thinking about it all. She was my assistant. I'd never fucked assistants before. This was different. Our professional ties should reign me in, but I knew they wouldn't. If only I hadn't seen how responsive her body was during that interview. I was already imagining harnessing it—controlling it. Belle Stuart wouldn't be a simple fling. Not with the things I wanted to do to her.

Which is exactly why you need to take a cold shower.

I yanked the pillow from under my head and threw it across the room. Apparently I had a half hour to get my head—and my dick—under control.

She's a means to an end, I reminded myself as I started the water a few moments later. As long as I remembered that, I could keep myself from touching her. It was that simple.

"Who are you kidding?" I asked the empty bathroom. "It's that complicated."

Then I turned the heat down a few more notches and stepped inside.

CHAPTER FIVE

I needed to quit this job. That much was already clear. Smith Price might get his rocks off on ordering me around, but there was no way I was going to let him. The trouble was that I needed this job and its completely ludicrous salary.

The salary page from yesterday's contracts floated to mind. So many zeroes behind that two.

Okay, so I couldn't quit. Not yet. A few months of putting up with his bullshit, and I would have the capital I needed to finance my business plan. In the meantime, I would be setting up some clear boundaries, like more than a five-minute notice that he expected me dressed and ready to head out the door.

Jane appeared in her doorway and rubbed the back of her neck. "Starting this early? We shouldn't have had so much wine last night."

"Apparently I'm on call at all hours," I grumbled as I

shoved bobby pins in my hair. There was no time to wash it. I had no intention of actually meeting my new driver outside in five minutes, but I didn't want to risk being later than ten minutes. Checks and balances. "I'm sorry I woke you up. Mr. Price needs his morning coffee in bed."

"A demanding man waiting for you in bed." Jane bit back a smile. "If you decide to quit, I'm available for the position."

I held up a finger in warning. "Don't. I'm not sleeping with him."

"That's a pity," she said with a yawn, "because you need to get laid."

"I'm not justifying that with a response." I planted a kiss on her cheek as I swooped past her.

"Have a lovely morning," she called out, her voice tinged with amusement.

I'm sure there were a lot of women who would jump at the chance to serve coffee to Smith Price in bed. They'd probably offer to serve him a lot more. I just didn't want to be one of them. Sex and Belle Stuart no longer mixed. I had a vibrator I wasn't afraid to use and a plan. Screwing Smith wasn't part of that equation.

But the site that greeted me at the door stopped me in my tracks. A sleek, silver Mercedes AMG idled in front of the building. Holy fuck, it was hot. I said a silent prayer that Smith hadn't been here to witness my reaction. He didn't need to know I had a penchant for luxury cars.

The driver side door opened and I braced myself. I half expected it to be Smith himself, come to drag me to his house to make him coffee. But the fiery red hair didn't belong to him. An unfamiliar face smiled in greeting.

"Garrison?" I asked, shouldering my purse as I fought to regain my composure.

"Miss." Garrison tilted his head in greeting and opened the back door.

I slid in, allowing my fingers to caress the buttery leather seats before I settled back. This car was power. And sex. Maybe it made me a gold digger, but I loved it.

"This is...nice," I said conversationally, aware that Garrison might be wondering if I was having some sort of fit in the back seat. "It's an AMG, right?"

"An AMG S-65. Mr. Price has excellent taste in cars." Garrison turned out slowly, making his way into the morning traffic of East London.

"Yes, he does," I murmured to myself. Expensive taste, inhuman good looks and an asshole to boot—it was the trifecta of hotness. And three big red flags. Smith Price was dangerous.

"Will you be requiring me for the rest of the day?" Garrison asked as we made our way toward Knightsbridge. I made a mental note to ask more about what area of law he practised as the houses grew larger.

"I don't know," I answered truthfully. "Do you drive Mr. Price?" I didn't think his excellency would want to be parted with his servant much today.

"Mr. Price drives his own car," Garrison informed me as he turned toward a gated drive. "I drive him to social functions in whatever car he puts me in. Today he asked me to pick you up in this car."

My thoughts jumbled together as I took in the house that loomed overhead. Maybe it was more than one flat. Surely, it was more than one flat. Deciding that, I was finally able to process Garrison's last statement.

"This isn't his personal car?" I asked in surprise.

Garrison shook his head as the gate opened to allow us entrance.

"I'm sorry. I assumed it was." It made sense that Smith would use a company to pick me up. I could only hope whatever Smith drove was somewhat less extravagant. I didn't want to think about riding shotgun with Smith manoeuvring a stick shift next to me. I might come on the spot.

"That's why I asked if you would require me the rest of the day." Garrison's kind eyes caught mine in the rearview mirror. "Mr. Price would prefer that your car be garaged privately overnight."

"My car? I don't have a car," I informed him.

"This is your car. Mr. Price acquired it yesterday," Garrison continued as if this wasn't a complete bombshell. "I will pick you up and drive you home each day. It's up to you if you would prefer I drive you throughout the day. He keeps me on retainer, so I will be available when you decide."

"I'll be sure to let you know," I managed to squeak. My car? I might have to have a few minutes alone with it in the garage. I shook my head, recovering some composure as

Garrison pulled up next to a black Bugatti Veyron. One of just over four hundred models in the world. I ogled it as the driver popped out and opened the door for me. Smith and I clearly had one thing in common.

"The lift is to your right." He gestured to the side of the private garage.

"Thank you." My head was still swimming when I reached it and realized I had no idea where I was going. "Um, which flat is Mr. Price's?"

Garrison's eyebrows knit together. "This is his house, Miss. Kitchen's on the lower ground floor. His bedroom is on the second."

"Of course. That's what I meant." I beamed at him, wondering just how big of an idiot he thought I was.

A Mercedes for his assistant. A Bugatti for himself. And a house roughly the size of Harrods. I'd known a few lawyers in my lifetime. They didn't make this kind of money. Maybe I should ditch the business plan and go back to law school, I thought as I stepped out of the lift into the entrance hall. I'd been in palaces for heaven's sake, but this place was impressive. Traditional eighteenth century architecture blended with crisp, clean decor. Grey marble complimented the modern furniture. I dropped the keys Garrison had given me on an empty console table that stretched the length of the foyer. It was the opposite of his office. How many faces did Smith Price have, and which one hid the real man?

Now if I could just find the kitchen.

As it turned out, the coffee maker was the one item that

was easy to find once I'd located the kitchen. It was the only item on his granite counter. I stared at it for a moment, wondering how to work the Impressa espresso maker.

"Use the auto mode. I'll teach you how to pull a proper shot sooner or later," a gruff voice instructed me.

I spun on my heels and nearly dropped the mug I was holding. I'd been worried about keeping my hands to myself when I brought Smith coffee in bed. Now I would give anything to have him tucked under his covers. It seemed infinitely...safer.

Apparently Smith had occupied himself in the shower, and now he stood before me with a towel hanging loosely on his hips. Damp hair had fallen across his forehead, dripping down his face. Smith pushed it back with one hand, the other tightening over knotted fabric at his waist. Drops of water glistened over his broad shoulders and chest. Chiseled abs tapered into narrow hips. I'd guessed he was powerfully built when he was fully clothed, but I had no idea how much. He watched me, his eyes smoldering with a raw authority that unnerved me. He was temptation in a towel—a masculine trap that sent prurient thoughts flooding through me.

I had to push the brew button four times before I actually hit it. I was pretty certain I looked like I was drunk. My first official day of work was going to consist of confusion and incompetence. Fabulous.

Smith accepted the coffee without comment when I passed it to him a minute later. He cupped the mug with both hands, allowing his towel to hang suggestively off his hips.

Do not look at his abs, I ordered myself even as my eyes drifted to the perfect slab of muscles on display.

"Is your car acceptable?" he asked after he took a long, slow sip.

"Yes-s-s," I stammered. "Um, actually, I'm a little confused about that."

His eyebrow raised as he took another drink.

"When you say my car..." I trailed away as embarrassment overtook me. I'd had a proper British upbringing, which meant I'd been taught never to talk about money. Or ask questions, for that matter. I'd had no problem eschewing those rules until today. Now I twisted my fingers together and hoped he wouldn't make me continue.

"The car is part of your compensation package," Smith explained with a shrug.

The nonchalance with which he responded bolstered my confidence. "Daily transportation is part of my compensation package."

He smirked. "You're not driving my car."

My thoughts flashed to the sports car in the garage.

"The Bugatti?" I guessed.

"Yes," he said, surprise flitting over his features. He was impressed. "Need I say more regarding the possibility of you driving it?"

Not impressed enough.

"Maybe someday you'll trust me enough to change your mind on that," I countered.

"There's no one I trust that much." He took a step closer, bringing his nearly naked body too close for comfort. "But I'll take you for a ride."

Smith Price needed to be schooled on where I stood on cars—and him. "As long as you drive in manual, I'll consider. I'm not a girl who rides an automatic."

Smith's eyebrow cocked up at my blatant double entendre.

Oh God, I was flirting with him. Shamelessly flirting with him. So much for keeping my thing for cars under wraps. I might as well have stripped naked and climbed into his back seat as an offering.

Smith rubbed a hand over the stubble on his chin. "Let me get dressed, and I'll show you around. You'll need to know the entire house for when we have guests."

There was that we again. I couldn't quite figure out if this was standard personal assistant fare or if I'd been hired to play house. "You know a wife might be a cheaper option for you."

Lightning flashed across his green eyes, a fleeting thunderstorm of anger that was quickly replaced by calm. "Until she divorced me and took half of it."

"I believe that's why they have pre-nups." I crossed my arms over my chest and took a step away from him. This wasn't the first time Smith had displayed a volatile mood swing. At least, it had passed quickly. "But I'm not a lawyer."

"You seem intent on proving yourself unnecessary to me, Belle," he said, bypassing my jibe.

That wasn't my intention at all. Or was it? Why was everything so confusing in the presence of Smith Price? "You haven't fired me yet."

"Yet," he repeated with meaning.

My attitude hadn't gone unnoticed it seemed. Well, then I figured he was also aware of how often he was flirting with me, or rather, sexually harassing me. It was best to think of it in those terms. Flirtation was too welcome a concept.

"Follow me." He motioned toward the lift.

I stared at him, trying to comprehend. I couldn't handle Smith giving me the grand tour in that towel. "I thought you were going to get dressed."

"I am, but we have things to discuss. You'll find there isn't much downtime in my life. I already wasted half an hour waiting for my coffee."

"Maybe next time you could get up and make it yourself. You seem to know how." I shrugged but forced the haughty smirk on my face into a false smile.

"Don't do that," he ordered in a stern voice, catching my elbow and tugging apart my still crossed arms.

I swallowed hard and forced myself to be honest. "I tend to be a little snarky when I'm nervous."

"No, not the snark. Don't force yourself to smile. I didn't hire you to be a puppet. Although I would request a little less of the biting remarks in the presence of clients." His tone had softened, and my heart did a strange leap.

"I'm sure I won't be nervous then at all," I said dryly.

"Do you drink wine?" he asked as we stepped into the lift.

"Um, yes." Apparently we were changing floors and topics.

"Then I'll have some brought up from my private stock. You should have a glass or two before client dinners to help ease your nerves." Smith lounged against the mirrored glass of the lift.

Drinking around him seemed like a very bad idea, but I kept that to myself and nodded, determined to contain some of my snark. What I couldn't quite ignore was the way his towel had split open in the front, revealing too much of a muscular thigh. An inch or two higher and the towel would become obsolete. Smith crossed his legs, breaking the spell, and I looked sheepishly back up at him. A crooked grin carved across his face.

Suddenly the lift felt too small, as if it was closing in on me, pushing me closer and closer to him. I locked my legs into place and hoped for a miracle that didn't include me pinned against the control panel. His head tilted, studying me, and then he slowly licked his lower lip.

In that moment I had no doubt what he could do with those lips, and more than ever before, I wanted to find out. I needed to know how that tongue would taste in my mouth and what it would feel like on my skin—how it would feel between my legs. I took one step closer just as the lift dinged and the doors slid open.

"After you." He held an arm out past the door to prevent it from closing. The gesture did nothing to allay the steady pulse growing in my core. There was a promise in his words—a knowingness that hinted at an intimacy we hadn't yet shared but would.

I did my best to brush it off as I exited into a plush hallway.

Smith led me through a set of French doors into the master suite.

"Excuse me." He sauntered across the room to another door. My gaze followed the swagger of his hips. The towel was even more low-slung now, showcasing his taut back and perfectly carved tailbone. I nearly followed him through the closet door.

Instead I hung back until he reemerged carrying a slate grey suit and a precisely folded oxford. He laid them across the bed then tossed two ties on top.

"Choose one," he instructed me before he disappeared into the attached en suite.

I could no longer see him, despite the fact that the door was wide open. Forcing myself to get a grip, I picked up the silk ties and turned them over in my hands. The differences were subtle. Both blue. A slightly checked pattern to one, a thin red threading artfully embroidered in the other. I wrapped them around my hands, savouring the smoothness of the fabric. The strangest desire to press them to my lips came over me, but I threw one down and stepped away before I gave in to the urge.

A low buzzing vibrated from the loo as Smith called out, "Do you have your phone?"

I stepped closer, trying to hear him over the sound of

the electric shaver. Movement caught the corner of my eye, and I realized he was now visible through the crack of the door. When I saw the towel puddled around his feet, I wanted to look away. Instead I drank in the pronounced curve of his ass matched along with the muscular arch of his thigh. He shifted, revealing more of his groin and the carved v that pointed down to the top of a dark patch of hair and the very root of his shaft.

I stumbled back and pressed a hand to my chest before he noticed me staring.

He called out again.

"Yes," I responded, mentally berating myself for peeping on my boss. Then again, he was the one who invited me into his bedroom.

Not a good reason! the persistent voice in my head screamed.

"We have a dinner tomorrow at seven."

Typing while in heat turned out to be more difficult than I expected. My fingers kept finding the wrong buttons, but I finally got it in the calendar on my mobile.

"We're running later than I thought," he continued, "so I'll show you around the house tomorrow morning. Can you be here with my coffee at seven-thirty?"

Was that actually a request? "Yes."

"This afternoon, I'll have you copy my date book for your own reference. Doris will see that you're listed on my important accounts." He strode through the bathroom door a moment later.

The only thing that registered was the lack of towel.

And wow.

He walked into the closet and returned slipping into a pair of black boxer briefs, seemingly oblivious to the fact that he was on display. I needed to look away. I couldn't be sure, but I was pretty certain staring at your boss's dick— his beautiful, perfect dick—on the first day on the job sent the wrong message. Then again, it would be an injustice to the female race if I didn't look. It hung low, brushing several inches down his thigh.

God, if it looked like that right now—

A warning bell rang in my head, cutting me off from that line of thinking. Nothing good would come out of it, although someone would probably come of it.

I blurted out the first question that came to mind. "What do I wear?"

"Come again," Smith said as the briefs slipped over his hips.

Good job, Belle. Mention clothes while he's naked. That's not obvious at all. "Tomorrow. What do I wear for dinner tomorrow? Is it formal? Cocktail?"

"Don't worry about it." He wandered closer to me and my breath caught. He'd seen me watching, and there was no way I was going to put up a fight. The only thoughts racing through my mind were whether to start on the bed or the floor. But he brushed past me and picked up his dress shirt. His fingers nimbly undid the buttons, and he slipped it over his broad shoulders.

"I need to know what to wear. If I show up in cowboy

boots, no amount of wine will save me from my nerves." I planted my fists on my hips and stared him down.

"We have an appointment at Harrods tomorrow at ten sharp. I'll pick something out then."

Not this again. "I actually have an excellent wardrobe."

Smith turned on me, and before I could process it, his hand had covered the one on my hip. He tugged slightly, and I stumbled forward breathless—waiting—until he released me. He held up the second tie. I'd forgotten I had it wadded in my fist.

"I think I'll wear this one," he said in a low voice that shivered over my skin. "You have delicious taste, Belle. But given your financial portfolio, I imagine you don't have the latest pieces. We need to look like we're doing well at all times."

This time I ignored the we and went straight to the point. "My financial portfolio? You've been looking at my bank statements."

"And your debt," he said. "It's standard. I need to know who I'm getting in bed with—metaphorically speaking."

So he knew I was broke. Was that why he chose me? Because he knew I was desperate enough to do anything he asked? Worse yet, did he think I was desperate enough to sleep with him?

"I don't think any less of you," he added as if he could read my mind. "Most recent graduates have debt."

I didn't want to press the issue. I had no idea how far he had looked into my personal circumstances. Obviously he would know that I hadn't been gainfully employed previously. He would know about the engagement to Philip. He'd already admitted to knowing I had a relationship with Clara and Edward. It was a perfectly reasonable thing for a prospective employer to do a background check, but that didn't stop my stomach from tying into knots.

But there was one thing I needed to be clear about. "I don't want charity."

"I'm not offering it." He looped the tie around his neck and crossed it. "I told you I would work you hard."

Somehow I still suspected there was a double meaning there, but all I said was, "good."

"Did I choose correctly?"

It took me a moment to realize he was talking about the tie. My hand reached out absently and smoothed it down. Even through the layers, I could feel the hardness of his body underneath. "I chose."

"Ah yes. Beauty's privilege." His eyes sparked as he spoke, and I sensed he was looking past the words we exchanged and the few moments we had shared, searching for a place I'd locked away.

I turned away, afraid to let him find it.

CHAPTER SIX

*B*elle stood at my bedroom window, enveloped in the first light of dawn. The warmth of it wrapped around her, making her porcelain skin glow pink. Her simple ivory sheath dress hugged her body, revealing her slight curves. The ensemble was relatively chaste, if suggestive, save for the leopard print heels she'd chosen— yet another sign of a wild side that she tried to hide. As she stared, her expression changed from fascination to sadness. I still couldn't read her. She remained an enigma, but part of me empathized with the sudden bouts of melancholy that seemed to color her world.

I cleared my throat politely, not wanting to scare her. "Good morning."

She spun around to greet me, a look of relief crossing her face. "Oh, you're dressed!"

Had she hoped I wouldn't be? Was she as preoccupied with what was beneath my clothes as I was with what was beneath hers? Her gaze swept over me appreciatively. She liked suits, and I had a fucking closet full of them.

"We have lots to do today." I pointed to a coffee mug sitting on my bedside table. "Is that for me?"

"No, it's for me. I thought I'd drag myself across the city to make myself coffee." She rolled her eyes as she picked up the cup and brought it to me.

"Not a fan of coffee?"

A slight grin played at her lips, but she held it back. "I'm a Brit. I drink tea."

"I suppose us Scots are less discriminating," I said, before taking a hesitant sip. I hadn't been there to oversee her use of the machine.

"I didn't poison it." She twisted her hands, undermining her antagonistic facade.

She wanted to please me, even if she pretended otherwise. Things were getting interesting.

"It's good," I reassured her. "Precisely to my preference."

"Black coffee isn't that hard." She shook her head with a disapproving sigh.

"I suppose you take your tea with milk and sugar?"

"You suppose correctly. Do you find that repulsive?"

"No. I might bring you tea one morning." I made a mental note to have my housekeeper pick up bags.

She cast a dubious glance at me but said nothing.

"Let's get on with the tour," I snapped. Since she didn't respond to kindness, there was no point in operating under false pretenses. We both seemed to prefer when I was an asshole.

"Shall we start at the bottom?" she suggested.

Beautiful, you're staying bottom, I thought. Outwardly, I jerked my head and strode toward the lift, pleased that she had to run to catch me. You have no idea how hard it's going to be to keep up with me.

As soon as the lift doors shut, the space contracted and I had to inhale deeply.

She eyed me in concern. "Are you okay?"

"I'm fine," I replied in a clipped tone. I kept my gaze and thoughts on her tits until the doors slid back open.

Belle darted out and headed into the garage—the only area she was familiar with. I didn't bother to correct her. Instead I headed left, banking into a hallway. She didn't like to be told what to do. I appreciated that in a woman, but she needed to learn that I was the one in control.

"Where are we going?" she demanded when she finally caught up to me.

I smirked but didn't stop to acknowledge her. "On the tour."

"I thought maybe you would take me for that ride in the Veyron." She took a step closer, crossing her arms behind her back and drawing attention to her breasts.

A simpering request. Well-played. I'd been impressed that she knew the make and model of my personal car yesterday. This morning's initiative sealed what I already suspected.

I turned on her. "You like cars."

"I guess," she hedged, but it was written all over her body—flushed cheeks, quick, shallow breaths. Unrestrained lust practically dripped off her. She ran her tongue over her lower lip, leaving her sinfully red lipstick glistening while proving my point. An image of her mouth closing over my cock flashed to mind.

"You do." I stepped closer, noting how her body shifted toward mine. "I said I'd take you for a ride. Now you have to earn it."

I walked away, leaving her panting in the hall. Surreptitiously, I adjusted my hard-on before opening the door at the end of the passage. I could fuck her right here. Or take her back to the garage and screw her against the Bugatti. She'd like that. There'd be no fight. That car was a guaranteed leg-spreader. There would also be no chase—and I loved the pursuit.

I chose to start with my least favorite feature of the house. The faint aroma of chlorine seeped through the open door as I showed her my private lap pool. The smell made my stomach roil. but I'd learned to ignore that.

"You have a swimming pool?" she shrieked.

Despite myself, I grinned at her enthusiasm. "It was added in the seventies. You're welcome to use it."

We continued our progress through the house, which somehow felt more extravagant with Belle struck silent with awe at my side. I'd never looked at the property as anything more than a showpiece—a relic meant to project a familial grandeur that never was. Now I couldn't help seeing it through her eyes.

"We need to purchase some art," Belle said, noting the bare walls that accompanied most floors.

I allowed a tight smile. Perhaps I was being too encouraging of her enthusiasm. "I recently painted. I prefer an uncluttered space."

"That's a shame. This place is practically a gallery." She spoke wistfully as her eyes continued to scan the blank space. "Maybe—"

"Out here is the garden," I interrupted her. Watch out for the hole I'm currently digging myself into.

She took the hint and lapsed back into silence. My gaze darted to her periodically as I continued the tour. Her initial shock over my house had dissipated. I'd assumed that she'd been in grander estates, given the company she kept. Her amazement had been directed at me. No doubt she'd begin to ask unwanted questions soon.

On the third floor, I ushered her through a cluster of guest rooms.

"Does anyone actually use these?"

"My housekeeper sees they're kept fresh." It wasn't exactly a lie. Mrs. Andrews did dust and change the sheets purely out of compulsion. Most of the rooms hadn't been slept in for years.

"Do you have guests stay often?" Once again Belle seemed psychically in tune with my inner thoughts. I couldn't deny her mysterious insight made her more alluring. Perhaps that's why I kept her around. I was hoping to discover the trick behind the magic.

"Very rarely." I opened a door at the end of the hall. "This is your bedroom."

"My bedroom?"

I couldn't resist. "Unless there's another room you'd prefer to sleep in."

"I have a flat," she said, bypassing my insinuation.

"Believe me, I'm not asking you to move in." I couldn't think of anything I wanted less in the world. Mrs. Andrews nagged me enough during the hours we were both on premises. Two ladies of the house would be untenable. "There will be times when I need you until very late or I require you here very early. You may choose to use this room on those occasions if you prefer."

Belle stepped inside the suite and pivoted slowly around, taking it in. The room was decorated in hues of champagne, from the creamy silk curtains to the oversized king bed made up with a golden coverlet. Sunlight shimmered across the gilded damask wallpaper. It was an elegant space—understated while still opulent. She belonged here.

"There's a private bath attached." I motioned to a door in the corner. "You may keep anything you wish here."

"I'll consider your offer," she said as she exited. She paused in the corridor, her attention focused directly across from her on the only closed door in the hall. "Another guest room?"

I didn't look at the room "No."

She walked past me and jiggled the handle. "Locked?"

"I prefer that room remains undisturbed." I gestured toward the hall we had come down, trying to ignore the faint memories forcing themselves to the front of my mind.

"What's in there?" she pushed.

"Nothing that concerns you," I snarled.

"You've made it pretty clear that I need to know everything about your life, so I can only assume you keep your murder weapons in here!" She huffed as she finished her rant, waiting for me to respond.

I stalked away, laughing humorlessly at her suggestion.

"The tour's over," I called over my shoulder as I dashed off a list on my mobile. "I'm sending you a to-do list. Finish it and meet me at Harrods at ten sharp."

"Yes, sir," she hissed.

Sir. I'd pressed her buttons. "Garrison will drive—"

"I can drive myself," she yelled.

I knew she could, because she'd been driving me crazy since we met. "I don't care who drives you. Just leave."

"Gladly." Her tone was flat as she pushed past me and smacked the button for the lift.

She entered it and turned to glare at me. Neither of us made a move to prevent the doors from sliding closed. I stayed there, eyes transfixed on the lift. I was caught in limbo. All it would have taken was one act to move forward and away from the ghosts lingering at the end of this hall. I couldn't turn to face them and I couldn't walk away. Belle had seen that, but she didn't understand it. She never could.

I wouldn't let her.

CHAPTER SEVEN

I stepped through the glass door of Harrods and breathed in the familiar smell. Some people might not believe shoes and designer dresses had a scent, but they did. The rich aroma of soft-grain leather and linen mixed with floral notes from the department store's display of fine teas and the perfume counters. With any luck, I had a little credit on my account and could pick out a treat to celebrate my new job. I hadn't charged anything for months, not since I'd found myself suddenly single. But surviving my first days working for Smith Price deserved a reward.

Before the glass door had shut behind me, a woman swooped over, dressed in an unapologetically plum dress suit that matched her lipstick. A large Harrods' badge pinned to her lapel read Harriet. She offered me a tentative smile. "Miss Stuart?"

I froze in place before nodding.

"I've been waiting for you." The hesitancy in her expression vanished, replaced by a warmer, if slightly less than genuine, smile.

"I must be later on paying my charge account than I thought if you're meeting me at the door."

"What?" she asked, the joke whizzing right over her smooth black hair. She tilted her chin, as if to puzzle me out.

"I usually don't get met by name at the door somewhere unless I'm in trouble." I tried to sound light-hearted, but inside my stomach churned. There had been a time when I was met at restaurants and parties by people eager to introduce themselves. Or rather to meet Philip's fiancée. That time had passed.

"Oh! Nothing like that!" Her polite laugh tinkled like a bell—too high and practiced. She'd obviously been working here a long time. "Mr. Price informed us you would be arriving."

"Did he send over my mug shot?"

"You're so funny." She batted my arm as if we were life-long friends.

I hated her already.

"Mr. Price described you—in perfect detail, I must say." Winking at me, she motioned for me to follow her toward the lift. "You're quite lucky to have a man who is so attentive."

"He's my boss," I said flatly, even though butterflies fluttered in my stomach as I spoke.

That revelation shut her up, and we enjoyed a blissful

silence as the lift carried us to the fifth floor. The opening of the doors broke the magic spell, and she began to chatter again. Something about starting with the base pieces and building toward ensembles. I stopped listening to her. I had more important things on my mind.

Smith Price had described me in perfect detail. What did that mean? My height and build? Any stranger could do that. But I had hardly been the first petite blonde to walk through Harrods' doors this morning. He had to have told her more.

"Excuse me," I said, interrupting her blather about the rising importance of proper stockings. "How did Mr. Price describe me?"

She paused as if to recall. "I believe he referenced you as a sophisticated blonde. About eight stone with a 32B breast size. He also guessed you'd be wearing Louboutins."

This circus trick obviously impressed her, but it only surprised me. He'd perfectly sized me up, down to noticing my shoes.

"Of course, he didn't know they were Louboutins. He mentioned the red sole," she continued, adding, "He did ask that we pull a selection. I was truly sorry when I told him we didn't carry them."

"Me too." I didn't know what else to say. Not with my head swimming over the fact that Smith had been so attentive. Then again, after yesterday's show in his bedroom, I could guess his shirt size...amongst other things.

Harriet led me past the front desk of the Penthouse, where By Appointment, Harrods personal shopping service, was housed, to a private fitting room. Sleek leather armchairs clustered around a large turquoise ottoman, and against the wall not one rack, but three racks of clothing waited. They must have pulled every piece in my size that the store had. This was hardly the first time I had been to Harrods, but it was the first time I was treated like royalty —and I'd been here before with Clara.

"Does Mr. Price do this often?" I asked. The whole spectacle smacked of the sort of privilege afforded to wealthy men that readily flashed their wallets.

"I've never worked with him before, but my manager was very clear on Mr. Price's expectations. She was also clear that we meet them all."

Enough said. Then again, I'd thrown on clothes yesterday to attend him on a whim. Smith Price might simply be a man who got what he wanted.

Except me.

I wandered over to the racks, brushing my fingers across the silky fabrics. Shopping had been a luxury I couldn't afford the last few months after cutting up Philip's credit cards. Although he'd left me with a stocked closet in addition to my broken heart, I had grown tired of window shopping. Enough so that I'd hatched a business idea. A company that catered to women with tastes that exceeded their bank accounts. Women like me.

A tag snagged against my palm, and I flipped it over absent-mindedly. My mouth fell open when I saw the price. There was taste like mine and then there was taste like Smith Price's. I shouldn't be shocked given that I'd seen his house, but even I had never spent such an extravagant amount on a piece of clothing.

"Did he give you parameters?" I tucked the obscene price tag inside the neckline, unable to look at it.

"The most expensive pieces from our top lines," Harriet answered as she joined me. She pushed apart the gowns to reveal the one I'd just stumbled upon. I glanced over to tell her to take it away and spotted him. Harriet rattled off more particulars, but I didn't hear her.

Smith was in the doorway, his eyes studying me intently. He'd looked at me this way each time we met, as if I was a puzzle he was trying to lock into place. Or maybe he was hoping to fill a certain open slot. I turned back to the racks, my face burning. I told myself it was embarrassment that a man I barely knew thought I needed a new wardrobe. But that wasn't it. The heat I felt had nothing to do with my emotions. No, it came from somewhere deeper—a place I'd sealed away with my own psychological chastity belt.

I sensed him behind me before he spoke, his presence silently urging me to step back and close the space between us. It took a record-breaking amount of willpower not to do just that.

"Belle." He said my name softly, as though he was tasting it.

Closing my eyes, I took a steadying breath before I turned to greet him. "I thought you said ten sharp."

"A client needed a moment of my time." The answer was final and more than a tad bit dismissive.

"That reminds me." I switched the topic to business, eager to clear the tension in the air. "Exactly what area of law do you practice?"

"The gray area," he replied in a clipped tone.

A tingle danced up my spine. Suddenly the house, the cars, the extravagance made a little more sense. Terrible people needed lawyers who could be paid to look the other way. Before I could attach judgment to this revelation, I realized I was no better than he was. Not while I worked for him.

"Will you require a model, or do you want to try on the garments personally?" Harriet broke in. This time I was grateful for her obliviousness.

"She'll try them on," Smith decided for me.

It irked me that he'd made the call, even though I had the same preference. "Exactly what I was thinking."

"You two must have a wonderful working relationship," Harriet gushed.

I grabbed something from the rack and dashed into the attached dressing room before I laughed. Tense? Yes. Awkward? Yes. Sexually volatile? Hell yes. But wonderful? No. I hung the dress on a hook and sank against the wall, staring at it. Simple, black but with a cut that made it something more than a little black dress. No, this was a statement. It was exactly the kind of thing I would pick out.

Harriet poked her head through the curtain. "May I?"

I waved her inside. She bustled in, carrying an armful of

other options and began to place them on the rack in the corner of the space. Meanwhile I stripped down.

"Do you require any special undergarments?" Harriet asked.

"I think I'm fine," I said, allowing a little sarcasm to slip through.

I caught her glancing up in the mirror and surveying the validity of my claim. Her mouth fell open a little when she saw the Lucille London garter set I was wearing. Lingerie as distinctive as this had that effect regardless of gender or sexual preference. My lips curved a little in challenge, and she quickly looked away, busying herself with removing the black dress from the hanger.

Philip's bank account might have supplied my shopping habits, but he had personally supplied my lingerie drawer. Each week he'd brought me something new, dressing me up like a paper doll. My belly tightened at the memory as a wave of nausea rolled through me. I'd been his plaything while he'd bided his time waiting for Pepper Lockwood. Now I was expected to do the same thing for Smith. By the time Harriet had helped me into the dress and zipped up the back of it, I was fuming. I barely had the presence of mind to slip my heels back on before I strutted out.

If Smith Price wanted a show, I would give him one.

He looked up from the business section of The Globe as I came closer, his expression changing from distracted to keenly interested instantly.

Planting my hand on my hip, I turned for him and then flourished my arms. The dress had been little more than a fitted black sheath on the hanger, but it dipped low in the front, revealing the valley between my breasts. It was understated but very sexy. "Does this meet your approval, sir?"

Smith frowned and motioned for me to turn once more.

So that was how he was going to play it. I remained still and stared him down.

"Most women enjoy shopping," he said, his voice so cool that I shivered.

"I enjoy shopping," I spit out. "I don't enjoy being a toy."

"I needed to be present to make certain we were on the same page regarding your appearance, given how often you'll be accompanying me and, at times, representing me." Smith paused to let this sink in.

"You gave me that line before."

"Do you like this dress?" he asked.

"Yes, but—"

"Enough." Tossing his newspaper aside, he stood. He tipped his chin toward the corner of the room, and Harriet scurried over. "Miss Stuart desires a private shopping experience. Please place her purchases on my account."

"Of course," Harriet said, a bit too eagerly. But then her eyes darted over to me like she was being left with a rabid animal.

Was it so crazy for a girl to want to try things on and consider them by herself?

Smith reached for the suit jacket he'd laid over the back of his seat. He slipped it on, buttoning it over the matching charcoal vest. As he adjusted his cufflinks, I realized he was actually going to leave. Heat crept over my cheeks and across my chest. This had to be the tenth time I'd blushed in front of him. If I were smart I'd lay outside until I had a sunburn that might hide future instances.

"Wait," I blurted out.

He stopped a few steps from the door. "Yes?"

"Stay." I managed to force out the request despite the rapid pounding of my heart. "I get a little defensive when I feel like a charity case."

"And when you feel like a toy," he added, a thoughtful gleam in his green eyes.

Most of my life had been spent occupying one of those two roles. If I was going to strike out on my own I wanted another option. "Can you blame a girl?"

His jaw visibly tensed. It took a moment for me to realize he wasn't angry, he was trying not to smile.

Taking a deep breath, I crossed the room and stuck out my hand. "Let's start over."

"Why would we do that?" he asked.

"Because I've been provoking you since the moment we met," I admitted.

Smith took my outstretched hand, but he didn't shake it. Instead he drew me slowly to him, close enough that I felt the heat radiating from his body. I'd never been this close to him before. I caught faint traces of leather and bergamot on the air around me, forcing me to fight the urge to melt against him and breathe in his warm, rich scent. Smith leaned closer until his breath tickled my ear and whispered, "Continue to provoke me, beautiful. I like it. But you're wrong about one thing: I don't look at you as a toy. Although I should be so lucky to play with you."

My eyes closed involuntarily as my body took over, but he didn't pull me closer. I ached for him to, caught up in the irresistible draw of his presence.

"You've been fighting me. This. We both have, and it's for the best. We have a professional relationship," he continued quietly. "I don't know if you like me, Belle, but you shouldn't."

"Do you like me?" The question slipped effortlessly off my tongue. I didn't want it to matter. I wished it didn't.

"Very much. Too much." His thumb rubbed circles on my palm as he admitted it. "You're smart to keep me at a distance. Don't try to fix us. Do your work and keep hating me. Protect yourself."

"Or what?" I stepped away from him, jerking my hand free from his hypnotic touch.

"I might bite." He clicked his teeth on the final syllable. "Consider that a warning."

He nodded a farewell and disappeared out the door, leaving me to wonder if I should heed his advice or if he was trying to get under my skin. My gut had told me to stay away from him since the moment we met, but I couldn't deny my body had other ideas.

AN HOUR LATER, I decided to give up. There was no way I

could choose between the amazing pieces in here, especially with my head still spinning over Smith's warning. Dropping onto one of the plush chairs, I waited for Harriet, who'd insisted on bringing in a selection of accessories. The trill ring of my mobile shattered the temporary silence I'd been granted in her absence. I fished it from my purse, groaning when a picture of my mother flashed across the screen.

"Hello, Mum," I answered, knowing I couldn't dodge her any longer. Avoiding my mother was like trying to stay dry under water—completely impossible.

"Where are you at?" she asked suspiciously. "I hear music."

"A strip club. I got a new job."

"Don't be vulgar. It's not that kind of music." Her voice carried the weight of years of disappointment in it.

I sighed. "I'm at Harrods, Mother."

"Is that in our budget?" she asked. Budget had become my mother's favorite word since the death of my father.

"It's in my budget."

"Do not take that tone with me," she warned, and suddenly I was ten years old again. "I called because I heard about your new job. You hadn't mentioned it."

So much for keeping that a secret. I considered asking who had ratted me out, but she'd always been protective of her sources. I could only imagine she had an entire network of spies in the London area dedicated to the task of tracking and reporting my every move. "I just started, and honestly, I'm not sure it's going to work out."

"Not with that attitude."

Harriet bustled into the room, holding up a few different belts. I never thought I'd be happy to see her. "Mum, I need to go. The shopgirl is here."

"Come to the estate this weekend. We should discuss how this impacts Stuart Hall," she ordered, revealing the real reason she'd bothered to ring me in the first place.

"I think I have to work." That probably wasn't a lie. Over the last couple of days I'd gotten the impression that Smith expected me at his beck and call at all hours.

"What kind of job is this?" She didn't bother to hide the distaste in her voice. Considering she'd never held a position outside of wife and estate manager, it didn't surprise me. Even if it stung a little.

"I already told you: stripper."

"Belle!" Admonishment rang in her voice.

"Sorry, Mum, gotta go!" I hit the button to end the call and turned the ringer off, thankful she didn't have the number to the phone Smith had given me.

Yet.

Undoubtedly she would before the month was out. I smiled weakly at Harriet. "I'm not actually a stripper."

"I knew you were joking." But something in her voice told me she suspected I must be in some type of unsavory business. Perhaps she's misread today's dress-up session. "I've arranged to have your items delivered to your flat this afternoon. Will you be there to sign for it?"

"I won't be, but my aunt can sign for a delivery."

"Perfect. Have you decided?" she asked.

"Harriet, this has been the most tiring day of my life, and it's not even one in the afternoon. Choose for me. Everything is lovely. I'm certain it will be fine."

She raised her overly plucked eyebrow dubiously. "I'll see to it then."

Something told me that was going to be the last easy decision I made for a while.

onight was a test—an important one. Not only for my associates, but for me as well. No matter how much I liked Belle, if she couldn't be docile for one evening, I couldn't justify keeping her around. I'd given her enough slack as it was. It was obvious she was going to continue to ask question and push the limits. The issue was that I enjoyed it when she did.

She appeared at the building's entrance as soon as the Veyron parked. Determined to set the right tone for the evening, I climbed out of the car, rounding it to open the door for her. I stopped with my fingers on the handle.

I hadn't approved this dress. I would never approve this dress for an appearance outside my bedroom floor.

Silky white fabric clung to her exquisite body, fluttering down her legs, draping low between her breasts. Despite the gown's off-the-shoulder sleeves, there was nothing remotely reserved about this dress. It poured over her like creamy milk, highlighting the curves of her breasts and hips. Pert nipples poked through the thin fabric, and I knew with absolute certainty she didn't have a stitch on underneath. Her hair was tucked into a small knot at the nape of her neck. Other than dark lashes and red lips, she wore no makeup. She didn't have to. She was a walking wet dream.

Belle accepted my hand as I helped her into the passenger side of the Veyron, flinching slightly as I slammed the door shut behind her.

I was too pissed for words the entire way to the Carlton. I shifted hard, punching the paddles behind the steering wheel furiously as we zipped in and out of traffic. Belle held her tongue, but I got the sense she was enjoying having provoked me more than ever before. Why on earth had I told her to continue doing so?

Because you want a reason to punish her. There was no denying that was truth as my dick stiffened in my trousers. I wanted her over my knee with her smooth alabaster ass presented for my palm. But that was a desire I needed to keep in check. Our lifestyles were incompatible in more ways than one.

My cock hadn't come to the same conclusion by the time we pulled up to the valet stand. Getting out of the car, I buttoned my suit jacket, knowing it wouldn't remotely cover my bulge if anyone was looking.

"My message told you to wear something modest," I hissed in her ear as she pushed herself out of the car.

"You should have seen the other dress I considered."

She smiled serenely at the valet, ignoring me. I passed the key fob to him, catching his sleeve before he could turn away.

"I know, I know," he said with an unimpressed groan. "Your car is worth more than my salary."

"That car is worth more than your life," I corrected him. I didn't bother to measure his response. I didn't care, so long as he knew where he stood in the pecking order.

"Somebody's concerned about the size of his dick tonight," Belle muttered as I held open the door for her.

Placing one hand on the small of her back, I guided her inside before leaning down to her ear. "That is one thing I never worry about, beautiful."

And Christ, she was as beautiful as her name advertised tonight. The dress was revealing—too revealing, given the company we were keeping this evening—but it skimmed softly down her body, rippling over her toned thighs with each step she took. Upright, the neckline was less risqué. I just had to make sure no men stood over her this evening, which meant marking her as my own. The fact that she was my assistant might have been a boundary to the rest of our party until she showed up looking like forbidden fruit.

The silky fabric felt like nothing under my palm. My hand was warm, but she stiffened the moment I made contact before relaxing into my touch. Her reaction pleased me a bit too much.

"Anything else?" she asked under her breath. "Should I only speak when spoken to?"

"If you're going to behave like a child then I suppose so."

The maître d' bent toward the back of her chair, but I stepped in front of him and pulled it out. Belle didn't speak as I greeted the others already present. She nodded and shook hands as I introduced a half dozen people to her. When I finally took my seat beside her, I reached for my napkin and came up empty-handed. Belle dangled it in the air between us. Turning I took it, temporarily mesmerized by the radiance of her smile. No one would guess that we'd spent the last twenty minutes arguing with one another or that we'd fought all morning. As I'd suspected, she knew exactly how to maneuver this situation.

For the next half hour, I made small talk with the rest of the table while Belle gossiped politely with the other escorts. A hush swept down the table as the final guests arrived. Belle's eyes flickered to mine as a few of the others stood in greeting, but I shook my head. There was no need for us to do so.

Jack Hammond paused at my seat as he made his way to the end of the table.

"Smith," he said, shaking my hand.

I raised an eyebrow at the jovial greeting. It had been four days since I last saw him. Longer than usual but hardly a record. Then I realized his attention wasn't directed at me. Hammond's smile was focused over my shoulder.

I stood, pushing my chair back so that I could block him from getting too good of a view. But Hammond merely dropped an arm around my shoulder and drew me close.

"Goddamn, that's a pretty piece of ass you've brought this evening," he whispered.

"Hammond, this is my new assistant," I said in a stiff voice.

Belle held out her hand, splaying her polished fingernails in a gesture as timeless as femininity. Hammond caught it, but instead of shaking it, he bent to kiss it. The bastard's gaze traveled down with him. Judging from the intrigued look he shot me, he'd gotten enough of a glimpse.

Fuck.

I cleared my throat, and he relinquished his hold of her. Sitting quickly, I replaced the napkin on my lap and then slung an arm over the back of her chair. Her eyes darted to the side, but she didn't question me.

Dinner arrived in courses, Hammond having a penchant for ceremony. When they served the salad, Belle's hand bumped mine as she picked up her fork. She jerked it swiftly away, but we had both felt the subtle shot like an unexpected jolt from a power outlet. We spent the whole meal speaking to everyone but each other. As my conversation died down, I began to eavesdrop on hers.

"I'm certain we've met," she said to the woman on the opposite side of the table. "If only I could place you."

Georgia Kincaid shrugged, a demure smile pinned to her face. "I'd remember you."

Demure and Georgia were mutually exclusive concepts. She knew exactly where she had met Belle, and she wasn't going to remind her. That meant it had been business, and any business involving Hammond's right-hand girl was bound to be dirty. Georgia's eyes flashed to mine, narrowing into catlike slits for a moment while Belle handed her glass to the waiter. I shifted my chair over so that my shoulder brushed against Belle's. She froze, her hand poised in midair, before she regained her composure.

Every touch between us this evening had been innocent, and yet none of them had. Each graze of our skin was accidental. Unplanned. Uncomplicated.

At least, it should have been.

I restrained myself from pushing closer to her, from making more extensive contact. I'd invited her into the lion's den, and she'd shown up looking like a piece of meat. It was my duty.

But it was a problem I was unfamiliar with. I had no doubt Hammond had fucked my assistants in the past. Hell, Georgia probably had as well. It was a nonissue unless their loyalty to me was compromised. But the thought of either of them laying a finger on Belle drove me to move even closer until we were no longer sharing unavoidable bumps of the hand or legs. Under the table I swept my knee along the side of her thigh, my eyes trained on the naked flesh of her shoulders. The goose bumps that surged over her skin enthralled me.

I stayed that way, my leg pressed to hers, and began a new conversation with Hammond regarding an investigation into his jewelry store's payroll. We spoke in a code long established between the two of us. I was so absorbed in the discussion that I nearly startled when I felt a hand squeeze my knee.

I glanced over at Belle, who shot me a pointed look.

Final warning.

Moving my leg away from her, I noticed Hammond studying us intently. All my attempts to claim her had only brought more attention to her.

"Belle, how old are you?" he asked.

"Twenty-four." Her smile was dazzling.

"About the age of my daughter." He reached over and took Georgia's hand, but instead of a quick, fatherly squeeze, he clasped it. Georgia placed her free hand over his and held it there.

"I had no idea you were related." Belle somehow managed to sound polite even though her eyes shone with dismay.

"There's not much of a resemblance," he said seriously.

I sighed, shaking my head. "Georgia is adopted."

"Oh!" Belle looked somewhat relieved, but not entirely.

"I have a large adopted family," Hammond explained. "I was raised to believe it was one's civic responsibility to help those who needed it."

"And Georgia needed it?" Belle asked, a sharp current running under her words. Her innocent expression hid it, but I hoped no one else could read her as well as I could.

"Georgia came to me when she was fifteen. Bad home life. She's worked for me ever since." Hammond tipped his wine glass slightly at the lovely brunette.

"She worked for you? But she's your daughter."

"Hammond believes in helping oneself," I interrupted, concerned at where this line of questioning might lead. "He simply gave many of us a leg up."

"Us?" Belle repeated, glancing from Georgia to me.

"At one time even Smith needed help," Hammond said good-naturedly. "Although you'd never know it now. Is he as stubborn with you as he is with me?"

"I imagine more so," she said dryly.

"Some things never change," Georgia added, her mouth coming to rest in a perfect pout.

Or rather a suggestive pout. Belle stiffened but kept the smile on her face.

"You'll have to excuse them. Those two grew up together." Hammond's words should have sounded like the equivalent of an affectionate ruffle of the hair. But, like Hammond himself, they came out twisted. Wrong. A perversion of what a normal man might mean.

I couldn't explain to Belle that Hammond was exactly that. A perversion. There had been no possibility of keeping her away from him. Some ties ran too deeply. The kind of ties that bound and gagged and suffocated more when you tried to fight them.

"Wait!" Georgia exclaimed, her hand flying to her chest. "I do know you!"

I gritted my jaw, bracing myself for whatever new move she was making.

"We have mutual friends," she continued.

"We do?" Belle countered, no longer trying to mask her disbelief.

"Alexander and Clara." The names gushed from Georgia's mouth. It was obvious that she had been waiting to reveal this all evening.

"Alexander and Clara? Um, how do you know them?" Each syllable was carefully chosen. Belle had begun to see the eggshells lining her path.

"Hammond is a jeweler," I interjected. This time when I moved my chair closer to hers, she didn't shrink away.

"I made Clara's ring," Hammond said.

"That was Alexander's mother's ring." Belle was testing him just as much as he was testing her.

"I made it for his mother. As well as Alexander's wedding ring and the one for young Edward's friend."

"Fiancé," Belle corrected him coldly.

"Of course, I go back with Alexander almost as long as I do with Smith." Georgia rested her chin on her hand. So far she'd barely shown her true colors to Belle. She'd been friendly and gracious, but underneath it all she dripped venom.

Judging from how Belle shifted in her chair, my assistant saw through her facade nearly as well as I did.

Georgia knew it, too. Now that there was no reason to hide her fangs, she struck. "You were engaged to Philip Abernathy. Such a shame. What a cad. Already engaged to that awful Pepper Lockwood."

The intake of air beside me was audible. Belle's hand flew to her stomach. "I hadn't heard that news."

"It's a rumor, of course." Georgia made quote marks in

the air. "But Father designed the ring. I expect they'll announce it in the papers any day."

A poisoned silence fell over our end of the table before Belle pushed her chair back so quickly it nearly toppled over.

"Thank you for a lovely evening," she sputtered. "Please excuse me, I'm afraid I'm rather tired."

"Not at all." Hammond's grin showed too many of his crooked teeth. "Do drop into the shop some time. I'd like to get to know you better."

Belle's face turned green, and I half expected her to vomit on him. Before I was on my feet, she had hurried out of the private dining room.

"You can retract your claws now, Georgia," I said to her coldly.

"However did you find her, Smith?" She plucked at the tines of her fork. "Such a lovely, simple creature."

"Stay away, sis." I nodded tersely to Hammond, not trusting myself to say anything else.

Belle was waiting on the curb outside the Carlton with her arm extended out to hail a cab.

I pushed my valet ticket into the attendant's hand as I passed him. "Bring it around immediately."

There was a murmur from the small line waiting for their cars, but the man jogged off to bring around the Veyron.

"I'm going home," Belle called as I came closer. "Alone."

"Fine." I caught her upper arm and dragged her away from the side of the street. "But I'm taking you."

"What about your family?" She didn't bother to hide her disgust any longer.

"You don't choose your family, Belle."

"It sounds as if you chose them."

"No, I didn't." I glared at her, daring her to press me further.

The Veyron roared to the curb, and the attendant jumped out of it. I handed him a hundred pound note as I opened her door. She got in without a fight but as I shut the door, she said in a low voice. "How can I already know you better than I knew him?"

The statement settled heavy on my chest. She didn't know me. Not really. She knew nothing of my past. Little of my work. She knew how I took my coffee, and she'd seen me naked. That shouldn't have been enough for her to feel that way.

And yet as we took off, I had the most peculiar sensation that she was right. We didn't know all the minute details of our past lives, but she already knew what buttons to push. She could already anticipate my responses. She could give as good as she took. I couldn't say that about most women.

I couldn't tell her that she could never know more than that—that she wouldn't want to.

"I've been called out of town for a few days. I'll be back this weekend." I tapped the paddle shifters, and the Veyron revved into third as we merged effortlessly onto the motorway.

Belle continued to gaze out the window, but her throat

slid as she swallowed the news. Without thinking, I shifted the car into automatic drive and reached for her hand, hoping to draw her thoughts away from the past. Her head swiveled, revealing wide eyes framed by wet lashes. She looked at our hands, loosely clasped together, and then to me. Our eyes met, and past the tears, I saw confusion overtake the sadness.

The same turmoil seethed within me. Apprehension. Anger. Denial. But most of all: need. God, I wanted to take her to bed and show her what it was like to be possessed. Kiss away the tears trickling down her face and replace her fear with mind-numbing bliss.

She drew her hand back slightly, a signal that she'd made her choice.

Denial.

It was the safest option. But it was quickly becoming the least viable one. I had my own choice to make.

I tightened my grip, crushing her delicate fingers inescapably. She had made her move. I had made mine. This time she didn't pull away. We drove in silence to her flat, my hand clenching hers possessively. There was no turning back now.

I pulled the Veyron up to the curb, wanting to turn it off and take her upstairs. My body already coveted my new possession. I wanted to strip her down, rip off her panties, and show her what it meant now that she was mine.

But tonight wasn't the time.

"I'll be back by Friday," I told her in a low voice.

"Friday," she echoed.

Abandoning the wheel, I caught her head in my hands, turning her face up to mine. The tears had evaporated, replaced by a hunger that burned so fiercely that she moaned when we made eye contact. I caressed my palm down her cheek and captured her chin so she couldn't look away.

Those eyes. That mouth. The way her body angled itself toward mine. Every inch of her needed to be fucked. My thumb brushed over her bottom lip, and her mouth opened instinctively.

So receptive.

"Can you behave while I'm gone?" I asked sternly. My balls tightened at the thought of what I would do to her if she didn't.

"Yes, Sir," she breathed, her petulant nickname for me taking on a new, and much more welcome, meaning.

I smeared her lipstick with the pad of my thumb, enjoying the way she gasped and held her breath—as if her life depended on my touch "I have to get to the jet now. Go inside. Tonight I want you to dream about me and what I'm going to do to you when I return."

Her teeth bit down on the end of my finger. I slapped the side of her cheek softly until she released it.

"Friday," she whispered it like an incantation.

"No one touches you until I do, beautiful. Not even yourself." It wasn't a promise or a date. It was an order.

Belle wriggled in her seat, but for once she didn't challenge me. I released her, pulling away and breaking all contact. She opened her mouth to speak, changed her mind, and popped the handle on her car door. She slid out of the seat gracefully, considering how low the car was to the road and how high her heels were. She'd almost exited when my hand lashed out and caught hers. She turned hopefully back to me.

"What was in your past no longer matters," I informed her in a soft voice. "Now that I'm here, no one will hurt you, Belle. I won't allow it."

And if they tried, I'd kill them.

CHAPTER NINE

"No news?" I called over the frenetic pulse of Brimstone's sound system. The club was packed, making it as hot as the hellfire that decorated the walls. I wiped beads of sweat off my forehead, remembering guiltily that it had been my idea to stick to the main level where we could easily dance.

David gave me a thumbs down as he pushed through the crowd. Edward followed behind him, a cluster of shots held high over his head.

"I just want to know before Us Weekly," Lola grumbled at my side. Since Clara had officially gone on bedrest earlier this week, we'd all spent the last few days obsessively checking our mobiles for updates on the baby. The crisis, which the doctors assured all of us was completely normal, had provided a welcome distraction from Smith's absence.

Or rather Smith in general.

My belly tightened as I thought about him. I'd expected him home today, but still no word. It was beginning to feel like my life was measured out in texts and voicemails. I grabbed a shot from Edward and downed it. Now I could pretend the warmth spreading through my core was from booze rather than the conflicting emotions tumbling through me.

"Clara rang to tell me she requires a photo of you dancing, and I quote, with a man. Don't shoot the messenger!" Edward held up his hands, but the smirk spreading over his charming face undermined the effect.

"Not bloody likely!" Lola cried, coming to my defense. "She'll have to accept one of her best friend and her sister."

Lola took a shot, slammed the glass down on the table, and tugged me out onto the dance floor. Clara's baby sister had turned out to be wildly different than I'd expected. Any occasion I'd spent with her, either Clara or their mother, Madeline, had also been present. As she began to grind against a guy on the dance floor, motioning for me to join her, I realized it took a lot less to loosen her up than the other women in her family. Five minutes ago, I'd been casually picking her brain about up and coming grassroots publicity campaigns. She'd been focused, driven, and completely brilliant with her thoughts. Then she flipped a switch and turned into a party girl.

I had to admit I found myself liking her more.

She reached out, wagging her fingers for me to come closer. I giggled, the effects of the vodka already setting in, and pressed against her. The guy dancing behind her slid his hands from Lola's waist to her hips, then they disappeared. Lola pushed me gently forward and peeled herself off of him, shaking her head in annoyance. It was too dark to see his face in the club, but the man held out his arms.

Lola laughed as she hooked an arm around my neck and we pushed our way further into the crowd. I'd had my reservations about wearing a minidress in London's fickle autumn weather, but now I was grateful I had taken the chance. I lost track of time as Lola and I danced with each other, obliging various men who wanted to join in—until they became handsy. My black dress clung to my slick skin as the DJ morphed the music from a fast, electronic rhythm to a haunting, deep pulse. It was slower—languid almost—and it vibrated through my flesh into my bones. My head fell back as I let it undulate through me.

A pair of familiar arms circled my waist, and I relaxed against Edward. The perks of having a gay best friend included, but weren't limited to, always having a dance partner and always having a dance partner who wasn't trying to get his hand up your skirt.

The record merged seamlessly into a Lana Del Ray mix and I dropped lower, circling my hips against Edward. His strong arms supported my gyrations, but the closeness of his body was only making me warmer. I pushed my hair off the back of my neck and held it in a loose bun as we continued to move to the beat.

A third hand gripped my shoulder, and my eyes flew open to find Smith glaring possessively down at me. In his suit, he stuck out from the rest of the crowd. Then again he would have stuck out anywhere. But his tailored three piece was where the professional look ended. His hair was mussed across the top matching the wild look glinting in his eyes despite the club's dim lighting.

"Excuse me, mate." Edward shoved his hand off of me.

I snapped out of my shock and darted between them just as Smith's hand clenched into a fist. Placing my palms on each of their athletic chests, I turned to Edward and mouthed, "It's cool."

His eyes narrowed, but he stepped away. He tilted his head in acquiescence to Smith and shot me a look that said I'd be hearing about this later.

Smith's hand closed over mine, and he pulled me out of the mass of squirming bodies and toward the back door. Locking my knees, I forced him to halt in his tracks.

"Come. Now."

A quiver of anticipation snaked across my skin, but I shook my head. "I need to tell my friends I'm leaving."

I had meant to tell him to fuck off. I'd planned to. Now all I could think about was following wherever he led.

"They'll figure it out." He tugged on my hand, but I yanked it away from him again.

"They'll worry." I didn't wait for any more of his orders. Pivoting around, I made my way back to our table with Smith following behind me. He paused leaving some distance between himself and my friends.

"I take it that's Smith," Edward said, distaste coating his words. He studied him for a moment then frowned. "God, that man's dick must be a heat-seeking missile."

Lola bounced up to the table, dripping with sweat. She looked from me to Edward and back again. "What's going on?"

"Have you heard the one that starts 'two alpha males enter a bar?'" I bit out.

"Sounds like a one-hander!" She wiggled her middle finger suggestively. Her gaze traveled a few feet past me. "Speaking of killing kittens..."

"Meet Belle's alpha du jour." Edward nodded toward Smith.

Lola grabbed my arm and shook it. "Why are you not having sex with him right now?"

"Because we're in public." I removed her hand gently from me and patted it. "I'm getting out of here."

"Getting off, you mean." David made a kissy face next to Edward who swatted him on the shoulder.

"Don't encourage this behavior," he warned him.

"You've been praying she'll get laid for months and now you want to cock block here," David said in exasperation. "Not cool."

Edward looked over my shoulder. "I wanted her to get laid. Not make up for all the lost time in one night."

"How do you know—"

"Honey, I might be gay, but I'm still a male."

"Then I should get going. I have plans for the rest of the night." I stuck my tongue out at him as David passed me my wallet.

Displeasure radiated from Smith as I approached. I

stopped short and crossed my arms over my chest. I wasn't going anywhere with him until he cooled off.

"You need to get out of here," he informed me.

"Maybe you need to leave," I said haughtily. He'd told me that he liked it when I provoked. Considering it annoyed me when he gave orders, I'd have no problem giving him exactly what he wanted.

A low rumble vibrated from his throat. He'd actually growled. I did my best to look unaffected as I drenched my knickers. So much for holding on to my dignity. Smith lunged forward, catching me around the waist and crushing me against him. "Come. With. Me."

The club faded away. There was only us. Only the heat scorching through me where our bodies met. Only the air he breathed. Only him. I blinked and nodded. There was no point in trying to break the spell. I didn't want him to relinquish me back to the swarming crowd. I wanted him to carry me away and choose my fate.

Smith let go, seizing my hand as he turned around and led me toward the rear entrance. As we neared the door, a bouncer moved to the side.

"Mr. Price." He tipped his head and opened the back door.

An evening breeze sang along my damp skin, instantly cooling me down. I raised my face toward the stars and inhaled the fresh air greedily.

The Veyron was parked in the back alley, guarded by another member of the Brimstone security team. He took his leave without a word.

"Come here often?" I asked, watching the man disappear into the building.

"The owner is a client." He opened my car door, my hand still locked in his tight grip.

Maybe it was the fresh air, or finally being free from the noisy, packed dance floor, but the events of the evening began to click into place. "How did you know I was here?"

"That doesn't matter." His tone was thick with warning. "I've been trying to reach you for hours."

"A phone doesn't really fit in this dress. I left it at home." I shrugged.

It got the reaction I had expected.

Smith grabbed my hips and backed me into the brick wall behind us. "Your ass doesn't fit in that dress."

"You don't like it?"

"It's not a dress. It's a bandage."

"Actually it's a bandage dress." I bucked my hips against him, brushing across his stiffening cock. "Does it make you hard when I talk back?"

In a flash, he pinned my arms above my head. His face slanted over mine, hovering dangerously close before his mouth trailed along my jaw. "I told you to behave."

His teeth nipped my earlobe.

"I did," I moaned.

His mouth moved lower until his teeth sank into my shoulder. Hard.

"I saw another man touching you," he roared. "He had his hands all over you in this pathetic strip you call a dress."

I groaned, partially because he had gotten the wrong

impression and partially because his lips were on my collarbone. "Edward? He's as gay as a maypole."

"He was touching what is mine!" Smith exploded, slamming my body against the wall with the weight of his. There was no insinuation—no subtlety—to the act. He ground lewdly against my belly, digging his cock into the soft flesh.

"Yours?" I repeated breathlessly. "I don't belong to anyone."

"That's where you're wrong, beautiful." He pulled back, and we both went still as we regarded one another. The line was in front of us. We'd tiptoed around it. We had teetered on the edge. But we hadn't crossed it. Not yet.

Smith groaned, his eyes snapping shut for a brief moment, before he leapt over it.

His mouth collided with mine, mashing against my lips so forcefully that I tasted blood. I didn't know if it was mine or his. I didn't care. I only wanted more. More of his taste. More of his tongue. More.

I was completely under his control. My lips moved in sync with his. My mouth parted for his forceful tongue. He would take me when and how we wanted, but he would take me.

"Is this what you want, beautiful?" he asked as he licked the edge of my teeth. "Do you want me in your mouth? Where else do you want me?"

Here. There. Everywhere. My synapses fired rapidly, overwhelmed by the sensations crowding through my body wherever our skin met. I moaned, squirming closer to him. There was no chance of me processing words. I could only show him what I wanted.

"You're going to have to be clearer," he murmured against my mouth. "When I take you to bed, there will be no yes or no. You will belong to me. Now tell me, are you ready to be mine?"

He drew back and waited.

I struggled to tell him what I needed to say. In the end, it was five simple words.

"Shut up and fuck me."

CHAPTER TEN

*W*e made it as far as the garage.

Smith threw the Veyron into park and was out of his seat and at my door before I'd unbuckled. I accepted his hand, my legs wobbling as I pushed out of the car. The combination of excessive speeding and lust had left me shaky.

His arm hooked around my waist. Propelling me against the car, his lips crashed into mine. He tasted like bourbon and sex. My hand tangled in his hair, holding him to me. He was intoxicating, and I needed a fix only he could give me. I'd spent so long denying him—denying myself. Now I was ready to let go and shed my inhibitions and my clothes. The window was cool against my heated skin, and my other arm clutched the frame of the car. My fingers slid over the sleek metal, and I moaned into Smith's mouth.

He captured my tongue, sucking it into his mouth until I felt the sharp edge of his teeth.

He had promised to bite.

My body fought to get closer to his. There were too many clothes. Not enough skin. Smith drew away and spun me around, pushing me until my body molded to the curves of the car.

"Let me show you why I object to this dress," he murmured into my ear as he pushed his leg between my thighs and nudged them open. "See how easy your pussy is to access?"

I tried to nod, but my cheek was smashed to the top of the car, my breath fogging across the metal.

He grabbed a fistful of my hair and wrenched my head back. "I can't hear you, beautiful."

"Yes," I gasped.

"Yes what?" He yanked harder, forcing my neck to arch uncomfortably.

A warm gush of arousal coated my sex as I whimpered, "Yes, Sir."

"Good girl." He lowered my head gently, stroking the side of my face. Then he trailed kisses down the curve of my neck. "I'm going to claim your pussy with my mouth now, and I want you to stay right here like this. Do not move."

A desperate sob escaped my lips, and he pressed his mouth against mine as his hands wrenched my skirt up to my waist. "I know you want to give your body to me. No one's ever protected you before—treasured you, have they?"

My eyes closed as I shook my head.

"But that's what you need, isn't it?" He tucked a strand of hair behind my ear while he stroked his knee along my swollen mound.

I wet my lips as my eyes opened and found his. I didn't have to say yes. He knew.

"I'm going to take care of you, beautiful," he promised. "I'm going to make you feel so fucking good."

His fingers slid under the bands of my thong and twisted. They snapped hard, stinging across my hips as he ripped away my underwear. The lace grazed across my seam and I bit my cheek to restrain from jerking away. He tossed them to the garage floor. "I've thought about tasting you since the moment we met. Open wide for me, so I can."

I gripped the car as tightly as I could, tottering on my heels as I wriggled my legs open farther. Smith's hands ran down my body as he knelt between my splayed thighs. The tip of his finger traced my seam, sending a jolt of electricity sizzling through my swollen sex.

"You're so goddamn wet for me. Ripe and ready." His low voice raked over my skin. He pushed deeper, stretching me open as he thumb circled over my engorged clit. But instead of leaning into me, his arm hooked around my hips and yanked me down, forcing my knees to bend just enough that I was squatting over him. One more quick jerk, and he'd pulled me to his mouth. His tongue lashed out, stroking along my sensitive slit.

For all intents and purposes, I was sitting on his face, clinging to a Bugatti. The realization lit a fire that crackled down my nerves, setting my body aflame. My thighs burned with the effort of staying upright, but it only heightened my awareness. Pleasure curled inside me, winding tight as Smith sucked my greedy clit. When he flicked it with his tongue, I cried out, nearly losing my balance. I crushed myself to the car as Smith caught my hips to steady me.

"I won't let you fall," he assured me, his voice thick with desire, "but you're going to let go and come on my tongue."

I groaned, shaking my head, but he paid no attention. Or he didn't care. I couldn't hold myself up much longer—couldn't handle the overwhelming sensations taking over my body. Smith nipped my clit and I fractured. The feverish strain occupying my body morphed into ecstasy as he sucked it between his teeth. My arms fell away as I plummeted, pleasure echoing across my limbs.

But I didn't hit the ground. Smith's strong arms bracketed me. His tongue anchored me. I slumped against the car, numb, but he didn't stop ravaging me with his mouth. My thighs tried to shut against his persistence, but they proved too weak. He slowed his machinations, stroking gingerly along my pulsing cunt until I felt my muscles contract.

Impossible.

There was no time to filter more through my oxygen-drenched brain before my limbs spasmed as he coaxed me to another mind-blowing orgasm.

This time when my climax subsided, my muscles betrayed me entirely. But before I could stumble, Smith swept me into his arms and pinned me to the car, cradling my body against his. I was lost for words. He'd fucked them all right out of my head.

Brushing his thumb over my lower lip, he pulled it down until my jaw fell open. "Now I want to see your sexy mouth in action."

I reached down, fumbling for his zipper, but he shook his head. Smith kept his arm around me as he led me around to the driver's side of the car. "I'm not sure what makes you more hot—me or my car?"

My mouth opened in protest, but he pressed it shut with his index finger.

"I don't care what turns you on as long as it belongs to me, beautiful." There was a click, and the door swung open. "I want your knees on my driver's seat. Show me how beautiful your cunt is when it's naked and quivering in my car."

I stumbled back, grabbing onto the doorframe as I twisted around and climbed into the bucket seat. The steady pulse between my legs grew more demanding as my skin slid over the buttery leather.

"My most priceless possession and my most expensive one," he said, his words taking on a husky tone as he pressed his palm to my sex.

I didn't clarify which was which. I should mind that he thought of me as his possession, but I couldn't bring myself to. I only wanted to be claimed by him. Owned over and over. My mind had stopped processing anything outside of him, his touch, and wanting to please him.

Behind me, I heard the swish of a zipper. Angling my neck, I watched as he withdrew his cock. I'd seen it before but not like this. It jetted from his groin, majestically flanked by a heavy set of balls. I'd known he was endowed, but seeing it now, fully erect, thrilled—and terrified—me.

"No need to be scared." Smith seemed to sense what I was thinking. "I won't take you until you're ready."

I pressed my lips shyly to my shoulder. It wasn't like he was my first. Far from it. But it was clear he was in a different league than my past lovers. I wasn't even sure he was playing the same game.

"Don't hide your mouth," he ordered. "I want to see it in action. I told you I wasn't sure if you were fucking me or my Bugatti. Show me what that sweet mouth can do to my car."

Maybe it was because I was on display. Maybe the two orgasms he'd already given me had fried my brain. Maybe I'd held out for so long that I no longer knew the difference between what I wanted and what he wanted. But instinct took over. I moved farther onto the seat, crawling closer to the steering wheel, until my tongue touched the soft leather. It tasted expensive, like luxury and sin. Shifting my eyes over so that he was in my sight, I dragged my tongue along the circumference. The warm natural musk of the leather mingled with faint traces of salt from Smith's hand. Angling my head, I ran it over the stitched interior of the wheel, savoring each bump.

Out of the corner of my eye, I saw Smith's hand close tightly over his shaft. I moaned as he began to stroke himself off. I was torn between wishing it was my hand and wanting to continue my performance for him.

Creeping up the steering wheel, I brought my lips to the dashboard, taking time to kiss each button.

"That's it, beautiful. Show me how dirty you are." The hand on my ass pressed hard, increasing the pulsating rhythm of my clit from a faint tick to a drum solo. His reaction spurred me on and I dropped lower, lifting my ass into the air as I pressed my mouth to the center console. The shiny chrome left a metallic taste on my tongue. The car—like us—was the perfect union of opposites, both luxuriously rich and undeniably modern at the same time. I drew my tongue up the metal of the gear shifter, circling the tip of it around the knob before popping my lips over it and swallowing it deep.

Smith released a groan behind me. "I can't wait any longer, but I'll be gentle."

The warm crest of his cock nudged against my entrance, and I bit down onto the leather knob in anticipation. He waited a moment, allowing me to adjust—or, at least, prepare myself. Then he began to push inside. My folds, still swollen with blood, ached as they stretched to accommodate his considerable girth. God, his shaft was impossibly thick. I drew back, abandoning my vulgar exhibition so that I could catch my breath as he buried himself deep inside of me.

This is what I'd been fighting. Pleasure. Indescribable pleasure.

"I'm going to fuck you hard, Belle," he growled.

My breath caught and I waited. When he didn't begin, I pushed my hips back, trying to take his dick deeper.

"Not yet." He petted my back as he continued with shallow, leisurely pumps. He was taking his time with me even though I kept trying to race forward ahead of him. When suddenly he withdrew, he left a hollow craving in his wake. "I want to see you when I come."

I manoeuvred onto my back as he pulled a condom from his pocket. He ripped open the foil with his teeth, stroking himself as he pushed the condom over his tip and rolled it down. "If you aren't on birth control, you will be by next week." Another command. "I want to see my cum dripping from that pretty pink pussy."

I nodded, my teeth sinking into my lip as I tried to resist the urge to jump him. I considered telling him I was on birth control, but I couldn't wait any longer to have him back inside me. Smith was running things tonight. I could only imagine what would happen if I tried to take the reins. When he'd finished, he extended a hand. I placed mine in his tentatively, and he pulled me to my feet. But as soon as my shoes touched the floor, he scooped me up, holding me against the car and over his shaft.

"When you're ready, beautiful."

My hips immediately dropped lower, taking him to the root. I might be sore in the morning, but for the moment, I was going to savor all eight delicious inches of him. Smith didn't miss a beat. Wrapping his arms around me, he cupped my ass and carried me to the front of the Veyron. Laying me gently over the bonnet so as not to break physical contact, he flashed me a wicked grin. "I just lived out one of my adolescent fantasies."

"Me, too." I hooked my thumbs over the straps of my dress and shoved it down to expose my breasts. My nipples beaded in the cool air. "Let's see what we can do about the rest of them."

His mouth closed over the pert furl before I'd finished the thought. Squeezing my breast, he retreated for a second before plunging his mouth over the other nipple. God, I hoped he had good insurance, because there was going to be a dent from where he'd fucked me so relentlessly into the hood. My back arced off the car and he seized me, using my body as leverage to pound deeper. Harder.

He didn't give me an orgasm, he captured it. Claiming my pleasure as if it was his own, and this time as I splintered around him, there was no light. No sound. No fireworks. He'd wrecked me entirely, and I came with a scream that shattered the air surrounding us. Smith's face tensed, his jaw contracting, as his arm snaked up and held my neck.

"Look at me," he ordered, his pace never faltering as he shifted me in his arms.

I tried to open my eyes, but they no longer seemed to work. My head felt heavy, my brain drenched with too much oxygen. When it lolled to the side, he forced it back up.

"Look at me." This time an angry edge glinted from the command. His fingers fastened around the back of my neck and my eyes flew open as the pressure increased. "This is it, beautiful. I'm about to come, and when I do, this pussy will belong to me. You will belong to me. You can still say no. Tell me to go fuck myself if you want. This is your only chance."

His mouth smothered mine for a brief, heated instant.

"Once I come, there's no turning back for either of us," he warned, his green eyes sure and steady. They didn't waver even as he thrust tirelessly. "Choose now and never look back."

Even if I could think, I didn't have to. I'd made my decision the moment he held my hand in this car. I might have made it the first time I saw him.

I wound my fingers in his hair and brought his mouth to mine, sealing my choice with a kiss, as he took what was his.

CHAPTER ELEVEN

*S*he felt good in my arms.

I'd fucked women recently, but putting your dick in an available slot wasn't complicated. This was complicated. This was different.

I'd wanted her from the moment I saw her, but I hadn't anticipated what would happen when I finally had her. The last few days away from her had been a blur, stuck in Paris, conducting a deposition with a hard-on. I guessed there were worse places to have a perpetual erection than France.

"You made me crazy when I couldn't reach you earlier." She was in need of a far less gentle reprimand, but this time I'd let it slide with a tongue-lashing. My expectations, while firm, were new to her.

"I didn't know when you were coming back."

She tucked her head under my chin, close enough that I caught the scent of lilac in her blonde locks.

"You didn't have your phone." If I stuck to the facts, I could be stern. It was best to set a boundary for myself until personal limits could be discussed.

"No pockets," she mumbled dreamily, cuddling closer to my chest as I pushed the button for the lift.

"Planning on going to bed?" I asked dryly.

She stifled a yawn, shaking her head.

I backed into the lift, hitting the second floor button with my elbow. Tilting her chin up with my little finger, I continued, "If you'd had your phone, I could have reached you earlier. I could have been fucking you for hours. But you didn't have it, did you?"

"No," she whispered.

"You were unavailable at my convenience. Now I'm going to be forced to keep you awake for hours."

Her blue eyes rounded as she grew more alert.

"I haven't had my fill of you yet. Neither of us are sleeping until I do."

"You're saying I won't go to sleep until you're satisfied?"

"No, beautiful," I corrected her gently. "I'm saying neither of us are going to sleep until we're satisfied. I spent the last few days plotting what I was going to do to you. We're just getting started."

I didn't offer her another option. I'd given her a choice in the garage. Hell, I had been offering her outs since her interview. She'd given herself to me. That would be the last decision she made this evening.

"I understand." Her lips split into a tentative smile.

I raised my eyebrow. "Do you?"

She lifted her soft fingers to my cheek, hesitating until I shifted my face against her palm. Holding her hand there, she met my gaze. I saw questions in her eyes. There was fear and confusion, but also hunger. "Yes, Sir."

Her whispered response told me what I needed to know. She understood, on some level, what she was getting into. Although I would need to take it slowly with her.

But for now, I would take her to bed.

SUNLIGHT CREPT over her peaceful face. Her blonde hair fanned out, haloing her head, and making her look even more the part of an angel. She shifted in her sleep, curling a hand under her cheek.

What was she doing to me?

Some broken things could never be fixed. I knew that. I'd witnessed it over and over again. I had watched as the cracks of time and heartbreak destroyed people. It was too much of a burden to bear—to try to pick up the pieces and heal. I'd always believed it was safer to shield your wounds and arm yourself against future attacks.

But last night I had laid awake and counted her breaths, catalogued each of her movements. The serenity she found in her sleep radiated from her. I could almost feel it seeping through my skin.

I told myself that sleeping next to her left me unguarded. Vulnerable. But the truth was that I didn't want to close my eyes.

Belle's lips began to move although she was still asleep. I propped myself up on my elbow, torn between waking her and hoping she would settle back to sleep. Instead she flipped onto her back, her body stiffening. Tossing her head against the pillow, a small cry escaped her lips.

The anguish of that sound wrapped itself around my heart and squeezed. She was mine to protect, even in dreams.

Laying a hand against the side of her face, I caressed her skin, calling her away from the nightmare and back to me. Her eyes fluttered open, filled with terror. They darted over to me, fear turning into confusion.

"I've got you, beautiful."

Relief washed over her gorgeous face at the sound of my voice. The pressure in my chest relented, and I leaned over her, pressing a kiss to her forehead. She relaxed against the pillow, making no move to pull the covers over her body or draw away from me.

Her reaction felt dangerously like trust.

"Are you watching me sleep, creep?" she murmured sleepily.

"You were having a nightmare." My protective impulse urged me to take her in my arms and lock her away. Instead I brushed hair from her face. "Does that happen often?"

"Isn't one bad dream enough?" She rolled toward me, pushing her face against my palm.

She was avoiding the question...but why?

I had no right to push it further. Instead I slid an arm

under her torso and drew her close. She curled into a ball, and we fell into a dark, dreamless sleep together.

CHAPTER TWELVE

She was gone when I awoke. A mixture of anger and panic rose in my chest, but I pushed it away. There was no reason to believe she had left—unless she'd finally figured out that she'd wandered into the wolf's den. Unlocking my mobile, I checked the garage security cam. Her car was still parked there. I fell back against my pillow.

Belle Stuart was going to be a handful.

When she was naked and writhing for it, she'd do anything I asked. That much I knew. The rest of the time she was a wild card.

If only I was attracted to more predictable women.

Swinging my feet over the side of the bed, I spotted her dress wadded on the floor. That made me grin. She obviously hadn't gone far. I tossed on a pair of boxer briefs and went on the hunt. When I found her, I'd show her what she missed by crawling out of bed early.

A quick search of the kitchen and living room yielded

nothing. She hadn't gone to the bedroom I showed her. I stopped and stared at the door across from hers.

There was no reason to check in there. I'd warned her about the consequences.

I finally found her gliding along the bottom of my pool. Stark fucking naked.

I watched her move effortlessly, water rippling across her curves and her blonde hair billowing behind her. It wasn't a terrible way to spend a Saturday morning.

When she pushed her upper body up and over the side, she shot me a wicked grin. I held out a towel.

"I'm not quite done here. Why don't you join me?" She pushed onto her back, allowing her perfect tits to float to the surface. It was an enticing offer.

"I don't swim," I called out.

She giggled. "Then why do you have a pool?"

"So pretty girls will get naked and go for a dip." I squatted closer to the edge so I could get a better view of the rest of her.

"Why don't you come in and show me what you do to those girls?" she suggested, batting her eyelashes.

"Why don't you come out?" I countered.

"Because I'm the one that's naked." She dove back under the water, giving me a view of her ass.

It was almost enough to convince me to jump in. Instead I stood my ground. When her head broke through the glassy surface of the water, I crooked my finger and beckoned her back to me. "I need room to achieve all the ways I'm going to fuck you."

Her arms swept over the surface. "There's plenty of room here."

Fine. If that was how she wanted to play it. I turned and headed toward the door, dropping my shorts on the way out.

Belle was in the hall before the lift arrived. Water trailed over her body and her hair snaked down her neck, dripping wet. Her lips were purple, but she showed no other signs of being cold. She sashayed past me as the lift doors opened. "Going up?"

"I was thinking about going down." Prowling in, I pounced on her, pushing her arms over her head. Her wet body sent droplets of water cascading down the mirrored surface. "Turn around, beautiful."

She obliged, bending so that her ass became an unmistakable target. Christ, the things I was going to do to her. But for now I wanted to try something else. I knew it would elicit a reaction.

I stroked my palm over her perfectly round rear and then smacked it hard enough to leave the imprint of my hand. Five unmistakable red lines on her fair skin.

Belle yelped, but she didn't pull away or turn around. She kept herself ready for whatever I decided to do to her next.

"I warned you to get out of the pool," I said in a husky voice, stroking the mark I'd left on her ass cheek.

"You asked me to," she purred.

"Never mistake my commands for a request, beautiful. Or there will be consequences."

"What do you mean by—" Her question was cut short by a stinging slap to the other side. "Oh!"

"Starting to get the picture?" I asked in a rough voice. "I wanted to fuck you, and you played coy. This is what happens when you don't listen."

She curled up on the balls of her feet. I couldn't tell if she was bracing for the next blow or hoping for it. I also didn't care.

"Your body has been responding to me since the moment we met, begging me to tame it." Hooking an arm around her, I wrenched her to me and pressed my cock against her stinging backside. "Do you want to be tamed?"

She mumbled something, her ability to speak reduced to unintelligible whimpers. I thrust my arm up her body and wrapped my hand around her neck. "Do you want to be tamed?"

"Yes, Sir."

"Very good," I murmured my approval in her ear as I pushed my knee against her bare sex. The moisture I felt there had nothing to do with the pool. "Did I make you wet when I spanked you?"

She bobbed her head as best she could with my fingers clenching her neck.

"I'll teach you how to please me, beautiful, but for now, if you ask nicely, I'll fuck you." I pushed my dick harder into the fleshy mound of her rear.

"Please fuck me," she choked out.

I waited. She knew what I wanted without me having to

remind her. But she said nothing. Disappointing. I'd counted on her instinct to submit to me to kick in.

I felt the slide of her throat as she swallowed, and then she whispered, "Please fuck me, Sir."

That was the missing piece. I wanted her to beg for it, and someday she would. For now a polite entreaty would do the trick. Reaching down, I grasped my cock in my free hand, guiding it to her sopping slit. "I don't have a rubber."

"Don't care," she gasped, widening her stance to give me better access.

The warm head of my cock skimmed along her slit as I coated myself with her arousal. "I received your medical report in the profile I ran on you. Clean and still on birth control despite your claims that you had sworn off men. If you have an objection to continuing without condoms, I would state it now."

When she remained silent, I continued, "Why stay on the pill? Was it because you wanted to fuck me the first time we met?"

She sucked in a breath, unable to answer me. She had wanted me the first time we'd met. She'd told herself she wouldn't let her guard down, but she hadn't stopped taking her pills. She'd known all along that we would wind up here. It was inevitable. That a man like me could never be completely denied.

"I need to see this," I groaned and released my hold on her. With both hands, I spread her cheeks open and watched as the tip of my dick breached her perfect cunt. The pink tissue stretched over it as I sank inside her. I pulled out slowly, marveling at how her sex rippled over my shaft. "I could do this all day. I love watching your greedy pussy take my cock."

"Please," she cried as I continued my slow assault.

My fingers slid to her hips as I rammed into her with quick, deep strokes. "I want to see my cum dripping from inside you."

"Oh god," she called in a strangled voice. "Fill me with it!"

It was a request I was more than happy to oblige. As the first hot spurt of my seed lashed inside her, she came. She tightened over me, her body beginning to shake from the force of her climax. The warm constriction of her pussy milked more, squeezing jet after jet and draining me entirely.

We collapsed together against the wall of the lift, my dick still pulsing within her.

"Don't move," I ordered. Withdrawing slowly, I watched as cream dripped from her quivering cunt. "You're so lovely with my cum leaking from you."

Belle didn't move or speak. She simply stayed smashed against the wall until I drew her away from it on wobbly legs.

"Can you feel it?" I asked.

I wanted her to tell me that she loved it—that she was every bit as filthy and lewd as I'd hoped she would be. She nodded, a numb expression frozen on her face.

"It's hot," she whispered.

"Touch it."

She slid a trembling hand down, parting her folds with her fingers.

"That's it, beautiful," I coaxed, placing my hand over hers and smearing the thick liquid across her swollen sex.

Her head fell back as I helped her caress her overwhelmed pussy.

"I want to watch you come again," I growled, adding pressure to her hand.

She bit her lip as her hips began to buck against our fingers.

"Let go!" I demanded.

A guttural cry ripped from her chest as she exploded. When the tremors started to fade, she fell silent, her mouth still opened in a perfect O. Angling down, I took a kiss and then another until I felt myself begin to stiffen again.

"Are you ready for me to show you now?" I asked again. "Are you ready to be tamed and at my mercy? I assure you that you'll enjoy every moment."

She brushed her mouth against mine, then bit into my lower lip, tugging it gently between her teeth. "I'm ready to please you."

I crushed myself against her as I felt for the control panel. I didn't care where the lift took us.

I was only ready to begin.

BELLE CRAWLED across the bed and dropped onto the mussed-up sheets. Before last night, it had been a long time since I took a woman to my bed. I'd preferred hotels simply for the sake of discouraging any unwanted attachments. Belle looked like she belonged here, as though she already owned the place. That should bother me more than it did.

Crossing to my closet, I opened a small box that had been left undisturbed for years. I knew exactly what I needed from it.

I returned to the bedroom, holding it in my hand. She raised a curious eyebrow when she saw the long red feather attached to a leather wrapped wand. I'd always appreciated the juxtaposition. With one end I could provide a woman's flesh with the faintest hint of pleasure, with the other I could turn her backside red. I could only hope Belle would appreciate both sides it had to offer.

"Roll over on your belly," I instructed as I took a seat on the edge of the bed. I grabbed a pillow and wedged it under her head. She watched me as I caressed the silky plume with my fingers. "Do you understand what I mean when I say submission?"

"I have an idea," she said dryly.

"You've been submitting to me since last night," I explained. "What went through your mind when I told you to bend over or when I instructed you to fuck my car?"

"I wanted to please you," she whispered. Her breathing came in short, shallow pants now. She wanted it as much as I wanted to give it to her.

"Submission is about control. My control over your

body. I enjoy possessing you nearly as much as I enjoy giving you pleasure. Have I given you pleasure?"

She nodded, the cheek pressed against the downy pillow growing pink.

"Now for some people it's about pain," I explained, smacking the leather end against my hand.

"Is that what it's about for you?" There was fear in her voice now.

I brushed a reassuring finger down her cheek. "For me, it's about pleasure. There is a fine line that exists between the two. When I spanked you in the elevator, it made you wet. Why?"

"It excited me." The fear had been replaced by embarrassment, and she hid her face.

"Don't do that," I ordered. "Look at me. I don't want to hurt you. I want to make you feel alive. You were excited because of how it made you feel."

"Free," she said.

"And owned at the same time. When people say opposites attract, I think they're really talking about sex. When you give control over to someone else, it allows you a freedom to experience total bliss. If I strike you with this end, it will sting. The other end will soothe. By combining the two opposites, the sensations overcome you. They liberate you so that all your body can understand is pleasure." I drew the feather along the curve of her spine, watching as her body tensed from the sensation. "Last night I warned you that once I took you, I would claim all of you. Do you still consent to giving yourself—your body, your power—over to me?"

For the moment I would continue to ask until I was positive I had her trained.

She licked her lips before replying softly. "Yes."

"Taming you isn't about changing you. It's about teaching your body to restrain itself until I command it otherwise. Only I can free you, and you can only be freed by allowing me that control." The tip of the feather tickled across her still glowing backside. "Right now you want to respond to this. Push it away or beg for more. I decide when it stops, just as I decide when there will be more."

I shifted farther onto the bed until I was kneeling beside her. "Get up on all fours."

She pushed up on her hands and knees as I stroked her back with my hand.

"I haven't told you how perfect your body is–smooth and soft. I pictured what you looked like naked the first time I saw you, but my imagination failed me. The reality is so much sweeter." I took the feather and placed it against her bare shoulder. "You'll feel this moving over you, but you aren't to budge. Can you do that? Simply respond 'yes, sir' when I ask a question, unless you want me to stop."

"Yes, Sir," she murmured. Her hips wriggled a little as she spoke, but I stopped them with a quick smack.

"Don't move. I'm training you now, showing you how to be tame so that you can please me. That's what you wish to do, right?"

"Yes, Sir," she answered more quickly.

Trailing the feather along her shoulders and up the back of her neck, I watched for a sign of movement. When she stayed still, I continued, drawing it lower until it caressed between her shoulder blades. I ran it down the curve of her spine, pleased to see she could control herself.

"I want you to open your legs for me." I moved the feather lower until it brushed her ass. Belle pushed her knees to the side. "Wider."

Her sex was swollen from our recent lovemaking, still engorged with desire. I placed the plume against it, running it quickly back and forth until I was positive she could feel the delicate fibers through the sensations crowding through her body. Belle's thighs began to shake, but she held herself motionless.

"Right now, you want more. I decide when you'll have it. I decide when you'll orgasm. Do you want to come now?" I asked, continuing my gentle assault of her pussy.

"Yes, Sir," she moaned. I could hear the strain in her voice.

"Not yet. There's so many things I want to show you," I told her in a soothing voice. "How good it will feel to crawl to me and ask for my cock. How well I'll treat you when your body obeys me. Sometimes though, I'll want to take you to the edge. Right now, it must feel like torture, having this soft feather whispering promises on your skin, but if I do this"—I flipped it over in my palm and smacked the leather end across her folds—"it makes you want it even more."

I continued to do this, brushing the soft tip over her

fevered flesh and then slapping the other end roughly until her mound had plumped even more. A trickle of arousal seeped through her seam, but she remained in place.

"You're learning your lesson well. I am very pleased with you." Bending down, I traced my tongue along her wet slit. I could feel her fighting to remain still, and I pulled back. "I wanted a taste, beautiful. I know it's hard. I don't expect you to learn it all at once."

Dropping the feather tickler on the bed, I scooped her up and turned her into me. Her legs spread, but she stopped herself before she slid onto my cock.

"Is this what you want?" I asked, pushing my shaft toward her aching entrance.

"Yes, Sir," she breathed.

"Then get on me, beautiful. I want to watch you ride my cock."

She lowered herself slowly, impaling her body on my shaft. I rocked into her until I was buried so deeply that she froze in my arms.

"Are you sore?"

She nodded.

"Then let's go slow and make it last." I cradled her back as she leaned away from me and began to circle her hips. "But you should know, I'm not nearly finished with you."

"Promise?" she whimpered as her breathing sped up.

"Yes," I reassured her, rolling my groin against her. "Now fuck me, baby. I want to hear you scream."

CHAPTER THIRTEEN

a change of scenery and clothing seemed the best way to start Monday morning. I dropped a note onto Smith's nightstand telling him to make his own coffee, and I'd see him at his office at eight. Then I headed across town, thankful that I was getting a head start before the streets turned into parking lots filled with morning traffic.

It took me all of two seconds to pluck the tailored black dress that Smith had seen me try on at Harrods from my closet. A sentimental gesture, perhaps. But then again, if my experience with men had taught me anything, it was that he probably wouldn't even notice.

Then again, Smith wasn't most men.

I had time for a quick shower but little time for additional primping. Thankfully, this weekend's nonstop cardio session seemed to have given me a permanent after-sex glow. A coat of mascara and a swipe of nude lipstick and I was all but ready for the day.

Coming out of the bedroom, I jumped, temporarily surprised to see Jane waiting for me in the kitchen. Her unstyled platinum hair stuck up even more than usual. That and the loose fuchsia kimono she wore belied that she'd just gotten up. She smiled at me as she took a kettle off the hob and poured water into two waiting cups.

"You look refreshed," Jane said, passing me a warm cup of tea.

I stirred in some sugar and milk, studiously avoiding her eyes, and shrugged. "I didn't have to work much."

"Apparently you didn't have to sleep either," she said in a knowing voice. There was a point hidden under that statement. I was expected to spill as to my whereabouts for the past few days.

But what had happened between Smith and me was too new for me to share. It might have meant nothing. Just a case of two consenting adults finally giving in to their more carnal natures. Still, I'd never been with anyone like that. Raw. Unfiltered. Up for anything he suggested. It had been like tuning into a private frequency. I knew what he wanted from me and I did it. No questions asked.

I sipped my tea slowly to avoid burning my tongue and considered how I felt about all of it.

"You're overthinking things," Jane informed me, breaking through the wall of thoughts I'd constructed in a matter of seconds.

My eyes flickered to hers. I had no doubt that Jane

would think nothing of my sexual escapades. I'd been treated to the dulcet sounds of some of hers over the last few months. She could help me understand how to feel about the shifting dynamic between him and me.

"Maybe I am," I admitted. This weekend was still ours. It belonged to Smith and me. I didn't want to share him, not even the memories he'd given me. It was a possessive streak I didn't realize I had.

I abandoned the cup and leaned over to kiss her on the cheek. "Why are you up so early anyway? I've never seen you out of bed before ten."

"My flatmate finally came home. I thought I'd better say hello before she disappeared again." Jane pursed her lips. She'd checked me, but I wasn't about to give up my cards.

"Did you worry?" I asked apologetically. That hadn't been my intention.

"Not at all. I received your text." She waved off my concern before turning a piercing stare on me. "So you aren't going to give me any of the juicy details, huh?"

A sly smile crept over my face. I couldn't hold it back.

Jane merely laughed, winking as if I'd just given her all the dirt. "I think that's detail enough."

THERE WERE terms for what I'd done with Smith. Ones I'd only read about in books. None of my past lovers had a penchant for dominance, which might have been why I never suspected I would be so open to it. Now I felt myself hungering for his hands on my body in ways no man had ever touched me. The slaps. The fingers around my neck. The desire to hold myself on edge and be restrained. It was all new to me, and I found myself wondering what it said about me. Part of me worried that it was seriously fucked up to crave his control, but the stronger half of me didn't care.

When I finally arrived, breathless, at work. I waltzed past Doris and went straight to Smith. He'd said I belonged to him now and I was eager to be back in his possession.

If I'd expected an affectionate greeting when I reached the office, I would have been disappointed. But because I was still growing accustomed to Smith's mercurial moods I'd prepared myself. Still his cold reception hurt.

"You weren't there when I woke up." He didn't bother to look up at me. His tone was so cold that I half expected ice crystals to form in the air.

But they only fired me up. I'd given my body to him but not every waking moment of my life. Perhaps allowing him so much authority over me in bed had given him the wrong idea about where we stood. No matter how much I'd enjoyed our weekend, I was still the same girl he'd hired a couple of weeks ago. Mostly. "I left a note. I needed to go home and change."

Smith continued tapping a message into his mobile. He frowned slightly but said nothing more to me.

Was he really that pissed off to wake up alone? "I'm not sure what I did wrong. I needed to change. I was under the impression that clothing-optional weekends ended before

Monday morning, but maybe you need to send an office memo."

His lips twitched but he didn't smile. A few moments later, he dropped his phone on the desk and finally shifted his focus to me. "I'll see that a few items are delivered to my house."

Sheesh, down boy. How had he managed to go from dismissive to giving me a dresser drawer so quickly? It was enough to drive a girl to drink.

"I don't think that's necessary. I have my own place"

"On the contrary." Smith leaned back in his chair and steepled his fingers. "You have a room at my house that you may have occasion to use. You should have some things there. It's unnecessary for you to drive halfway across London to pick up fresh clothes."

His purely pragmatic response left a funny taste in my mouth. I crossed my arms over my chest and glared at him. "Would you prefer if I use that room?"

"Clearly, I prefer you naked in my bed. But since you clearly want to establish boundaries, I merely pointed out a practical solution where both our needs can be met." Smith grabbed a stack of folders and stood. With one hand, he buttoned his suit jacket before he strode out of the door of his office.

I could hear him instructing Doris on what to do with the files, but I didn't care. Maybe I was being just as hot and cold as he was. But he had to see how ridiculous it was to expect a woman to go to work in the dress she'd been clubbing in the Friday before.

"There's also the issue," he continued as he reappeared in the doorframe, "that occasionally we might want to go somewhere that requires you be dressed on these, what did you call them? Clothing-optional weekends. But if you'd prefer to go all the way home with no knickers, so be it." He paused, mid-stride and took my hand. "And since I didn't get to say it this morning. Good morning, beautiful."

He pressed his lips to my knuckles, trying to charm his way out of this discussion. That was not about to happen. Smith needed to understand that regardless of how much he paid me, he couldn't expect to cage me entirely and that there were certain things I wouldn't budge on.

"I tend to always wear knickers in public," I said, not bothering to hide the caustic note in my voice.

"Not around me." He sank back into his seat, a devilish grin carving over his face. "I want your pussy bare, and if I find anything covering it, I'll just rip it off."

"I hope your clothing allowance will cover new under-garments." I refused to play into his game. At least, I wanted to believe I could refuse. But somehow I found I'd taken a few steps closer to him.

So much for willpower.

"It doesn't seem like you'll need many." His index finger rested thoughtfully over his lips.

Fire burned in my core. All he had to do was look at me and I was ready. It was going to be hard to stand my ground on any issues if his mere presence turned me into a puddle of arousal.

Smith had been in control since the moment he showed

up at Brimstone. Maybe he needed a taste of his own medicine.

"But when you aren't around," I whimpered, prowling closer to him, "I'm not certain I'll be able to control myself."

Smith raised one eyebrow as I leaned down on his desk, giving him a full view of my rack.

"I'd be disappointed in you if you couldn't," he responded in a serene tone, but I caught a blood vessel twitching in the side of his neck.

"What would happen if I didn't? If I lost control?" I sauntered around the desk and pushed myself up on its top. Crossing my legs, I gave him my most dazzling smile.

"I'd advise you to never let that happen." His hands dropped to the arms of his chair, and he clutched them, angling his upper body closer to me. The space between us was growing smaller by the second. "Or I would punish you."

"Punish?" I repeated, more than a little shocked to hear such an archaic term from his lips despite our foreplay over the weekend. "Would you spank me again?"

"For starters. Then I'd make you suck my cock until you were so wet, you were begging for it to be inside you. But you know what happens to bad girls, beautiful."

"Enlighten me." I drew the words out, allowing them to linger on my tongue far longer than necessary.

"When you disobey me, I can't give you what you want." He gripped the thick bulge in his trousers, stroking down the hard length of his cock for emphasis. "I can't give you this."

I wasn't about to give in so easily, even though the thought of him denying me pleasure set my heart racing. "Good thing I have a battery-operated boyfriend."

"That would be a very naughty thing to do. And you wouldn't need this then, would you?" he prompted as he unfastened his belt. "Except we both know that you can play with all the toys you want, and they'll never make you come like I will. Do you remember what it was like? How you screamed?"

My ass squirmed higher on the desk. I tried to make it look purposeful, but the truth was that I was losing my control of this situation and I was losing it quickly. There was only one thing for it.

Gripping the edge of the desk with my palms, I pushed myself off and immediately dropped to my knees. Scooting between his legs, I stroked the back of my hand along his hot length.

There was one sure-fire way to regain the upper hand over a man. My fingers deftly unbuttoned his fly, but before I could pull down his zipper, the phone on his desk rang. Smith's hand shot out and caught my wrist as his other picked up the receiver.

I leaned down and pressed my mouth to the bulge in his pants, but he moved his chair away. With a flick of his chin, he mouthed, "Get up."

I yanked my hand free and continued to work on his

pants, but he stood, nearly knocking me over in the process.

"No, I'm available to discuss the clause now. We all need this merger to go through as smoothly as possible," he said into the phone as he took a step away from me.

The message was loud and clear. My advances were unwanted. I scrambled to my feet, embarrassment flushing across my cheeks as I tugged down my skirt. Smith leaned over and scribbled something on a piece of paper.

At least if he was going to be a dick, he was going to explain himself. But when he handed me the note, there was only one word scribbled on it.

Coffee.

Motherfucker. That was the note I wanted to pass back to him. Instead I crumpled up the piece of paper and marched out of his office, slamming the door behind me.

BY THE TIME I'd gotten through the line at the coffee shop on the corner, I'd considered a hundred different ways to murder him. Poisoning his espresso seemed the easiest and most poetic, but it was definitely the fastest way to get caught. Although I thought a police officer might let me off when he heard my reasoning.

Smith had refused my blowjob.

That was obviously grounds for some type of extreme reaction.

Stopping at the corner newsstand, I grabbed a copy of

Trend magazine and began to page through it. If I wasn't going to poison him, I was going to make damn sure that his coffee was cold before it hit his lips.

Revenge was best served cold, right?

An article on the perfect little black dress caught my eye and I flipped to it. The pages were stuck together, changing the article headline to "Bless."

I smiled at the thought. Any girl would agree that the right black dress was definitely a blessing.

Meanwhile, I ignored the shrill ring of my text notification at first but finally dug my phone out of my purse when it sounded for the second time. But there were no messages. Wrong phone. Digging my personal mobile out of the bottom of my purse, I nearly dropped it when I saw the note from Edward.

EDWARD: We have contractions! Get to the hospital.

I turned, stuffing the magazine into my purse and nearly spilling the coffee in the process.

"Miss! Miss!" The newsstand's owner gestured wildly to my purse.

"Oh, here!" I passed him the coffee and dug out a five-pound note. Tossing it to him, I took off down the street before he could hand me the change.

I was nearly to the carpark when my mobile began to ring with an incoming call. It took me a moment to realize it wasn't the one in my hand. I pulled my work mobile out. Smith's name flashed across the screen. I took one look at it and hit decline.

Then I turned it off altogether.

CHAPTER FOURTEEN

*N*orris, Alexander's personal security guard and oldest friend, met me in the parking garage, ushering me past the swarms of well-wishers and paparazzi that had shown up for the blessed event. As far as I knew, only three people were on the guest list. Me, Edward, and Alexander.

And the baby, of course.

All the frustration and embarrassment I'd felt when I left Smith's office had vanished, leaving only excitement that I was about to meet my new, if unofficial, niece. Half of the Royal Protective Services were parked at various entrances to St. Mary's. I could hardly blame Alexander after the year he'd had. But despite the massive available security, he was a mess when he met me at the door.

"How is she doing?" I tried to peek around him, but Alexander caught my arm.

"She's having a rough time. I finally convinced her to have some pain medication."

I squeezed his shoulder in support. "You should be in there. Edward and I will wait out here."

"Actually, she's pretty put out with me at the moment."

"So you want me to go in and remind her that you hung the moon?" I guessed.

He smirked, but the grin quickly fell from his handsome face. "She didn't take my joke about being her lord and master all that well five minutes ago."

"She must be in a lot of pain." I didn't bother to remind him that he had gotten her into this mess in the first place.

"Look, she coped with this pregnancy for far too long without my support. I'm going back in there in ten minutes whether she wants me to or not."

"I'm fairly certain that as the ruling King of England, you can go anywhere you want."

"I didn't think she'd like it if I reminded her of that either."

"Give me a few minutes." I ducked inside before he could keep me there any longer. Alexander had become the center of Clara's world, but she was the center of his universe. I didn't always appreciate feeling like I was in the middle of that, but I also couldn't deny that he made her happy. No matter how frustrated she was with him, there was no way she was this without him at her side.

"Thank God. The testosterone level in the room was beginning to make me ill," Clara announced when I entered. She held her hand out to me just as the monitor at her bedside spiked. Clara let out a strangled cry, her hand still extended, and her other clutching her swollen belly.

I rushed to her side and took her outstretched hand, wondering if the contraction was as painful as the death grip she had on my fingers. "Breathe."

She shot me a warning look.

"Or don't," I said flatly. "But I don't think not doing it will help."

Clara exhaled forcefully and dropped back against the bed.

"I think you broke some of my fingers," I informed her, trying to wiggle feeling back into them.

"Sorry," she said sheepishly.

"No problem." I passed her a cup of ice chips from the table next to her bed. My experience with childbirth was limited to what I had seen in movies. As far as I knew, women screamed, cursed, and sucked on cubes of ice. There were more bizarre rites of passage but not many, in my opinion. "Now why has Alexander been banished."

"Because I'm going to take this"—she held up her IV line—"and strangle him with it. He seems to have forgotten which one of us is birthing this baby."

"What does the doctor say?" I switched the topic away from her husband quickly.

"I'm not dilating fast enough. They gave me some useless pain pill, and now they're monitoring the baby. Oh and a nurse told me half of the damn country is outside waiting for me to push her out."

"Keep things in perspective," I said soothingly. "A couple

hundred of years ago and they would have all gotten to be in here watching you."

"That might be the only thing that's changed for the better," Clara muttered, catching her breath as another contraction hit her. "Distract me."

"I slept with Smith." I blurted out the first thing that came to mind. So much for keeping the news to myself.

"I know," Clara cried. When she went limp again, she gave me a weak smile.

"News travels fast."

"Edward said you two practically shagged on the dance floor at Brimstone," she said breathlessly

"Edward is a cad."

"He also said Smith almost punched him." Clara threw me a pointed look

"Yes, Edward and I were dancing too suggestively. Smith must be the only person in England who hasn't heard the prince is gay."

"I am?" Alexander's deep voice called as he appeared in the doorway. "Then how did we get into this predicament?"

The effect of his presence on Clara was immediate. Despite her big talk about being tired of his over-protectiveness, her whole face changed when he entered. It lit up the room. Even when she was annoyed with him, he still had that effect on her.

It had been one of the first warning flags to me that Philip and I might not be the right fit. I'd chosen to ignore it at the time. Now I wondered how I'd ever been able to.

Maybe because I'd been so desperate to find someone who loved me even a fraction of the amount that Alexander loved Clara.

A nurse followed Alexander into the room and shooed me out. "I need to check her progress. You can come back in a minute."

"I'll go find Edward." I squeezed Clara's hand, but when I went to release it, she gripped it tighter.

"I'm not sure I can do this," she whispered.

"That makes one of us, because I know you can." I gave her a quick kiss on the cheek and turned on Alexander.

"Try not to piss her off."

"I think I missed that boat nine months ago," he muttered.

I pushed him toward her. In my experience, neither of them could stay mad at each other for very long.

THE HALLS of St. Mary's were empty. The entire Lindo Wing had been cleared out with limited access to staff and visitors. My phone chirped, and I caught a message from Lola.

LOLA: Madeline is threatening parental divorce if she's not admitted.

BELLE: Do you want me to speak with Clara? She might let her in.

LOLA: Definitely not. There's not enough pain meds in

the world to get Clara through that. I've got her under control. But let me know what's going on in there.

I promised her I would and then continued my search for Edward. Rounding a corner, I caught sight of him in a lounge. His fiancé David grinned at me as I entered with my hands planted on my hips.

"Are you hiding?" I accused them.

"Nappies. Bottles. I'm game for any of it," Edward explained, "but I was in there for ten minutes and that was more than enough."

"He just told me he was glad neither of us could give birth," David told me.

"Not going in with the surrogate?" I asked.

They both responded at the same time.

"Maybe."

"We're not having kids."

I put my hands up in surrender. Apparently I was starting fights all over London today.

"What do you mean we aren't?" David demanded.

"Have you seen how screwed up my family is?"

David crossed his arms and grinned as he shook his head. "If I recall correctly Alexander said the same thing about children."

"Thankfully, you can't get knocked up," Edward bit out.

"This is not the last time we're discussing this," David warned as he stood up. He gave me a quick hug before he headed toward the door, calling over his shoulder. "Talk some sense into His Highness."

"Apparently that is my official job title for the day: She

Who Talks Sense Into the Monarchy." I grimaced. "Exactly how have I wound up being best friends with half the royal family? The lot of you is completely cocked up."

"How's it going?" Edward asked. He patted the now empty seat next to me.

"I think it would be going better if my life made any sense," I admitted. "I'm not sure how I'm supposed to offer advice when I'm busy making all the wrong choices myself."

"Things didn't go well with Smith?" Edward guessed, wrapping an arm around me.

I shook my head, leaning into him. "Things went too well with Smith."

"I wish I had your problems," Edward teased.

"I'll trade you," I offered. "I think David and I would have beautiful babies."

"Keep your hands off my man," Edward said in mock-warning. "Besides, it looked like you snagged one of your own the other night."

"I thought I had." At least, I could go into this with Edward without giving him all the dirty details. Normally I might have tried to talk with Clara, who knew a thing or two about getting involved with a complicated man, but she had other things to worry about at the moment. "I don't know. He's so demanding."

"In the bedroom?" Edward asked, his eyes glimmering mischievously.

"Everywhere." I didn't add that no part of me minded his compulsive attention to detail between the sheets.

"Well, I learned how hard that can be watching the couple of the hour." Edward paused, rubbing his chin thoughtfully. "I think you have to decide if you see a future with him."

"I don't know him well enough," I admitted. "But I wouldn't mind spending a couple of weeks in his bed."

"Then make that boundary clear. Look, Belle"—Edward leaned forward and squeezed my knee—"we both know you can be a little resistant to the idea of a relationship."

I snorted. "Can you blame me?"

"Not one bit, but don't get so caught up in keeping things safe that you stop taking chances. Take it from a guy who made his boyfriend pretend to be just friends for years."

"Yeah, you might not be the best person to give relationship advice now that I think about it," I teased.

"I went legit!"

We were both laughing when David popped his head in.

"They're taking Clara into surgery."

I was on my feet in an instant. "Is everything okay?"

"The baby is showing signs of distress."

He didn't have to say any more before we were all booking it back toward her room. We arrived just in time to see them wheeling her out into the hall.

"Belle!" she called my name frantically.

I rushed over to her.

"If anything happens—"

"Nothing is going to happen," Alexander interrupted her.

"If anything happens," she continued, tears sparkling in her eyes "take her shopping. She's going to have a fantastic dad. I want to make sure she has some girl time, though."

I swallowed back my own tears that threatened to spill down my cheeks. I didn't need to encourage her by showing her I was scared. "We'll take her shopping. Who do you think taught you how to dress? Or have you already forgotten?"

"Sir," the doctor interrupted, "we need to get her down the hall."

Alexander's and my eyes locked and then he was running along her side, hands clasped. His mouth was moving, but even though I couldn't hear what he was saying, I could imagine.

Life might not be counted in moments, but that was only because in times like this, moments seemed to stretch into hours. Edward and I took turns pacing by the entrance to the surgical room. No one had told us how long it might take.

"She's going to be fine," David assured both of us as he rubbed Edward's shoulder. My friend caught his hands and held them tightly.

We'd lost so much already this year. It seemed that every moment of joy was overshadowed by tragedy and horror. My called-off engagement. The attack at the wedding that had resulted in Edward's father's death. The car accident. It seemed that fate kept trying to take Clara from all of us.

She might have grown tired of Alexander's obsession

regarding her safety over the last few weeks, but personally I was glad he was in there now. I'm pretty sure death himself couldn't have gotten past him to get to her.

Behind us, a door opened and we all spun around, hoping to finally have some news. But instead of a doctor, Smith stood there with his tie loosened and his hair disheveled.

"How the hell did you get in here?" I demanded. I didn't want him here. Not now. Not while I was feeling vulnerable and certainly not after how he'd dismissed me earlier today.

He held up a bag. "I brought you some food."

I crossed to him, my arms clamped tightly over my chest. "That doesn't explain how you got in here."

"I represent a few of the physicians here," he explained. "I called in a favor."

"You should have saved it, because I don't want you here."

"Too bad," he said dismissively. He shifted his focus to Edward. "They told me she's been in surgery for about a half hour?"

"Yeah." Edward's eyes narrowed. Smith's memory might be short, but Edward clearly wasn't over their showdown at Brimstone.

"There'll be news soon. It takes a while to get everything sewn back up."

My stomach lurched at the thought. I hated that my best friend was in there and I couldn't be. Then again, clearly I didn't have the constitution to be at her side.

I grabbed Smith by the arm and dragged him into the corner. Everyone had enough to worry about without adding our bickering to the list.

"How did you know where I was? This is the second time you've mysteriously shown up where I'm at." He'd found me at Brimstone as well. Either he really could read my mind, or I should probably be considering a restraining order.

"Your aunt told me where you were on Friday," he explained, tugging his sleeve loose from my grasp and smoothing it back out. "And today? Well, it might have been harder to figure out if every media outlet wasn't reporting that your best friend is currently pushing out the country's next monarch."

"Thanks for the food, but I'm not hungry." I started to turn away but he stepped closer, rooting me to the spot.

"That was an important phone call earlier," he explained. "I wasn't going to be able to concentrate with your lips around my cock."

"I promise to never bother you in that way again."

He tilted his head. "Like it or not, you do work for me, Belle. Sometimes I have to handle things privately."

"You told me I would be there for everything," I reminded him. "But the truth is you haven't shown me one thing about yourself. I know nothing about you, Smith."

"It takes time to know someone." But his eyes lied.

"Yeah, it does, but you have to show them the truth," I reminded him softly.

Smith leaned closer until his lips brushed my ear. "Have you shown me everything yet, beautiful?"

I jerked away. He'd hit a nerve I didn't want plucked today. Or ever. Some memories were best left in the past. What I couldn't get over was that he was purposefully keeping certain elements of his business from me. I could understand client privilege, but he wouldn't answer a simple question about what type of law he specialized in. Now he was trying to twist my words. Just like a lawyer. "I've had enough experience with men that turn things back around on me. I'm not interested in that game, Mr. Price."

"I'll leave this here." He set the bag of take-away on a nearby chair. Inclining his head politely toward Edward and David, he turned to go. "Take a few days off, Miss Stuart. Spend time with your friend. I'm sure she needs you more than I do."

I wasn't sure what stung more: that he'd dismissed me or that he'd let me win.

"Wanker," I screamed as the door closed behind him.

"That is the second time someone has yelled that at me today. So much for commanding respect," Alexander said behind me.

I spun around, not realizing my little scene had drawn more of a crowd. But all my fury evaporated when I saw a tiny pink bundle in his arms.

"Elizabeth, meet your Auntie," Alexander cooed, bringing her over to me. "She has a very dirty mouth."

I nudged him the ribs. "You're one to talk, Daddy. How's Clara?"

"Resting," he said, his eyes never leaving his daughter. "Both of them are perfect."

The look on his face said it all. His world had just gotten a little larger. He had more power and money than most of us could ever dream of, but all that mattered to him was the tiny baby girl in his arms and her mother down the hall.

My heart constricted. That was love. As I took Elizabeth carefully from him, I experienced my own awakening.

I did know what love was. I'd seen it. I felt it now toward the people in this room. Maybe that was as much as some people got in a lifetime, and really, wasn't that enough?

I glanced back at Alexander and saw the pure joy written across his face.

Not everyone could have happily-ever-afters. Clara and Alexander deserved theirs. I'd just make certain my little godbaby didn't fall victim to the idea of fairytales.

"Once upon a time, there was a beautiful princess," I whispered, giving her soft, pink forehead a kiss, "and she could do anything she wanted without a man..."

CHAPTER FIFTEEN

Spending the week holding the new addition to my life did wonders for my soul, but it did little to allay the ache of absence I felt elsewhere. Smith had sent food and flowers, but he hadn't shown himself again at the hospital. I'd been grateful for that. It had given me the time I needed to realize the mistake I had made by letting him into my life—or at least into my panties.

By Friday, Clara was back home, adjusting to her new life as a mother, and I had to face my boss.

Boss, I reminded myself. That was where our relationship began, and that's where it needed to end. If I couldn't control my feelings about Smith, I would have to walk away. The income I'd get from a few weeks pay would be enough to get my business off the ground floor, and if working for him meant continuing to put my heart in jeopardy, then I would find another way to get it started.

His face registered no emotion when I strode up to his

desk and handed him a cup of black coffee on Friday morning. He looked good—too good—and I silently cursed him for wearing a navy pinstripe suit that fit his athletic body like a glove. His hair was neatly combed back, and I longed to reach out to muss it up. I'd seen what he looked like after my hands had held onto it for traction as he fucked me. Part of me missed it. I missed the primal, raw beast that had taken over my world. But Smith was a wolf hiding in a tailored three-piece suit, so why was I so determined to offer myself as his next meal?

"I'll pick up your suits from the cleaners this afternoon. I've arranged for the penthouse at the Plaza when you go to New York next month." I continued to rattle off the list of things I'd taken care of or would by the afternoon.

"Can you have Doris file these for me?" He passed me a large stack of folders.

I hadn't known what to expect when I returned today. I'd expected to want him. Part of me had wondered if I would fall into his arms. I hadn't expected the distant professionalism he was exhibiting now. Not after he'd spent a small fortune delivering food and gifts to the hospital.

"Is there something else?" he asked, tapping his chin with his index finger impatiently.

It was like nothing had happened between us. But if Smith thought he could just ignore what we'd done and the lines we'd crossed, he had another think coming.

"Let's get one thing straight," I hissed, clutching the pile of folders in my arms tightly. Air stung my index finger, and I realized I'd given myself a paper cut, but the sharp, if insignificant, discomfort was only a reminder that men equaled pain. "I hate you."

Smith leaned back in his leather chair and crossed his arms behind his head, regarding me with an arrogant smirk. "Do you always let people you hate fuck you, Belle?"

What I wouldn't give to wipe that smug grin off his face, but doing so would put me in dangerous proximity to his lips. Unfortunately, I didn't trust my body to not betray me, especially since it knew the mind-blowing orgasms he was capable of giving me. "Hate-fuck is exactly the right term," I said, purposefully mishearing him. "I hated every minute of it."

There was a pause after the words fell from my lips. The office was entirely quiet, neither of us moving. Neither of us breathing. It was a dangerous silence. The kind that followed a lie. The moments seemed to slow until Smith's hand swung out, sweeping across the paperwork on his desk and sending his lamp flying across the room. He was on his feet before I had processed his reaction. This time when his fingers lashed out, they caught the waist of my skirt as he yanked me against him, knocking the folders to the floor.

"Don't lie," he warned me. "Don't fucking lie to me."

"I do hate you," I breathed, even as the words hitched in my throat. Could he hear my heart pounding? It felt as if it was going to burst from my chest. My body was strung out on the strange cocktail of hate, lust, and hope.

Smith pushed me down, so that I was seated on top of

his desk. His phone began to ring, but I barely registered it as he reached under my skirt and yanked off my thong.

This was where I was supposed to say no. Hit him. Scream. But I realized then that I didn't want any of that. I didn't want to deny him. I only needed him to show me he still wanted me after our fight earlier this week.

And now that he had, I could see how stupid the fight had been. I'd been petulant. He'd been condescending. We both needed to make amends and this was the perfect way to do it.

He didn't miss a beat as he clicked the speaker button on his office phone. His eyes were trained on me and the intensity of his gaze sent my shallow breaths into full-blown pants. Stepping between my legs, he urged my thighs open wider as he reached for the scarf tied loosely around my neck. Bringing it to my lips, he held it there until my mouth parted as willingly as my legs. I bit down on the knot, grateful to have something to stifle the gasps I knew were coming.

"Hammond," he said in a clipped tone, his hand sliding under my skirt. "I was under the impression we were speaking over dinner tonight."

He traced along my seam, his feather-light touch sending a pool of moisture gushing to welcome him. My eyelids clenched shut as I waited, spread in invitation, for him to fuck me however he saw fit. All I cared about was that he filled this desperate ache building in my core. But his other hand curved around my neck and squeezed, forcing my eyes to fly open. My startled gaze met his.

There was no question who was in charge here, so when he withdrew his hand, he mouthed, "Eyes open."

"I merely wanted to discuss our plans," Hammond answered. "Is this a bad time?"

Thanks to the knot blocking my mouth I couldn't yell yes, but Smith merely smiled wickedly at me and shook his head. "It's the perfect time."

Smith pushed a finger between my wet folds and circled my engorged nub, drawing a smothered moan from my lips.

Oh god, I wanted him inside me. I wanted this torturous game of foreplay that had coloured our time together to end. I wanted to be fucked, and Smith knew it, which is why he continued his teasing strokes along my pussy. I was a trapped animal, cornered by a predator I had no hope of escaping, because I didn't want to be freed. I wanted to be devoured.

"I want this meeting to be between the two of us," Hammond informed him. "Leave your toy at home."

I was dimly aware of the fact that I was the one being uninvited, but I didn't care. I couldn't care about it at the moment. Not with Smith's fingers working their clever magic on my clit. The man was infuriating. He was a connoisseur of the slow burn, and I was learning quickly that he didn't mind taking his time when it came to pleasure. What he didn't seem to understand was that sometimes a girl needed a quick, rough shag.

"Miss Stuart is my assistant. She comes when and where I tell her to." His eyes landed on mine, and the implication was clear. He wasn't speaking to Hammond now. He was instructing me. I wasn't getting off until he said I could.

"This is a private affair. I assure you that you will have no need for her," Hammond argued, growing agitated but still trying to stay cool. I recognized the sound of it because it was exactly how I felt.

"I always have a need for her." Smith's finger plunged inside me, followed by a second one. He rolled and kneaded, coaxing me closer and closer to the brink. I held on through sheer force of will, not allowing myself to fall over the edge. My hands clutched the edge of his desk frantically, searching for an anchor as his touch set me adrift at sea. The water was calm, but the current warned of oncoming waves—the kind that would push me under and hold me there.

Hammond's tone switched from businesslike to snake-like instantly. "Need I remind you that she's connected to some very important people."

Smith shifted forward, pressing his weight against my body as the pad of his thumb settled over my clit again. A shudder wracked my body, and my legs coiled around his waist. His breath was hot on my face, his lips inches from mine. I longed to kiss him—to close the gap that always stretched between us. Between his words and the magnetic pull of his body, it seemed possible. But it wasn't, especially given the scarf wedged between my teeth. No, another kiss was dangerous in more ways than one. Kisses were expectations, and I didn't dare expect anything from Smith Price.

He was sending me mixed messages: controlling me, controlling my body. Protecting me while pushing me away. Keeping me close even as he shut me out. And maybe I was reading this one wrong, too. Maybe what he was trying to tell me was lost in translation, twisted by the heady pleasure he was ravaging on me. Smith leaned down and brushed his lips briefly over my forehead as he increased the pressure of his hand between my legs. "And now she's connected to me."

It was in his voice—the command to let go—and I plunged headfirst into his storm. Pleasure battered me, tightening across my limbs until my skin felt as though it would snap from the pressure, and then...release. I climaxed in bursts, clutching the desk while my legs snapped shut like a sprung trap around his body. The fingers inside me, the hand continuing its tireless siege, were my anchors. My whole being centered around him and the pleasure he could give me.

Or refuse me.

I could hear the voice on the other line, but it had faded, lost in the rush of blood and pheromones coursing through me as I endured each crest and crash. Smith murmured something I couldn't comprehend and hit the button on the receiver. In one swift motion, he tugged the scarf from my mouth, freeing my final few gasps of pleasures. He held the loose scarf by the knot and drew me forward. There was no resisting his pull, not while he had me—for all intents and purposes—collared. And certainly not while I was still throbbing with the memory of his touch.

The orgasm had only succeeded in making me crave him more. All the rational reasons to stay away from him—to keep myself emotionally detached—vanished as he pulled me roughly to his lips, still gripping the scarf. He'd released me, but he still had me caged. And with each day, the possibility of escape—the possibility of leaving him—grew more incomprehensible. Couldn't he see that he didn't need to trap me? To control me? That I was becoming his?

That I already was his?

Our lips crashed together, and I lost myself in him. Resisting him was like holding my breath and this kiss was the gasp following its release. I wanted to swallow him, consume him, let him infect my blood—and god, I hoped he felt the same way.

He pulled back slightly, his mouth still grazing mine, and tightened his hold on the scarf until there was no slack left. My hips squirmed forward to seek contact with him. The orgasm had been mind-blowing but not altogether satisfying. His closeness coupled with the spots where we touched only made me want more.

"You liked it when I played with you, beautiful." His teeth nipped at my lower lip, sending a shock of desire jolting through me. "You're such a good girl. Always doing as I say. Feel how hard that makes me."

I pried my fingers from the edge of the desk and

gripped the erection tenting his slacks. He was firm and hot, and I involuntarily caressed the hard length, imagining how it would feel inside me. Smith groaned and pressed closer as he unfastened his pants with his free hand.

"I'm going to take you, Belle," he growled, "and I won't be gentle. I'm going to fuck you hard."

I opened my mouth to welcome the scarf, knowing I'd need it to muffle my screams, but he shook his head.

"I want to hear you while my cock is inside you. No holding back or I'll punish you."

"Punish me?" I repeated, half fearfully and half hopefully.

"You like that, don't you?" he asked as he shoved down his boxer briefs, allowing me full view of his generous length.

I grew wetter at the sight and at the thought of what a real punishment from Smith might entail.

"It depends," I hedged.

"I've spanked you before."

A blush crept over my cheeks and I nodded. "Only playfully though."

"This won't be playful," he said in a low voice as my fingers closed over his shaft. He rocked against my grip, stroking himself with my clenched fist. "It will burn and sting and I won't stop until your ass matches your pretty pink cheeks. You won't be able to sit down without remembering my hands."

Oh my god. I refrained from turning over and presenting my buttocks to him. I wanted to know what it would feel like to be completely possessed by him, knowing any true pain I experienced at his hands would be matched by pleasure. I needed his hands on me—violently, passionately, any way I could have them.

His eyes hooded thoughtfully as if he could hear what I was thinking. "Not yet. You haven't earned a punishment."

"What have I earned?" I asked in a breathless voice.

"This." He rocked against my hand, sending his hot velvet shaft against my palm. He grabbed my hip, digging his nails into my tender flesh and urging me roughly around. My scarf slid loosely around my neck, still gripped by Smith. His palm spread across my back, and he shoved me down, flattening my breasts against the cold, smooth surface.

"Spread your legs and show me your pussy," he ordered.

My legs parted willingly. I'd been with other men, but none of them had ever produced such instant, wanton reactions in me. I couldn't refuse his demand, even though I felt a tingle of self-consciousness as I put myself on display.

"I've told you about how I wanted to fuck you the day we met," he reminded me as he nudged open my folds. He paused there, torturing me with a patience I didn't share. "I wanted to twist those pretty pearls around your neck like this"—he tugged the scarf sharply—"and watch your red lips gasp for air while I screwed you. I wanted to know if I could turn a good girl bad. You've proven to me that I can, haven't you?"

He already knew the answer. He already knew how to

159

undermine my self-control. All he had to do was ask and I was his. My screams. My body. My pleasure. It had all belonged to him since the first time he took me in his sights.

"Put your hands behind your back. I'm in control."

I did as I was told, crossing my wrists over my tailbone and tilted my head so that my cheek rested on the desk. I could see him out of the corner of my eye, still in his suit, his tie still knotted at his throat.

"I'm going to fuck you hard, beautiful." His cock slid a fraction of an inch inside me, stretching my hole until I'd been reduced to a consuming ache at my core. "You're going to walk around the rest of the day full of me, and you're going to feel it. Do you want that?"

I nodded, my teeth instinctively finding my bottom lip.

Smith jerked the scarf, raising my head from the desk. "Answer me when I ask a question. Properly."

"Yes, Sir," I breathed as my heart raced, already anticipating what was about to happen.

"Oh, beautiful"—he pushed me gently back down to the desk—"I love it when you call me by my proper name. It reminds me that you're a lady even when you're being a slut. It tells me you know who you belong to and what I expect. Your behavior deserves a reward, so ask me for what you want."

I licked my lips, my eyes closing in expectation. "I want you to fuck me, Sir."

My response was met with a stinging slap across my ass.

"Ask," he repeated.

"Please, will you fuck me, Sir?" I squealed as the heat of his rebuke spread through my bottom.

"Yes, beautiful, I will." He thrust his length roughly until he was pounding deep inside me. His hold on the scarf tightened, lifting my head until I was staring blindly at the ceiling, too lost in the rhythmic strokes to see anything but stars. His other hand left my hip and closed over my wrists. Smith tugged them back, raising me higher so that my breasts bounced against the cold wood. He plunged in and out, alternating between slow thrusts and violent ones that lifted my feet from the floor. As his pace quickened, so did my breathing until I could no longer hold back my cries. They spilled from my lips in anguished sobs.

It was too much. The control. The way he dominated every inch of my body and mind. It was everything I'd ever wanted and never knew I needed.

Smith drove deep, impossibly deep, and buried himself against my soft cervix. Circling his hips, he pushed the small of my back with my pinned wrists and manoeuvred my body so that my clit pressed against the crisp wooden edge of his desk. It dug into the pulsing bud. Then he began to screw me again with deliberate precision, grinding it as I swelled over his punishing cock. My mind went blank except for the vibrations of pleasure that burst from my core and rippled through my body. There was only his cock. Only him.

"Come," he ordered gruffly. His voice strained from the nearness of his own climax. "I want to hear it. I want everyone in this building to hear it and know that you belong to me now."

As if to prove his point, his body crushed against mine, impaling me on his cock. My head snapped back, allowing his lips access to my neck as a scream ripped through my throat. I cracked along with the howl, ecstasy spilling through me and igniting the nerves that ran like fault lines across my flesh.

Smith growled, his teeth sinking into the curve of my neck, as the first hot jets lashed against the battered entrance of my womb. His hand released my wrists, allowing me to catch myself as I fell forward. And then the fullness of his cock vanished, replaced by the last spurt of his seed onto my tailbone.

The sensation of him lingered inside me. Before him I'd never allowed a man to come anywhere but my mouth. Now I wished Smith would mark me every day. He stepped back and I felt his eyes surveying his prize, but I was too blissed out to move. Not that my legs would be steady enough to hold me anyway. His fingers skimmed across my swollen seam, spreading me open so that the evidence of his climax leaked down my sex.

"Do you feel that, beautiful?" he asked in a husky tone. "Your pussy is full of me. Who do you belong to?"

"You, Sir," I mumbled, the production of complete thoughts still proving difficult.

Smith slid an arm under my torso and drew me up. I turned into him, nuzzling my face against his suit jacket and breathing in his spicy cologne. He pushed my skirt down and pulled me closer, tipping my chin up so that our eyes met. The hunger that had shone from his eyes was sated, and he kissed me softly.

"The car will pick you up at seven."

I blinked, trying to clear the fuzziness in my head. "I thought I wasn't invited."

"Your place is at my side. I've missed having you there this week, and I won't be without you this evening." There was no mistaking the finality of his words, and I wasn't about to argue. Not when it was exactly what I'd longed to hear. "Be ready by seven."

"I'm always ready for you." I flushed as I spoke. There would be no mistaking what I meant either.

"Talk like that will get you bent back over this desk, beautiful," he said gruffly, "and we both have work to do."

He released me and I looked away, suddenly overcome with shyness. There was still so much I didn't know about Smith—so much I didn't understand about him and his job —and yet I'd given myself to him fully. He rested a hand on the small of my back and I could sense that he wanted to reassure me. Neither of us spoke as I buttoned my blouse, but when I was finished he leaned in, his mouth brushing my ear.

"It's a formal dinner. Wear stockings, and heels tall enough that I can fuck you when I need to, but leave your pussy bare," he ordered.

My breath hitched and my mouth went dry, but I forced myself to respond. "Yes, Sir."

"I want you to come home with me tonight," he continued, and his cool eyes studied me as he spoke. He pushed a lock of hair out of my face. "Cancel your plans for the weekend, you're going to be rather tied up."

A spasm of excitement shot through my core, but I did my best not to show him how aroused the thought of another weekend in his bed made me. As much as I lusted for his body, I needed to maintain some control of our relationship. I might turn into a reckless addict when he touched me, but I wanted the balance of power to remain equitable the rest of the time.

"I'll do my best to clear my calendar." I wouldn't promise him more that that, even if I knew there was no way I could resist his request.

"Clear it, beautiful. I plan to spend the entire weekend making you come and I'm not taking no for an answer."

His head slanted, crushing his mouth to mine, and I melted into him. In the end, I didn't say yes. There was no other choice.

Who was I kidding? This wasn't equitable. Not even a little. I was falling for Smith Price. Hard and fast.

I just hoped wherever I landed, I wouldn't find myself there alone.

CHAPTER SIXTEEN

*L*ondon traffic turned into a nightmare midday, so despite the fact that Smith had left the Veyron keys sitting on the reception desk—an act I took as an invitation—I decided to hit the pavement to finish out my to-do list. I made a mental note to thank Smith for keeping all of his personal and business needs in a relatively compact geographic area. But heading out on foot meant that I had considerably less time to deal with things before tonight's dinner plans.

I hoped this evening ran as hot as this morning had. Smith and I seemed to be stuck on a perpetual roller coaster, vacillating between on and off, hate and affection, hot and cold. When we were apart, I couldn't decide if I actually liked him, but when we were together, I needed him.

I always wanted him.

"Belle!"

I froze on the spot. There was no way I'd just heard his voice, but turning, I discovered I was wrong.

Philip stood on the walk in front of the law office and ran a hand through his floppy blond hair. He looked like the same lanky Harris Tweed ad. Although his hairline might be receding. With any luck, he'd wind up bald before his thirtieth birthday. Karma had a lot on her plate, but it appeared she had my back on this one.

"I'm sure you weren't expecting to see me," he said awkwardly.

"No, it's more like you're the last person that I wanted to see," I said coldly, before tacking on, "ever."

I had no idea what he was doing here. I'd spotted him at Clara's wedding before things had gone wrong. Retrospectively, I had considered it yet another bad omen. I'd managed to avoid him ever since.

Now he was standing in front of me. I waited for my heart to leap, waited for any sign that I still had feelings for him. Mercifully, there were none. All I felt was a pit opening up in my stomach. There were very few times in my life when I'd wished the earth would swallow me up. This was definitely one of them.

"I know things ended poorly between us."

I threw my head back and laughed at his choice of words. It felt liberating.

"I heard about you and Pepper. Congratulations." My voice took on a snide tone. "I hope you won't mind if I don't send a gift."

"Belle," he began, but I held a hand up.

"There's really nothing left for us to say to one another. I have errands to run." I walked away, ready to leave Philip behind—and all the baggage that came with him.

"I heard about your new job working for Smith Price," he called, stopping me in my tracks.

"It's going well." I shrugged as I turned back. So this was what we were reduced to—small talk about jobs. What was next? The weather? For the first time, I realized just how little we'd had to say to each other over the years. Maybe it was meeting Smith, but now I saw Philip for the bore he was. I'd spent the last few months believing he deserved a bitch like Pepper Lockwood. Now I realized she was getting hers as well. She had to put up with him for eternity.

"He represents a lot of bad people," Philip warned me.

Philip hated Alexander as well. In fact, he condescended to most people he knew, including me. But coming out of the woodwork to lecture me about my boss was the final straw.

"Don't you dare!" I exploded. "Don't come around here and pretend like you have something of value to add to my life. Your opinion no longer matters. It never should have in the first place."

Philip took a step closer to me, and the knot in my stomach tightened. "I care about you, Belle. I still love you. When I heard you were working for him, I had to say something."

"You lost the right to say anything when you cheated on me. And don't talk about loving me. You don't lie to the people you love." It wasn't an accusation. It was the truth, and we both knew it.

"Do you think he's being honest with you?" he probed. "Has he told you the crimes his clients commit? Who he's in bed with?"

I blushed scarlet at his choice of words, and Philip fell silent.

"I see," he said after a long moment. "You're in bed with him."

"That's none of your concern."

"He helps murderers go free, Belle. His father was involved in organized crime. I'm sure he hasn't told you what happened to him."

My blood turned to ice in my veins. His father was dead. I hadn't asked for details. Maybe I should have. "He isn't the only person with a dead father. That doesn't make him a criminal."

"Some people can have terrible fathers and come out unscathed. Smith Price isn't one of those people." His voice was low with warning, but all I could hear was the word terrible.

"My father wasn't a bad man." My lip began to quiver. Despite everything Philip had put me through, he had never once intuited that he judged my dad. Now I knew otherwise. "No wonder you decided to trade up. I guess you do care about who you're linked to. I would have thought you had better taste than Pepper."

"It's more complicated than that, Belle. I was trying to

end things with Pepper. You were the one I wanted to be with, and I'll never forgive myself for hurting you."

The excuses began to flow. I'd unleashed a flood of apologies that I didn't need or want.

"And now you're engaged to her," I reminded him.

"She told me she was pregnant," he said flatly.

"Then I guess more congratulations are in order." Acid rose in my throat, and I fought the overwhelming urge to vomit. At least he was close enough I could do it on him.

"She's not," he continued. "She's trying to trap me."

"Oh c'mon, Pip." I purposefully used the childhood nickname he hated, savoring how it felt on my tongue. "One blonde or the other. What's it to you as long as someone's willing to hang off your arm and pretend you're interesting?"

"I deserve that. But I know which blonde I want on my arm. I meant it when I asked you to spend the rest of your life with me. I don't care about your father or what happened in the past. We can get through anything now." He moved so close to me that I could smell the familiar scent of his aftershave.

"Why are you here? Because if you think I'm going to fall into your arms, I'd suggest you walk away before I cut off your balls."

"You weren't innocent either. I knew about Jonathan, and I didn't say anything. It really doesn't matter to me," he added quickly.

"It matters to me!" I cried. "I don't want a husband who's always looking for someone more spectacular."

"There's no one more spectacular than you," he said in a solemn tone, and then before I could process what was happening, I was in his arms. His lips sought mine, making contact. For a split second I melted into his familiar embrace. But almost instantly, my body rebelled, rejecting his touch. I realized I didn't belong to him anymore before I managed to push him away.

"When I said it was over. I meant it. I've never done second chances." I wiped the back of my hand over my mouth, smearing lipstick across it.

"That's no way to live life," he advised. "Sooner or later, you'll have to give someone a second chance."

"Later then, because that second chance will never be wasted on you." I spat the words. "I could have wasted my life with you in a loveless marriage in exchange for money and mediocre orgasms. You know what I realized since we've been apart? I never loved you. I loved the idea of a husband. I'll never make that mistake again. Life is too short to waste it on people who don't even know you."

"I know you," he pressed. "I know you like milk and two sugars in your tea. I know you prefer Kate-style Louboutins and that you secretly wanted to major in fashion but your mother wouldn't let you."

"That's not knowing me. When I have a nightmare, what is it about? What song instantly makes me happy? If I could have dinner with one person, who would it be? Answer those questions," I challenged him. When he didn't respond, I continued, "You can't because you don't know me at all. You want someone that never existed. That girl—that façade—is gone."

"You were never a façade with me."

"That you didn't even realize it proves my point." I shouldered my purse, shaking my head. "Have a nice life, Philip."

"Who was it?" he asked before I could go. "The person you would have dinner with. Do you even know?"

I knew exactly who it would be, but Philip didn't deserve an answer. He didn't deserve anything from me, especially not my time. I walked away, leaving him with the memory of a girl he used to know and nothing more.

My flat seemed deserted when I finally made it there with a pile of dry cleaning and my mail. Considering how much time I'd spent away from home between Smith and the baby, I'd half-expected to discover Aunt Jane had brought home a new lover. Her soft spot for artists and musicians meant that more often than not we had someone staying on our couch.

Jane stumbled into the kitchen with a sleep mask perched on her forehead. "Look what the cat dragged home!"

"I've been at the hospital with Clara and the baby."

"How is she doing?" Jane asked, her forehead wrinkling in concern.

"She's well. Alexander is over the moon, even if he's trying to act like a tough guy. They headed home this morning, so I'm back to work." I gave Jane a brief squeeze before I headed into my room. Tonight was an important date on two counts. Firstly, I had to find an appropriate dress to wear. Smith was potentially about to piss off one of his biggest clients, simply to prove I'd been wrong about the dynamic between him and Hammond.

"And getting laid," Jane guessed, following me into my bedroom.

"And that," I admitted.

Jane dropped onto my bed. "How are things going with your new conquest?"

My aunt had always had a way with words. "Conquest? I thought the woman was the conquest."

"Not Stuart women," she said, her mouth twisting into a wry smile. "Girls like us don't wait around to be caught. We take charge. We write the rules to the game."

"Maybe so." I didn't feel that way about Smith. He was definitely conquering me, but I hadn't exactly been easy prey. "To be honest, I'm not really certain who is capturing who anymore."

"When it comes to love, that's the best way to play it." Jane winked.

Sheepishly, I grabbed my leopard weekender and began to toss a few must-haves in it. My favorite face cream, a new toothbrush and razor. I hesitated when I opened my underwear drawer. If Smith had been serious earlier, I ran the risk of him destroying all my frilly, lacy thongs. I threw them in the bag anyway. He could afford to buy me more.

"Going away for the weekend?"

"No, I'll be here in London." I zipped the bag shut and

shifted my attention to my closet and what to wear this evening. "And I'll have my mobile on."

"I wouldn't dream of interrupting your plans." She laid a hand over my packed bag. "I know you're pretending to be busy, love. What's really on your mind?"

I plucked a velvet gown from my closet. "It's September. Can I wear velvet yet?"

Jane shook her head no, and I hung it back up. I stared at the rack for another five minutes before I realized that the reason that I was seeing no options was because I wasn't really looking. My head was stuck on Jane's question. I spun around and pressed myself against the door frame. "Philip came to see me today."

"I didn't see that coming," Jane admitted.

"Neither did I. It wasn't a welcome visit," I assured her.

"Good. Don't be that girl who goes back to a cheater. They never really change."

"Do you think that's true?" My thoughts drifted from Philip to what he had said about Smith. I knew he was keeping things from me, but it wasn't as if he knew my life story yet either. He hadn't answered my questions about the law he represented or how he had more money than ninety-nine percent of Londoners. I didn't want to believe what Philip had said, but if it was true, could I live with that? Especially if Jane was right and people didn't change?

"Oh, people grow up," she continued thoughtfully, "and where true love is present, there's always evolution. A good man will grow with you, walk beside you. That's not to say he'll be a saint."

I smiled at that. Sainthood wasn't one of my requisites for lovers.

"But when a man is out trying on different vaginas, that's not what happens."

"Have you ever considered writing a book?" I asked her, sighing as I went back to picking out my evening wear.

"I'm not sure people are interested in what an old woman has to say about love." She waved off the suggestion. "Particularly one who's left a string of broken hearts in her wake."

"I'm interested," I informed her. "I would be lost without you."

"In that case, spill. You've been holding out on me."

"I just...he's so..."

"Enough said." Jane patted me on the shoulder and swept toward the door. "Don't be scared to give someone a chance because someone's hurt you before. Just be smart enough to stay away from the ones who have."

CHAPTER SEVENTEEN

$\mathcal{I}$ expected to be a third wheel at dinner, and instead I was a fourth. Hammond smiled coldly as we entered the private dining room at La Rue. He rose, buttoning his blazer, and waited as Smith pulled out my chair. I took a seat, unfolding my napkin, and pinned a smile to my face. It was harder than expected, given that I was seated across from Georgia Kincaid. She didn't bother trying to look pleased to see me. Her dark hair was swept to the side, cascading over her shoulder. Her slinky red shift was more revealing than mine. The fitted grey dress I'd chosen revealed only my bare shoulders. It was clear she was a woman who drew power from her sexuality. I wasn't opposed to using such methods myself, but I had little doubt that my mere presence was statement enough regarding my influence over this situation. Georgia's eyes flickered to Smith. Their gazes met and something passed between them unspoken. I hadn't figured out their relationship yet, but I knew I didn't like it.

"It's so nice to have you with us, Miss Stuart," Hammond remarked as he sat back down.

Considering that I'd been present for his phone call with Smith earlier this afternoon, I understood that wasn't the case. "Thank you for inviting me."

Hors d'oeuvres arrived along with a selection of white and red wine. I brushed a piece of lint off the linen tablecloth, wondering if the whole evening would consist of us pleasantly lying to each other, or if they'd actually discuss whatever business Hammond wished to speak about with Smith.

A warm hand dropped onto my bare knee. My own found it instinctively. For a brief second, I wondered if that was too much, considering the newness of our relationship. Smith knitted his fingers through mine, our hands clasped under the table. It felt strange and wonderful—and far too promising.

"I assume you've had a chance to review the contracts," Hammond said as he speared escargot onto his fork. He brought the buttery morsel up to his mouth and left it hovering there.

Smith nodded as he set his wineglass down. "I have. It seems things are in order. Are there specifics that concern you?"

"There are, but I suppose they can wait. No reason to mix business and pleasure." His teeth clicked against the tines of the fork as he sucked the snail off it.

"I was under the impression this was a business dinner," I said in a soft but unwavering voice. I wasn't interested in double entendres this evening. He had wanted to see Smith for a reason.

"I would never dream of discussing something so boring in the presence of a lady," Hammond responded.

My eyes flashed to Georgia, but she seemed nonplussed by his use of the singular. In the few times I had met her, lady hadn't been a descriptor I'd applied to her. Still, it was another none-too-subtle reminder of my unwanted presence.

"Don't worry." I shrugged, tapping my fingers on the stem of my glass. "I'm certain it will go over my head. I'm not a lawyer."

Just a woman. I kept that thought to myself.

Hammond tilted his head as if to say well-played. He turned his attention back to Smith. "There are certain exclusions I want to see drawn in before I'll sign the papers. My control over my shares needs to be airtight."

"Understood," Smith said.

This was what he needed to talk to Smith about alone? From the way Hammond had spoken on the phone, I'd expected something much worse. Considering his attitude toward my arrival, I'd imagined he needed help covering up a murder.

"There's also the issue of the nondisclosure clause," Georgia added.

Apparently she was more than a pretty face. That didn't surprise me one bit. Everything about her rubbed me the wrong way. I could tell she wasn't someone to under-estimate.

"It's been dealt with," Smith said in a clipped tone. "The final documents should be ready by Monday."

Hammond shook his head slowly. "I want them by tomorrow."

"That's simply not possible." Smith leaned back in his chair, withdrawing his hand from my grasp so that he could cross his arms behind his head. "I won't be available this weekend."

"I pay you to be available at all times." Hammond leaned forward, placing his palms on the tabletop.

"I will be available for emergencies, of course. But I doubt a simple realty deal qualifies as an emergency."

The atmosphere in the room crackled with testosterone as the two men stared at one another. Neither looked prepared to back down.

"Boys, let's not be combative," Georgia suggested in a sugary voice. It was enough to make me nauseous.

But I took a cue from her. "I'll have Doris pencil in the changes for your review and fax them over. I assume you have no issue sending them to my email if they're simple contracts."

Every head at the table swiveled toward me. Georgia's expression had changed from practised disinterest to decidedly intrigued, whereas Hammond looked consti-pated. I couldn't bring myself to look at Smith. There had been a clear line in the sand, and I had crossed it.

"My job is to make Smith's life easier. I'm certain we

can find a solution that doesn't infringe on his personal time." I drew my mobile out of my purse and waited to see if Hammond would call my bluff.

"A lawyer doesn't have personal time, Miss Stuart." Hammond laughed as he spoke, but I knew it wasn't a joke. His dark eyes glittered with unrepressed malice. This was a warning.

"I can place a call to Richard. He should be able to review simple changes over the weekend," Smith offered. "If you don't mind someone else executing the contract."

Hammond's jaw tensed, and he took a moment before he spoke. "I suppose Monday will be acceptable."

"Excellent." Smith shifted in his seat and grabbed his fork. "Did you order the duck?"

Nothing had really been discussed. No important or confidential information exchanged, but still my pulse had rocketed into a frenzy. Pushing back my chair, I excused myself to the powder room. Smith glanced up at me but didn't move.

"I'll go with you." Georgia stood to join me. "Us girls should stick together."

Somehow having her with me didn't seem like it would be strength in numbers. I smiled graciously and paused for her to join me. I gripped my clutch tightly as we walked silently to the loo. Inside I ducked into a stall and sank down onto the toilet. I didn't have to go. I'd only come here to collect myself and sort through what had just happened.

"How long have you worked for Smith?" Georgia called through the door.

"Not long." Short answers seemed to be the best course. Giving up on my quiet time, I stood and flushed before joining her at the vanity.

"You appear to have a handle on him," she continued as she reapplied her lipstick in slow, precise strokes.

"Not even a little." Maybe a little casual girl talk would smooth the path between us. I tucked a loose strand of hair behind my ear and began checking my own makeup. "He's difficult to read."

"He is," she allowed. Spinning around, she settled against the marble counter and glared at me. "And how long have you been fucking him?"

I froze, returning her stare in the mirror. "Excuse me?"

"Smith knows better than to bring the hired help to a private meeting." Georgia arched an eyebrow in challenge.

"He prefers I attend all his dinners," I informed her. Smith had been quite clear on that when I took the job, but I had the sinking suspicion that his professional life wasn't nearly the open book he'd insinuated it was. "I'm simply doing my job."

"How interesting," Georgia purred. She moved closer to me, lowering her voice as she sneered. "I didn't know Smith employed whores. He's never needed to before."

"I'm sure your cunt has always been freely available," I hissed, officially losing my cool.

"Careful, princess, or I won't be so friendly in the future."

I snorted and grabbed my powder from my bag. Georgia wanted to make me squirm and that wasn't going to happen. I pressed the sponge to my nose, ignoring her.

"I know all about you," she continued. "Hammond is very particular about the people his associates employ. I haven't decided if you're as big of a gold digger as your friend, Clara. It would be hard to top that. But seeing as you're already sleeping with Smith, I imagine you'll give her a run for her money. Although you must have hated to lose out on your own crown."

"Clara must love you," I said flatly. "I'm already hoping you'll be my bridesmaid."

"Smith isn't the type that gets married. So if you're hoping he's going to ride in on a white horse and carry you away, I suggest you wake the fuck up." She planted her hands on her hips and waited for her last attack to hit.

"Your determination to rattle me is truly pathetic." I turned to face her. We'd see which one of us could be rattled. It wasn't going to be me.

"It's adorable how tough you think you are. Call me when you realize who he really is."

"He must be really good in bed," I said, feigning ignorance on the subject, "because you're clearly not over him."

"Smith and I have never been together. We grew up together. He's a brother to me, and any bitch who thinks she'll come between that is going to land herself in a rather large pile of shit." Georgia snapped the lid of her lipstick with a loud click and dropped it into her purse. "You know nothing about him."

"I will," I promised her.

"Allow me to offer your first insight." She pushed past me, purposefully knocking her hip into me as she crossed to the door. "He's the jealous type."

That I could have guessed, but I kept my face blank. She'd have to let me in on something more interesting if she thought I'd get upset.

"He wouldn't take kindly to finding out his flavor of the week is whoring around with her ex-fiancé."

From the corner of my eye, I spotted myself in the mirror. Face white. Mouth slack. So much for not letting her get to me.

"I pop by the office frequently. You might want to have your little sexcapades elsewhere. Unless you're hoping Smith will beat him to a pulp."

"My personal life is none of your business," I said through gritted teeth.

"That is where you're wrong. Hammond might not like to mix business with pleasure, but that's my primary job description. I collect sins."

"That sounds like a waste of time."

"I've found it to be quite lucrative." She tugged open the door and paused. "Your sins are in my files. Keep that in mind."

She left and I fumbled for the counter. I knew a thing or two about sins. So far I'd been outrunning mine. Now they were about to catch up with me.

When I returned to the table, Smith stood and caught me by the arm. "Our business is concluded."

Apparently the private dinner wasn't going to include

the main course. After what had happened in the loo, I was disappointed to cut the evening short. Between the cat and mouse game and the threats, my stomach was tied in knots. Hammond accompanied us to the exit. Taking my hand, he pressed his thin lips to it.

"Always a pleasure. Until we meet again."

I, for one, wouldn't mind if some time elapsed between now and then. Drawing my hand back, I forced a smile. Where was soap when you needed it?

Smith gave a curt nod and guided me out the revolving door. As it spun shut behind us, he grabbed my hand and strode toward the valet, dragging me behind him. He shoved his ticket into the attendant's hand along with another hundred pound note.

"I assume I don't have to tell you which car."

"No, sir," the boy said as he took off for the lot.

As soon as he was gone, Smith rounded on me, pulling me roughly against him. "You didn't correct him," he growled.

My mind went blank. Him? Had Georgia gotten to him in the few minutes before I'd returned from the powder room? I wasn't certain how to explain. I shouldn't have to, but judging from the possessive heat rolling off of him, he didn't feel the same way.

Any other man wouldn't believe he had a claim on me. Any other man I might have told to sod off. Why did Smith already have such a hold on me? Warning bells rang out in my head. This was exactly what I'd been trying to avoid. Now, not only was I jumping into the deep end, I found myself yearning to. The lines between us were blurred. I didn't know when I was crossing one, and I didn't know what the consequences would be when I did. All I knew was that I wanted to bend them. Break them. Just like part of me wanted him to break me.

"I'm sorry," I said softly. There were no other words that felt appropriate. I didn't owe him an explanation, and I wanted his punishment—wanted his hands to take control of my body.

"You don't need to apologize because he called me sir," Smith said, gripping my hips forcefully. "That title belongs to your lips."

It took me a moment to register that he was talking about the valet, not Philip. I breathed out, relieved and disappointed at the same time.

I wrapped an arm around his neck, drawing his mouth toward mine. "And what belongs on your lips?"

"This." He swept a kiss over my mouth. His hands drifted up, skimming quickly over my breasts. Despite the brief contact, my nipples beaded in expectation. The small flame of desire that had been stifled by my anxiety blazed into an inferno. "These. Your pussy. All of you belongs on my lips, beautiful."

The rest of my fear melted away in the heat that small word inspired. Until him, fantasy and reality had been separate worlds, lying far from one another. Now they both centered on him.

He leaned in, moving his mouth to my ear. But he didn't kiss me. "What did Georgia say to you?"

"Nothing that mattered." And none of it did matter. Not anymore. Not with him so close to me.

"Stay away from her," he advised. "She doesn't play by the same rules."

"And you do?" I asked, my focus shifting from foreplay to business.

"No, I don't," he confessed. "Does that scare you?"

"Yes," I whispered. If I wanted the truth out of him, I had to be honest myself.

"Good. You should be scared of me. Don't ever forget that, beautiful." He nipped my earlobe with his teeth for emphasis.

Breathing him in, I pressed an index finger to his chin and shook my head. "She told me you were the jealous type."

"I own many things. Most of them are replaceable. But occasionally, I obtain a priceless piece. Do you understand, beautiful?

I shook my head slowly no. The shades of it were there, but not the complete picture.

"You are priceless to me, so yes, I would be very jealous should someone try to come between us. I would hate to hear Georgia was trying to be that person."

The implication was clear. "She was warning me," I admitted as the Veyron zoomed to the curb.

Smith didn't move toward his car, his green eyes trained on me instead. I could lose myself in those eyes. It was a dangerous proposition. I'd been led astray before by a man. I was determined not to allow that to happen again.

I'd pushed him away but there had been a moment when I opened myself to the possibility. However fleeting it was, I'd allowed another man to touch me. It was only made worse by the fact that I'd sworn never to speak to that man again.

"She saw my ex kiss me in front of your office."

Smith moved then, catching my upper arm and hauling me to the waiting car without a word. His whole body was rigid. I sensed his barely contained fury seething within him, and I wasn't the only one. The people wandering past us stopped and whispered.

I knew I should pull away. Yell. Scream. Put a stop to this now before it got out of control. But I put up no fight when he opened my door. I sank into the passenger seat without a struggle. It wasn't reasonable. It wasn't smart.

And I didn't care.

CHAPTER EIGHTEEN

Smith didn't speak the entire ride. By the time he parked the Veyron in his garage, I regretted my decision to come with him. The fascination I'd felt in front of the restaurant had evaporated, leaving only trepidation. He'd spoken of punishment and submission before. I'd never really considered what that might entail.

He exited the car without a word and walked to the lift, leaving me to scramble after him.

That was your chance. He hadn't asked me to come with him. He hadn't demanded I follow him. And I still had. I paused a few steps from him. He stood with his back to me, and I considered my options. I could walk out now. Or I could see where this led. I'd enjoyed his teasing slaps and smacks. I'd wanted more.

But how much?

I closed the gap between us and followed him into the lift. Smith pushed the button for the second floor. We were headed straight to the bedroom. The ache of expectation built in my core, filtering slowly through the rest of my body, until I was practically humming with need. When the doors zipped open, Smith placed his arm across the threshold and waited for me to exit. I stepped into the hallway.

"Bedroom."

One word. It surged through me. Squaring my shoulders I marched inside his room, stopping just past the doorway.

"Strip."

My eyes locked with his, but he looked away immediately. What I had seen in those deep emerald orbs chilled me. Reaching under my arm, I tugged down the zipper of my gown, still watching him. Still hoping he would turn back to me. He didn't. My dress puddled to the floor, and I stepped out of it, wearing only a nude silk bustier and stockings. I'd left my knickers at home as he requested, but he didn't acknowledge that.

"Everything."

It took me a few moments of fumbling to unhook all the tiny fasteners by myself. Smith's gaze had returned to me—or at least my body. There was no affection in his face. He was vacant—a void. There was no way to read him, because there was nothing to read. When I'd pulled off my last stocking, I stood exposed before him.

Smith circled around me, studiously avoiding my eyes as he inspected me. Then he uttered one final word, "Flawless."

I blushed under his scrutiny, both pleased at the praise and nervous about what came next.

He snapped his fingers. "Kneel before me."

I dropped before him, one knee at a time.

"I'm attracted to a fiery woman. Some men aren't. They like their women quiet. Docile. But a woman with a sharp tongue—a defiant woman—that's what gets my attention. You've had my attention since the moment we met, Belle." He paused and ran a single finger along the curve of my shoulder. Then he stepped in front of me, putting me eye level with the unmistakable bulge in his trousers.

I barely resisted the urge to snap open his fly and take him in my mouth. He wanted a defiant woman and I could be just that, but something held me to the spot. Curiosity, I suppose. I was curious what he wanted to do to me. Even more curious if I would let him.

"Perhaps what happened today was innocent, but I'm going to need you to prove that to me. I'm a man who prefers evidence to hearsay. Call it a hazard of my profession. Proof is much more convincing than words." He peeled off his suit coat and loosened his tie. When he unbuttoned his top button, a small moan slipped from my mouth. Smith tapped my cheek with the side of his hand, reminding me to be silent. "Your body responds to my requests even when you don't. I've learned how to read it by watching you since that first day. It will tell me everything I need to know. Do you understand?"

I nodded, my eyes flickering up to stare at him. My

hands longed to reach for him. I wanted to touch him almost as much as I wanted him to touch me.

"But more importantly, do you consent?" he continued in a low voice. "You are free to leave at any time. You are free to tell me to stop. I won't prevent you from leaving. The things I'm going to do to you might feel demeaning. They're supposed to. But if I'm correct, you will enjoy them. Just as I'll enjoy bridling your defiance and seeing where your loyalty lies. Do you have any questions?"

"How will you know that I'm not performing?"

"You're clinging to your bravado, beautiful." A note of affection colored his tone, but it quickly shifted back to domineering. "No one performs that well. I'm going to strip you bare and make you squirm until your mind ceases to function except to follow my commands."

My body burned, my knees stinging against the marble floor and the rest of me aching from want. "I consent."

"Very good. Stay."

I didn't budge, but I felt him moving away from me. The room seemed to darken without his presence, and I resisted the urge to turn around and look for him. I understood the expectations of me even if they were difficult to follow. My body relaxed instantly at the sound of his footsteps but tensed again when I heard the soft clink of a chain.

Out of the corner of my eye, I spotted him drop into the chair by the window.

"Come to me, beautiful."

His request washed over me. I felt wanted. Alive. I

pressed my palm to the floor and began to push myself to my feet.

"Crawl." The word lingered on his tongue.

Instantly I shifted forward, placing my other hand on the floor. The hardness of it registered faintly in the back of my mind, but my only conscious thought was of him. Each shuffle of my knees, each clap of my palm against marble took me closer. Smith lounged back, his chin propped against his hand. Two fingers pressed thoughtfully to his mouth as he watched my progress. When I got to his feet, I dropped back onto my heels and placed one hand onto the chair cushion, carefully avoiding touching his thighs.

"You may come closer," he said in a gentle voice.

I pressed my cheek against his knee and breathed him in. His woody cologne flooded my nostrils and the warmth of our small contact seemed to both feed and quell the fire raging inside me. Closing my eyes, I understood the truth.

There was only him.

The heat of his fingertips trailed over my collarbone. His scorching touch was followed by cool, smooth leather. It wrapped around my neck tightly enough that I inhaled sharply. Fingers swept under the strap, reassuring me that I could breathe.

"Turn around and hold up your hair."

I looked to him then. Smith paused and cupped my cheek. "You're doing so well, beautiful. Now turn around."

I did as I was told. Resisting the urge to touch the leather fastened around my neck, I moved to face away from him and lifted my hair, exposing the nape of my neck. The sharp, distinct click of metal sent goose bumps rippling across my skin.

"Hands and knees," Smith instructed.

A cold metal chain snaked down my back as I lowered myself on all fours. A tiny voice inside me dissented to this and the rest of me—my muscles, my senses, my thoughts, my very soul—hushed it. My arousal surged so plentifully that I felt it trickle down my seam and drip to the floor beneath me. A shudder wracked my body, a trembling promise of things to come.

"That made you wet," Smith murmured, dipping a finger between my weeping folds. He lightly brushed it, releasing more fluid. "I leashed you and you nearly came. I took you over, took away your decisions, took away your freedom. And soaking your pussy with want is your response, beautiful. Do you know why?"

I searched for a no, but all I could force past my lips was a whimper.

"You've even given up your voice. Everything you are centers around me and what I will allow you. My finger." He pushed inside my sopping hole and hooked his finger to massage my g-spot.

"My mouth." Warm, soft lips swept over my swollen sex.

"The hand that holds your tether." He gave a tug, forcing my head back. "I took away everything and how do you feel?"

Liberated. It wasn't the word that flashed through my

head so much as the concept itself. I felt light, as if a burden I'd carried my whole life had lifted from my back. I nearly believed I could float away. But the chain that had freed me anchored me to Smith.

"You've given me something precious." Smith stood and moved to the front of me. Dipping down, he caught my face, granting me the first peek of the gold lead he'd attached to my collar. He drew me up by the chin, and I effortlessly returned to a kneeling position. Reverence smoldered across his beautiful face, light glimmering from his eyes. "Trust."

The realization crashed through me. I trusted him. I gave him the one thing I'd sworn never to give a man again, and I didn't even know why. We'd known each other such a short amount of time. I'd never been the type that believed in soul mates or love at first sight. But right here, right now, I'd handed him control. He could do with me as he pleased, and I wanted him to.

"But now I need to know if I can trust you."

The pleasant exhilaration his last insight had given me vanished. It wasn't that I feared him. It was that I was scared of what I was about to reveal to him—and myself.

"Hold this." He pushed the leash against my mouth, and my lips parted, instinctively taking it between my teeth. Smith rubbed a hand over the thick outline of his dick. "You're so pretty with your mouth dripping gold chain."

He lifted his foot up to me, and I tugged off his shoe, repeating the action with the other until his feet were bare.

With deft fingers, he unfastened his belt and dropped it.

Its buckle clattered on the floor next to me. The sound gave me an idea. I held out my hands, crossing them at the wrists. I would give him more. More of what pleased him. More of my trust. Smith was looking to make a judgment about me. I would make his decision easier.

"Please, Sir," I pushed the words past the chain in my mouth.

"You want those bound, too?" he guessed, bending over to pick it back up. "Hands behind your back."

I crossed them behind me, and Smith leaned over me, pressing his groin against my face as he looped the belt around my wrists. When he straightened again, he unbuttoned his trousers and pushed his pants and boxers off to reveal his erect cock. Moisture glistened on its crown, beckoning me to lick across its tip. I'd yet to have my mouth on him, but his fingers closed over it.

He smacked his shaft against my cheek, knocking the chain from my teeth. "Do you want this in your mouth?"

"Yes, Sir," I squeaked, not daring to act on the impulse.

"In your pussy? Between your tits?" he continued. "How about up your ass?"

I licked my lips and nodded.

"Now this is important, beautiful. I know other men have fucked you. I wish that wasn't the case. That somehow I'd found you sooner, because I want to own all of your pleasure. Since I can't, I'm going to have to spend a lot of time fucking their memory right out of your pretty little head. When I'm finished, your body will only remember me." He tipped my chin higher with his index finger. "Men have had your pussy, and judging from the way you licked your lips just now, they've had your mouth. Has one come on your tits before?"

I shook my head no. The Oxford boys I'd been with tended toward traditional sexual activities, like missionary position.

Smith leaned down, his face angling toward mine until our lips were nearly touching. "Has one been in your ass?"

"No," I breathed. I couldn't stop myself from squirming a little.

"Not tonight, beautiful," he reassured me with a gentle kiss. "Those things can wait until you're ready. You've saved them for me after all. I want to take my time when it finally comes. Now suck my cock."

Smith took hold of the leash again and stepped back, forcing me to move awkwardly to keep myself upright. It was more difficult than I'd imagined with my hands secured behind me. As I neared him, he drew the leash tighter until I was at eye level with his erection. He left little slack in the chain, and the message was clear: this was where I belonged. This was my pillar. Smith. His cock was simply the nucleus of his masculinity. Forceful. Strong. Unyielding.

I wrapped my lips over the tip and he groaned. I had what he wanted. Willingness. Resilience. Release. Part of me wished I could use my hands. I needed him to climax. I was eager to taste him and desperate to please him. Smith grabbed a handful of my hair, urging me lower.

"I'm going to come in your mouth and wash away

Philip's presence," he growled, tightening his grip on my hair until my scalp sung with pain. "You forgot who you belonged to today. That was an error that I can forgive, because you've proven you know now. But tonight I need to mark you with my teeth, with my palm, and most of all, I need to fill you with me."

He wanted to claim me—brand me—as his. Warmth spread through my chest, and I hollowed my cheeks, sucking furiously, determined to aid his mission.

Frantic.

Smith sensed this and pulled away. "Slowly. We have all night, beautiful. Don't wear yourself out, because you aren't going to get much sleep."

This time when he offered himself to me, my mouth sank slowly down as I savored his smooth, rigid shaft, curling my tongue around it languidly.

"That's better," he rasped. His hips rolled in circles against my mouth, urging himself farther. I relaxed, taking him deep in my throat.

It was a new experience. Smith didn't want quick shags or blowjobs. He wanted pleasure, the kind one could only find in a continual exchange of power. I was on my knees, but as his breathing sped up, I knew I was the one in control. When the first hot spurts shot down my throat, I finally understood.

We were claiming each other.

Smith groaned, bucking hard against my mouth as he came. I took it all, only releasing him when he finally guided my head away with a gentle touch. Reaching down, he dragged me to my feet. With a few swift movements, my hands were free. The chain dangled between my breasts, and he stared at me for a moment, his emerald eyes distant with thought. Then he scooped me off my feet and threw me over his shoulder. I'd barely processed the change in circumstances before he tossed me on the bed. Smith sank down on the ground and hooked an arm around my thigh, wrenching me to the edge of the bed while his other hand collected my leash. He yanked the chain down and inserted it along my seam. Moving it back and forth, he tortured my tender clit. My hands grabbed for the sheets, bracing for when he finally granted me relief. After a few minutes, he drew the chain away and plunged his tongue into my crease. I cried out, feeling the first emissaries of pleasure bolting through me. But Smith knew how to make it last. He licked and sucked me to the edge and then backed off, concentrating on another area until I came to the brink again. He settled over my clit and flicked it with his tongue until my body tensed, then he pulled away.

I was torn between crying and screaming, but I didn't have the strength for either. Instead I whimpered, hoping he would take pity on me. Every nerve at my core was enflamed. A gust of wind would have sent me over the line. But I suspected Smith would never allow that to happen.

"Hush, beautiful," he ordered, undoing the collar around my neck as I writhed. "I'm going to give you what you need, and then you're going to milk me with your perfect cunt."

His cock nudged against my cleft, and I flowered open

for him. Smith slid in with one powerful thrust, severing the ties that held me captive. I arched against him from the force of my climax, and he caught me in his arms, holding me up, as he continued to pound into me.

"You feel so tight," he whispered as he chased his own orgasm. "God, beautiful, your pussy is going to bleed me dry."

I was limp in his arms, boneless and soporific, but I clung to him, kissing his neck, brushing my lips across the stubble on his chin. My attentions drew his mouth to mine. We collided together, fighting to crush closer. Our tongues tangled, and I sucked his into my mouth. I didn't merely want to be owned by him. I wanted him to fill me. I wanted nothing at all to separate us.

Smith lowered my body to the bed, never breaking our connection. My hunger shifted from hopeful to inevitable as he rocked inside me with deep, precise strokes. I cried out against his mouth as tremors quaked through me. Smith's mouth opened wider, swallowing the sounds of pleasure that belonged to him.

When we finally collapsed onto the bed, Smith gathered me in his arms and tucked me against his body. We lay like that for a long time. My fingertips grazed his shyly. The world seemed as new as the bud of a relationship we'd nurtured to this point. Smith caught my hand and brought it to his mouth before withdrawing from me. I held back a sigh, but my disappointment was short-lived when he lowered himself and laid his head on my hip. He brushed his fingers over my sex before pressing his palm to it.

"I want to own this. What do I have to give you? I'll buy you anything. Your own Bugatti? Diamonds? Name your price."

He just had. "You. A Price is my price. Smith Price. That's all you have to give me, and I'm yours."

"An intriguing proposition," he said, his mouth curving into a teasing smirk. "May I counter-bid?"

"No." My denial was firm. Irreversible. This was an all or nothing relationship, and we both knew it.

"I was merely going to suggest a trial basis," he whispered, his attitude no longer joking. "You may think I'm equal compensation now, but we both know that between this gorgeous body and wicked mind, you're worth a premium."

I brushed his hair back from his forehead, shaking my own. "Your body is beautiful."

"The ugliness is inside," he said in a low voice. "When you finally see it—"

"Don't show it to me," I murmured.

"I wish it were that easy." His hands slid under my back as he coiled himself around me.

"It is. This is a fresh start."

"I've never been very good at starting over," he warned me.

"Neither have I." It was one thing I'd never admitted to myself before. "We'll hold each other to it."

"Belle, my tastes..." He trailed off. After a pause, he continued in a strangled voice. "I don't take a woman to bed. I take all of her. I've only shown you a sample of what I'll do to you. If that scares you, leave now. I'll let you go."

But we both knew that was an impossibility. "I've never done anything like that, but I liked it. I—I wanted more."

My cheeks flushed with my confession.

"Oh, beautiful, I'm going to give you as much as you can handle." He bit playfully into the curve of my hip, continuing lower until his tongue skimmed along my bikini line. "And then I'm going to give you more."

I wanted to ask him to promise me, but experience had shown me promises were as easily broken as they were made. A hunch told me he'd also learned this the hard way. Smith didn't offer me a placation. In the end, he crept back over me, and as our bodies joined together, we sought out the answers to questions we hadn't dared asked—the only way we knew how.

CHAPTER NINETEEN

*T*he room was cloaked in darkness when I rolled over, my body searching for hers. Coming up empty, I stroked my frustrated cock for a moment. I couldn't believe she was already out of bed after I'd practically fucked her into a coma last night. I found her writing at the kitchen island, wearing nothing but a button down, which displayed her toned legs. Her hair was slightly tangled, and she still glowed from last night. I allowed myself a moment to drink her in. She glanced up from her paper and grinned. I'd been caught ogling her, but I couldn't care less. The slight movement had revealed a navy necktie knotted loosely around the upturned collar of my shirt. Her fingers wrapped around it, and she pretended to adjust it.

Holy fuck.

"I wasn't sure if we were starting today with work," she purred. "I thought I better dress formally."

"We'll never work again if you continue wearing that," I informed her. Rubbing sleep from my eyes, I opened the refrigerator and fumbled for a few light breakfast items. Despite how little sleep I'd actually gotten, I felt refreshed in a way that only hours spent making a gorgeous woman come could. Pulling a carton of strawberries out, I eyed Belle, who hadn't stopped scribbling in her notebook. "Writing down the details, beautiful? I doubt you're going to forget a moment."

"'Then he placed his finger…'" she trailed away, shaking her head.

"How long did you let me sleep?" I asked, realizing it was nearly noon.

"A couple of hours." Her pen swept over the paper as she spoke.

I couldn't see what she was drawing. "A little bit bigger, beautiful."

"Actually, I'm working on something unrelated to your cock."

"That's unfortunate."

"Narcissist." She dazzled me with a wry smile.

"Looks like that make me want to eat you for breakfast," I warned her, sliding a knife from the block.

Belle sighed but didn't drop her pen. "My body cannot handle another orgasm before food. It might actually kill me. You drained every drop of energy I had last night."

"Noted." I went to work popping the stems off the berries.

She returned to her note-taking, making me even more

intrigued. If she had been as famished as she claimed, why hadn't she grabbed a bite when she came down here? Especially if she'd been in the kitchen for hours. I shifted the cutting board closer to where she sat and peeked across the counter. There was only one word on the page, although it was sketched out over and over. One with swirls. Another thin and modern. And a half dozen other iterations.

Bless.

Her palm flattened, obscuring the page, and I glanced up to discover her eyes wide with embarrassment.

"It's nothing," she said, quickly shutting the notebook.

"It looks like a logo," I guessed. That or she had gotten some serious compulsion issues past me.

She kept her hand over the book, neither confirming nor denying my suspicion. I sensed her hesitation to tell me any more. Best to drop it.

"I want to start my own website," she blurted out. "Company, really."

"You've never mentioned that before." I supposed it was natural that she hadn't until now, but some part of me wished I'd already known. I'd had to catch her in the act of working on her idea. Now telling me about it was less discussion and more confession.

Belle's eyes flickered away, her expression changing from guilty to haughty. She tugged a hair band off her wrist and twisted her golden hair into a messy knot. "You don't exactly like to talk about work-related issues."

Ah. This again. "Technically you work for me now, so isn't everything work-related?"

She lifted an eyebrow, as if waiting for me to explain how last night was work-related. Laughing, I tilted my head in surrender. "I suppose we've clearly crossed the professional and personal life boundary."

"I think we obliterated it actually."

"Speaking of." I prowled closer to her and pressed my lips to the space under her ear. She melted against me before pulling away. "Maybe we should obliterate it further."

"Eat. Food." She emphasized each word with a laugh.

"Okay. I shall make you a meal almost as delicious as you on one condition."

"Which is?

I let her question hang in the air a moment, knowing she assumed my condition would be wicked. I finally answered. "I prep and you tell me about your company."

"Technically, I don't have a company," she hedged.

"Beautiful, I love it when you play hard to get, but I don't like it when you underestimate yourself." I held a strawberry out to her, savoring how she caught it with her teeth. "That was a sample of what I can offer you. Now tell me about Bless."

She licked juice off her lips, nearly distracting me from my mission.

"C'mon, beautiful. I have other ways of getting it out of you." Part of me hoped this led to coaxing it out of her. "I promise once my tongue is on your cunt, you'll tell me anything I want to know."

"You are so full of yourself, Price." But her throat slid on my name, her mind obviously thinking about the other name she had for me.

"I know you'd like it if I fucked it out of you, but you also want this." I brandished another berry.

She swiped it from me with a grimace and flipped open the notebook to another page that featured a hand-drawn graph. "Bless is 'black dress' combined. You've heard the term 'little black dress,' right?"

"I think so," I said dryly.

She tossed the stem of her strawberry at me. "The idea is basically couture clothing for rent. A customer can sign up for a monthly plan and then put items into a wardrobe. We send them out. They send them back. Voila!"

"So it's a subscription service." I scooped up the berry pieces and dropped them into a bowl.

"Yes."

"Aren't there other companies that do that?" I asked. If I was going to be remotely helpful at getting this idea off the ground, I would have to ask every question that came into my head just like an investor. I hoped her answer proved she was prepared for the task.

"Yes, but," she continued swiftly, "none of them focus on couture and designer clothing."

"Is there a reason for that?"

"Because the clothes are ungodly expensive, which means you need lots of capital and insurance for the stock," she admitted. "Most of these other companies offer subscriptions based on number of items out at a time."

I crossed to the fridge and pulled out a bottle of heavy cream. "How will Bless be different?"

"God, you are a lawyer," she teased but immediately grew serious. "Tier-based subscriptions. Designer clothing pricing already falls into tiers. There's a difference between buying Michael Kors and Versace. There should be a difference when you rent them, too."

"It sounds like you have this all worked out." There were a million more things to consider, but only time and persistence were going to get her from concept to company. I poured the cream onto the berries.

Belle peeked into the bowl, her eyes lighting up. But she didn't steal it, instead she popped onto her feet and opened the cabinet. My shirt lifted along with her arms as she reached for the beans, revealing the curve of her butt cheek. "Coffee?"

I moved behind her, grabbing her around the waist and pushing my stiffening cock against her ass. "I think if you're going to wear that, we should avoid anything that could burn you. I can't guarantee not to spill if I catch another glimpse of your pussy."

"You promised me food," she reminded me even as she turned and buried her face against my chest.

My hand instinctively reached up to stroke her hair and pull her closer. She fit here—in my arms. The curves of her body molded seamlessly against me, as though God had created her just for me. But that was impossible. God didn't owe me any favors, and he certainly had nothing to reward me for. Perhaps I was her punishment, although there was no crime she could commit to deserve me.

Or maybe she was my salvation. I pressed my lips to her forehead.

"What are you doing to me, Belle Stuart? You're changing me—rewiring me," I murmured.

Belle tipped her face up, revealing eyes full of her questions that, at the same time, offered me answers.

"I need to feed you," I said in a soft voice.

"I'm not hungry anymore...not for that."

But despite the invitation, I couldn't see past my duty. When I'd taken her, I'd chosen her. I'd placed her under my care and protection. But for the first time, I truly comprehended what that meant. Sliding my arms down, I cupped her ass and lifted her. Belle's legs wrapped tightly around mine, but even the tempting heat of her pussy against my waist couldn't divert me. Carrying her across the kitchen, I lowered her onto the island.

Her eyes closed as she opened her mouth expectantly, but instead of my lips, I pushed a strawberry past her teeth. She moaned as she sucked it free from my fingers and swallowed.

"You're making me jealous, beautiful." I ignored how my balls tightened as her tongue swept traces of cream from her bottom lip. Her teeth tugged gently on the same lip before she opened her mouth wider.

This time when I brought it to her mouth, I held it back, waiting until the cream pooling on its tip dribbled down her neck and onto her collarbone. A spot landed on the tie around her neck.

"Better take that off," I suggested, feeding her another bite while my free hand unknotted the silk necktie.

Belle peeked down at the stain on my three hundred pound tie. "I hope it isn't ruined."

"Fuck the tie," I growled, wrenching it off of her. I brought a handful of berries to her, smashing them across her lips, savoring the way the juicy cream poured over her chin. It only made me realize how good she would look with other things dripping from her mouth. Belle grabbed my fingers and sucked them into her mouth, licking the remnants of her breakfast from them.

"Aren't you hungry?" she asked.

"Such a simple question from such a sinful mouth." I was famished actually. There was no point to trying to salvage the shirt she'd chosen, so rather than mess with unbuttoning it, I gripped the placket and yanked. Buttons scattered across the granite as the shirt slipped over her shoulders, revealing her pert breasts.

"The housekeeper is going to wonder what you were up to...oh!" Belle lost her train of thought as my tongue lapped up her neck and then forced its way into her mouth. She met my hungry kiss voraciously, weaving her fingers into my hair and dragging me closer.

When I pulled back, we were both breathless. "I'm not done eating yet."

Picking up the bowl, I spilled the remainder across her tits. Without hesitation, I bent to lick it off of her. My arms bracketed her back as my tongue sucked cream from the stiff tips of her nipples. Nothing had ever tasted so good. Cream pooled in her belly button, and I dragged the puddle down, tracking it to the swollen apex of her cunt. Slipping two fingers into her wet slit, I spread her open, allowing it to stream across her sex, coating the delectable pink bud as it ran down.

I wanted to suck it clean. I wanted to pull her clit between my teeth until she screamed for the release only I could grant her. But I needed her to beg. I derived my self-control from the promise that patience would yield her breathless and supple. If I had to adjust my whole life around this new compulsion I felt about her, then I would remind her that her existence centered around me from now on.

Keeping my touch feather light, I circled around the nub with the tip of my tongue. Belle's head fell back, and my arm braced her more tightly as a tormented cry burst from her. My lips twitched at the sound.

"That's right, beautiful," I grunted into her swollen sex. She writhed against the movement of my lips, but I drew away. Only far enough to prevent her from locking onto a source of friction. Dipping my tongue into her cleft, I flicked it, appreciating the faint contractions already beginning in her channel. She was close, but I wasn't nearly finished with her.

Abandoning her pussy, I returned to her breasts, closing my mouth over her nipple and sucking the soft tissue into my mouth. In a flash, Belle tucked up her knees and planted her feet on the edge of the counter as she sought relief between her legs.

"Get back down there." She barely forced the words past her breathless pants.

I couldn't have that. I tapped her chin lightly in warning, and her clenched eyes flew open. "I don't take commands."

"I'm sorry," she breathed. "Please get back down there, Sir."

"Not even if you command me nicely," I said, wrenching her hips forward so that her knees smashed against her breasts. I crushed my body against hers. "Do it again, and I'll have you on your knees, sucking me off, and then you'll spend the rest of the day with a bare, needy cunt. Do you know what happens then? No chairs. No sitting. No friction. All you'll do is wait until I allow you pleasure again. Now what do you want to ask me, beautiful?"

"Please may I come, Sir?" she shrieked as I circled my hips against her tortured sex. Her whimpers wracked through her as I held her trembling body.

"That's a proper request," I said, knowing praise would soothe her.

Her wild eyes met mine, and another plea fell from her lips. "Please kiss me. Oh God, kiss me, Smith."

My mouth collided with hers. She hadn't asked. She hadn't begged. Still the desperation in the request plucked a string in my heart I'd thought was out of tune. Instead the note rang through me, vibrating at a pitch I'd forgotten.

Her heels dug into my sides and pushed down my boxers, freeing my cock. In one smooth motion, I lifted her ass and slid inside her.

A strangled cry—half pleasure, half agony—ripped through her. I smothered her anguish with another kiss. Her hand slipped from my hair down to the nape of my neck as she clung to me. I straightened up, refusing to break the kiss, and her legs encircled my waist. Keeping one hand on the small of her back, I held her steady as she lifted her ass up and then plunged it back down.

I wanted to whisper dirty things in her ear and watch as her body reacted but not as much as I wanted my lips on hers. My tongue forced itself deeper into her open mouth. Every fibre of my being longed to fill her. My cock. My mouth. It wasn't enough. I needed more than her body. I coveted her soul.

Sensing her muscles tense, I thrust harder, hammering her toward devastation. She fell apart in my arms, crumbling into a wreckage of sobs and screams that exhorted my own climax. I cracked open at the core, erupting inside her until all that was left was a tangle of sweaty limbs. I held her there, unwilling to extricate my body from hers.

Because I no longer knew where I ended and she began.

CHAPTER TWENTY

I'd never considered having two sinks in my master bath an asset until this morning, but as Belle poked through the drawer looking for a spare toothbrush, the space felt like it had been made for the two of us. The white tiles on the walls and floor reflected the light from the windows, making the room as light and airy as her presence made me feel.

I grabbed my shaving brush and lathered my face before I slid open my straight razor. The method took a precision that I appreciated. One wrong move and I'd cut the hell out of myself. Belle paused and watched me intently.

"That looks dangerous," she commented as I rinsed the blade so I could continue.

"I prefer a close shave," I told her, flipping the straight razor closed and holding it out to her.

She took it cautiously and smiled shyly. "I rather like when you have a little stubble."

"Why is that?" I moved closer until our bodies lightly brushed one another's.

"What did you call it earlier? Friction?" There was a playful tone to her words. She'd become giddy at the memory of our kitchen encounter. If I had it my way, she'd look at every room in this house and feel the same exhilaration.

"It grows fast, beautiful," I promised her. "I'll show you just how fast tomorrow morning. But for now, finish this for me."

"Me?" She tried to push the razor back into my hands. "I don't know the first thing about how to use that. What if I miss and slit your throat?"

"Then I will die a happy man." I took her arm and guided her to the toilet. Sinking onto its lid, I tilted my face to expose the area still covered in shave soap. "Just like this."

I opened the razor and placed her fingers in the correct positions, noting that her hand was trembling. "Don't be scared. I'm not."

"You aren't the one wielding an eighteenth century street weapon." She sighed and held the blade closer to my face.

Turning her wrist so that it was at the proper angle, I guided her hand down, enjoying the slight tug as the blade swept over my skin.

"Your turn," I told her.

She moved the razor over and hesitated before pressing it gently against my face and repeating the motion I'd shown her.

"And I'm still alive," I teased her softly.

"Careful, Price," she warned me. "I'm still the one with the sharp object."

I lifted my chin, exposing the much more delicate skin of my neck. The wrong angle or a moment of panic and that would be the end of her shaving career. "Let the razor guide you," I advised.

She approached the task with more confidence this time, drawing the blade swiftly down until it was finished. I started to stand, but her hand pressed on my shoulder. "Wait. I missed a spot over here."

I turned my face, allowing her access. The blade glided over the curve of my jawline smoothly until it caught, sending a sharp twinge of pain ringing through my flesh. Belle startled away from me as apologies spilled from her lips. "I'm so sorry. Oh my God, you're bleeding."

"It's nothing. I've cut myself before." The sting had already dulled.

"But I haven't cut you," she whispered. Leaning down, she brushed a kiss over the wound. I watched her, mesmerized, as she licked the small smear of my blood from her lips.

Taking the straight razor from her, I snapped it closed and threw it into the sink. I reached for her, but she bounced away, breaking the hypnotic spell of the act.

"Uh-uh." She wagged her index finger in my direction. "I have a lunch date with your favorite person."

"Oh?"

"Edward, so I need to get in the shower." There was a mixture of finality and challenge in her tone.

"He's important to you," I surmised, which meant I needed to get a hold on my feelings about her being around other men. "We should have dinner with him."

"Are you going to hit him?" she asked in a dry voice.

I shrugged noncommittally and grinned. "Only if he deserves it."

"We could invite his fiancé, so you feel less threatened." Belle's eyes glinted with amusement. "But before we do any of that, I need to shower!"

I sprang to my feet and pounced on her. Backing her into the wall, I trailed a string of kisses along her jaw. "We'll both get in the shower," I suggested. "I'll wash you."

"The point of a shower is to come out cleaner." But she giggled, and I knew it was a done deal.

Stepping away from her, I held up my hands in surrender. "Get in the shower. I'll put on some music."

"Music, huh?" She scurried over and turned on the water.

"Music soothes my savage side. It's your best chance at controlling me if you're going to be naked and wet within a ten mile radius." Unlocking my phone, I accessed the house's sound system and chose a playlist. A few seconds later, a bluesy rhythm filled the air as Mick Jagger began to croon.

"The Stones?" she asked. "I pegged you as more of a classical listener."

"Beautiful, this is classical. I grew up with the Stones."

"God, for a second I thought you were going to tell me you're their lawyer."

"I'm not. " I winked at her. "But I know their lawyers."

"Of course you do." She brushed her lips over my shoulder. It was a relatively chaste kiss, but that didn't matter to my dick.

I swatted her ass, shooing her under the water. "Get in before I change my mind about joining you."

Returning to the sink, I splashed cool water on my face to rinse away any remaining residue. I fully intended to behave myself, but the reflection of Belle in the mirror gave me other ideas. She twisted under the shower stream, tilting her head back so the water washed down her hair. Steam had begun to fog the room when I slid open the glass door and joined her.

"I thought this was my shower," she called, blinking water from her eyes.

"It's a double shower. You're not the only one who needs to get cleaned up." I smirked as I switched on the set of shower heads on the opposite side. Leaning back into the warm stream, I reached for my dick and began to pump it with my fist. My eyes hooded lustily as I watched her soap up her tits.

"Are you enjoying yourself?" she called, lathering the flat plane of her stomach. Her fingers dipped between her legs, washing her pussy a bit too thoroughly.

"Are you?" I asked, massaging my balls as I continued to stroke myself off.

She shrugged and turned her back to me, rubbing lather over her round ass. I was definitely enjoying the show, but it seemed some audience participation was in order. I hooked my right arm around her waist and pulled her against me, guiding my cock to her slippery entrance. Pushing the crown barely inside her, I paused.

"Isn't it better to get dirty now when cleanup is so easy?" I said in a gruff voice, pistoning deeper into her channel.

She leaned into me, allowing my left arm to snake between her breasts. I shoved my cock fully into her, lifting her feet from the ground as she cried out.

"This is admittedly a bit slippery," I whispered in her ear.

She took the cue as I lowered her to the balls of her feet and bent forward, pressing her palms to the tiled shower wall.

"I can't decide which view I prefer," I said in a husky voice. "Your gorgeous cunt stretched over my cock or the look on your face when you come." I slid inside her, relishing how the velvet smooth walls of her pussy squeezed my shaft. It was good, but I needed more. Withdrawing, I spun her around and pinned her against the wall. In a swift motion, I'd hoisted her against the tile and thrust back inside her. Her arms splayed across the wall as I continued my relentless assault. In the background, a new song began to play, and I matched the tempo as water spilled across us.

"Tell me what you want," I growled, pounding roughly into her.

Her arm lashed out and grabbed my face. "You. I want you."

"Fuck, beautiful. I'm yours." We crashed into one another, our bodies sliding in frantic unison as we searched for release together. When her hold on me tightened, I captured her mouth, sucking the sounds of her climax into me. I felt her pleasure flooding through my veins as I unleashed my own, emptying myself into her tight cunt.

I helped her gently to her feet, keeping a hold on her so she wouldn't slip. She blinked at me, still lost in a haze of bliss, as I found the bar of soap. Reaching between her thighs, I ran it along her folds, washing away the cum spilling from her. She clung to me as I rinsed the lather off. I didn't release her as we stepped out of the shower. Wrapping a thick towel around her, I rubbed it roughly across her skin until it glowed pink.

I took her hand to help her into the bedroom, but she shook her head. "I think I can walk."

"I won't be satisfied until you can't," I warned her.

She disappeared through the door, swaying her ass saucily the whole way.

"Are you sure you have to meet Edward?" I called in to her. "If you stay here, I can make it worth your while."

The thought I'd be without her, even for a short period,

made me want to bend her over the sink and fuck her until she begged to stay. I'd endured our separation this week, sensing that she needed space. Now that she no longer required that, it was difficult to give her any.

Pausing in the doorway, I watched as she unwadded her gown from last night and studied it.

"I wasn't planning to do the walk of shame," she admitted with a grin. "And no knickers to boot."

"I'd prefer you wear knickers when you go to lunch with another man, even a gay man." I crossed to my closet and flipped on the light. "Come here, beautiful."

"I don't think I can fit in your shorts," she said dryly, but the sarcasm faded from her voice as she spotted the dress in my hands.

"I had a few things delivered here," I explained, stepping aside to display a rack of clothing selected by her stylist at Harrods. "Shoes are over there."

Her feet belonged in Louboutins, and I'd made certain she would have no shortage at her disposal. A dozen pairs in varying styles from sky-high to demure lined the shelf. She pranced over to them, trailing her fingers over the leather.

"I only forgave you yesterday afternoon." She rounded on me. "When did you order these?"

"Tuesday."

"You're awfully sure of yourself." Her eyes narrowed, and I sensed she was struggling between annoyance and delight.

"I hoped you would come back." I went to her and ran

my knuckles down her jawline. "And if you didn't, I was going to drag you back here."

"Has anyone ever told you that you're a bit of a cave man?" she said, her lips twitching with a suppressed smile.

"Beautiful, I'd be a happy man if I only had to fuck and eat," I admitted, angling my face to bite her shoulder.

"I think you also had to hunt and find shelter," she said, pushing me away and grabbing a pair of heels.

"I already have the biggest cave, and"—I grabbed my dick—"the best tool."

"Later, you can show me how to use it, but now I'm getting dressed!" She swiped the closest garment and dashed out.

When I'd finally picked out a casual pair of trousers and a tailored button down, I emerged after her. She was slipping a heel on, bent in a graceful position that was the very definition of sensual femininity. She straightened up and shot me a warning look.

"I'm going to dry my hair," she informed.

I grabbed her as she tried to pass me and kissed her. "Come back to my bed tonight."

"Wild horses," she whispered. I released her, smiling at the reference. I couldn't be dragged away either.

My mobile buzzed on the nightstand, and I realized that wasn't quite true.

"This is Price," I answered. My light mood vanished like clouds stealing across the sun. I listened intently as my mind started sorting through options.

By the time, Belle reappeared in the room, I was fully dressed. "I need to go into the office. I'll drop you off."

"Is anything wrong?" she asked, grabbing her purse.

Only everything.

I kissed her forehead. "No. Everything is perfect."

CHAPTER TWENTY-ONE

Smith insisted on driving me to my lunch date with Edward. He coasted through the streets of London, blaring the Rolling Stones. When we reached the restaurant, he put the Bugatti in park and leaned in for a kiss.

"Behave yourself," he advised me.

"I think you prefer it when I'm bad." I left him with that thought as the valet opened the door for me. I swayed my ass saucily as I climbed out, knowing he was paying attention. In the bedroom, he held all the power. Outside of it was a different story. A fact I was prepared to show him at every possible convenience. The uniformed man looked distinctly disappointed that he wasn't going to be parking the sports car.

Considering Smith hadn't relented on letting me drive it, I understood his pain.

The dining room was crowded with the afternoon

crowd, popping in to grab an early tea or a late lunch, but I spotted Edward's friendly face from across the room.

Edward set down his menu and rose to greet me as I neared him. Grabbing both of my hands, he studied me for a moment. "You're glowing," he accused. "Tell me that's a new skincare regime."

"No." I smacked him in the shoulder as I sat down. "I spent the night with Smith."

I reached for my glass of water, shrugging like this was no big deal. Edward tipped his glasses to the end of his nose and shook his head like a disappointed schoolmistress.

"I can't help it if I have needs."

"Needs which you denied for months," Edward reminded me as he perused his menu. "Then you picked the biggest todger out of the bunch and shagged him."

"I think Philip qualifies as the biggest todger." In fact, I knew he did. "Especially after yesterday."

Edward opened his mouth to beg the story out of me as the waitress appeared. I took my time ordering, having recently discovered the impact of being forced to wait for satisfaction. By the time she hurried off with her notepad, he was drumming all ten fingers on the table.

"Story. Now," he demanded.

"It's not much of a story." I pressed my index finger to the tine of my fork until a prickle of pain shot across the tip.

"Don't be coy with me, woman," he warned me. "I have access to people that can find out."

I snorted at this, trying to imagine sweet Prince Edward pulling such a corrupt move. He wasn't the type. His brother, on the other hand, would already have someone following me. "But then you wouldn't get all the good details like how I felt and what went through my head."

"What?" he pressed. "Why were things going through your head?" He pushed his glasses higher on his nose, looking as if he might explode any moment.

This really was kind of fun, but since I was still sorting through my own tangled emotions about the last twenty-four hours, I supposed I needed to come clean, particularly if I wanted his insight. Or, at the very least, a sympathetic ear.

"Philip showed up outside Smith's office yesterday."

Edward groaned and leaned back in his chair, scanning the room as if every patron in the establishment would simultaneously groan along with him. "I bet that went over well."

"Smith didn't see him," I clarified. "Not that it mattered."

"Oh?" His voice peaked on the word.

"Let's see. The abridged version is that he made a mistake, and he wishes he could take it back, but Pepper lied to him."

"How shocking," Edward said in a dry voice. "I swear those two deserve each other."

"I couldn't agree more. Then he kissed me, and I felt nothing."

"He kissed you?" Edward repeated.

"Apparently I'm very desirable all of a sudden." I wanted to tell him more. About the kiss. About Georgia's threat and Smith's reaction. But something held me back.

"You've always been desirable." The reaction reminded me of Smith.

"Smith does that, too," I said without thinking. "Gets on my case when I'm being hard on myself."

"I'll admit I like him a little more hearing that," Edward said, somewhat grudgingly.

"Me too. I think I might be getting in over my head," I admitted. "Our relationship is moving so quickly that I feel like I need to grab something and hang on."

"Sounds like you're falling in love."

I scoffed at this, shaking my head. It was way too soon for that, but my chest tightened a little as I considered it. "That would be terrible, considering my best friend hates him."

"Maybe he'll win over Clara," Edward teased. "But in all seriousness, if you care about him, he must have some redeeming qualities."

"He wants you and David to have dinner with us," I told him, waiting to gauge his reaction.

"Sounds like he's falling in love, too. Or at least he wants to be a significant part of your life."

"Maybe." It was all I could commit to for now. Although I suspected Edward was right. "I made the mistake of believing a man wanted that before."

"Philip was a prat. He never deserved you."

I raised my water goblet in toast to this. "That is definitely true."

Our food arrived a few moments later, and conversation shifted to talk of wedding plans.

"When are you going to set a date?" I'd been prodding him about this for months, adopting the philosophy that if pressure could turn a lump of coal into a diamond then I could exert enough force to see that Edward finally made it down the aisle.

"If only UK law applied to everyone equally."

I speared a Brussels sprout on my fork and waved it around. "Correct me if I'm wrong but isn't Alexander the one who grants permission in this case?"

"Yes," Edward said with some hesitation.

"Than I don't see what the problem is. He's going to say yes." I had no doubt about that. Both Alexander and Clara seemed as anxious as I was to see the two happily married.

"It's more about the court of public opinion." He held up a hand to stop me from interrupting him. "I know this is modern times, and there's been very little backlash. If it was my father's decision, it would obviously be a no-go."

"But it's not, so why are you waffling?" I abandoned my food altogether and stared him down.

"David went from being my secret to being in the public eye so quickly that I'm not certain he knows what he's getting into. You've seen what happened to Clara in the last year," Edward reminded me. "I don't want to put him through that."

"You should have considered it before you popped the

question, because that man is already picking out baby names." I'd seen how David's eyes had lit up when he held Elizabeth in the hospital. He was ready to be settled with a family of his own. "And Clara was the victim of a psycho and bad luck."

"Alexander thinks there's more to it than that." Edward's voice lowered conspiratorially. "He's been investigating what happened at the wedding."

My blood turned to ice. "I thought he dropped that."

"This is Alexander we're talking about. Clara is his world. Come on, Belle, there's no way Daniel could have acted alone, and until we have answers, all of our lives are on hold."

"Does Clara know about any of this?" My thoughts, which had been muddled for most of the morning, now came into precise focus. My best friend was home with her newborn baby while the people who'd tried to hurt her were still loose. "Or it possible Alexander's just being overly paranoid?"

"Not this time," Edward said in a grim voice. "Without knowing who was behind it, I can't risk another royal wedding."

"Elope," I advised. "Give David his wedding, and stay off the radar of whoever is behind this."

"I think David would like that idea even less than having to wait. You've seen his wedding planner."

I had, in fact, contributed to the bulky binder of ideas David had been storing since the proposal.

"Take it from someone who knows both of you. David

wants to marry you. He won't care how, and if that means giving up a dream wedding, he won't even blink." I continued, admitting something that I hadn't had the courage to before, "I wanted the dream. The dress. The party. The exotic honeymoon. I was so blinded by the perfect wedding and what I thought would be the perfect life that I didn't realize I'd chosen the wrong man."

"Speaking of the wrong man," Edward murmured, his gaze shifting past me. I followed his line of sight in time to see Philip and Pepper sitting down a few tables over.

It was as if I was looking into a carnival mirror. A year ago it might have been me being seated with Philip. Now the leggy blonde at his side looked like a sexed-up version of myself. Pepper was dressed in an ivory top with a black tulle skirt that was too short to be in good taste. Whereas I'd cut my hair, she'd kept hers long, styling it into the long waves I knew Philip preferred. Philip nodded noncommittally as she told him something, her hands gesticulating wildly as she spoke. The diamond on her left ring finger caught the light, sending dazzling sparkles shining off of her. I had to admit that I enjoyed knowing that he was looking for an out.

"Don't you own that outfit?" Edward asked, sounding as unimpressed as I felt.

"You're confusing the skirt and the man," I said dryly. Although, in all fairness, I'd never owned either of them.

"I guess the engagement is official." Edward kept his tone even, obviously not wanting to add salt to the wound.

"He admitted as much to me yesterday. I told him he

was getting what he deserved." I swiveled back in my seat, pressing a hand to my nauseated stomach.

Edward's eyebrows knitted together, creasing his smooth forehead. "You okay?"

"Yeah. I just feel like I have some unfinished business there." I knew I did. I'd spent the last half of a year wedging open the door for Philip to return. Yesterday I'd shut it, but now I needed to lock it permanently.

Edward shifted the conversation back to lighter topics, but even though I tried to relax, I could feel the two of them at my back. When I caught Pepper heading to the loo out of the corner of my eye, I stood.

"Excuse me a moment." I didn't wait for him to object. He had to have seen her get up, given that he was facing their table, but if he was going to stop me, I didn't give him the chance.

Pausing at the door, I said a silent prayer that no one else was in there and pushed it open. Walking to the sinks, I dug my lipstick out of my purse and applied it, scanning the mirror until I saw her heels in one of the stalls. I took a deep breath and waited. My stomach flipped over when I heard the toilet flush.

Now would be a very good time to run. I ignored the little voice warning me away. I wasn't running any more. Not from this anyway.

Pepper emerged from the stall, smoothing down her puffy skirt and froze when she caught sight of me. I smiled wickedly into the mirror and pivoted around to face her.

"Imagine running into you here." I dropped the tube of lipstick back into my purse and glared at her.

She crossed to the far end of the sink and turned on the tap. "If you're planning to break my nose again, I should warn you that this time Philip won't be able to talk me out of a lawsuit."

"I'm not, but seeing as I have my own lawyer now, it would be an interesting case." If anything, I didn't want to break her nose, I wanted to break her neck. Not because of what she'd done by wrecking my engagement but because of the havoc she'd inflicted on the people I cared about. She needed to be taught a lesson. The trouble was that I'd tried to teach her that lesson on multiple occasions, including the time when I slugged her. Some bitches never learn.

"That will come in handy when I break your nose, I suppose." She talked a big game, but I saw her hands shaking.

"Lovely ring." I couldn't help but notice it was much smaller than the one Philip had given to me. I supposed when you gambled and lost, you don't place as much money on the next bet.

"We're getting married this winter," she informed me, her voice taking on the catty tone she'd perfected through years of terror.

"I can see that. Cold-blooded people normally prefer chilly weather. Less jarring," I added.

This was going exactly as I'd imagined it would, but not how I had hoped. I'd gotten in my shots, now it was time to say what I came in for.

"Actually, I followed you in here for a reason," I began.

She picked up a paper towel from the basket and dried her hands. "Of course, you followed me. I don't know how to spell it out to you, but Philip belongs to me now. Please refrain from stalking me over it."

"Just like King Albert belonged to you? Or Alexander? You've certainly owned a string of men. At least this one is pretending you have a future with him." Damn it, I'd fallen right back into her petty trap. Squaring my shoulders, I refocused on my purpose for being here. "I wanted to thank you. If I hadn't caught you with Philip, I'd probably be married to the wanker right now—and I'm guessing you know how boring that would be."

"He never would have married you," she said, bypassing my jab at her fiancé. "You never would have married him."

"Then I guess I would have been thanking you either way," I said serenely. "The thing is that, until recently, I didn't know what a little man Philip was in every way. Now that I've experienced a real man, I know how deeply unsatisfied Philip made me."

"Perhaps the fault lay in you. I don't have the same problem." She tossed her hair over her shoulder and took a tentative step toward the door.

She might not have learned not to provoke me, but she clearly feared being in proximity to me. I tallied that as a victory.

"There was one other thing." This is where I was going to lower the bomb I hadn't intended on dropping. "Since technically you did me a favor by ridding

231

me of Philip's dead weight, I think I should return the kindness. Do you know where he was yesterday morning?"

Pepper's jaw tensed but she shrugged. "I don't have to keep tabs on him. He's completely loyal to me."

"Then you'd be surprised to hear he came to see me at work. He told me about your engagement and about how you lied about being pregnant."

"I didn't lie," she snapped, blinking away sudden tears. "I lost the baby."

As much as I hated Pepper Lockwood, my heart sank for her. Maybe a child would have forced her to grow up and see life outside of her own needs. "I am sorry to hear that. But you should know that he asked me to come back to him."

"Liar!" she shrieked.

I barely had time to duck before the basket of paper towels whizzed over my head. "And then he kissed me."

I was grateful that there was nothing else she could throw within reach. As soon as my words sank in, she straightened up and shot me a nasty look.

"You can lie all you want, Belle. I'm marrying Philip and you can't stop me."

"You have my blessing," I told her. "I've felt for a long time that you two are truly meant to be. I only hope you don't destroy everyone that gets in your path."

"Then might I advise you to stay clear of me." She ran past me and vanished out the door, leaving the truth hanging in the air behind her.

When I rejoined Edward at the table, he gave me an interested look.

"Whatever you said to her did the trick, because they left in a hurry," he informed me.

"I said what I needed to say." I left it at that. Edward knew all the details. He didn't need me to fill in the gaps.

"Well, half the restaurant heard what you said to her, because she was screaming it at him. It was quite the floor-show. I almost applauded." A smirk carved across his mouth, and he lifted his glass this time.

I tapped mine against it, appreciating the celebratory clink. Placing it back on the table, I smiled.

"Do you want dessert or was that sweet enough for you?" he asked.

"More than sweet enough," I confirmed, "but let's get dessert anyway."

EDWARD KISSED my cheek as we exited the restaurant, then hastily looked around. "Thank God, Smith isn't here."

"I told him there was nothing to worry about," I said as I shouldered my purse, feeling the vibration of an incoming text message. As Edward headed the opposite direction, I pulled my mobile out.

SMITH: All afternoon i've been thinking about your brown sugar.

I smiled at the lewd reference to this morning's unorthodox breakfast and our musical shower.

BELLE: Don't start me up or you won't be getting any work done this afternoon.

I kept the phone in my hand as I headed toward the Tube. Smith might not like the idea of me taking public transit, but it would be ridiculous to hail a cab to get all the way to my flat. Before I could make it underground, another message arrived.

SMITH: Have a little sympathy for the devil and come into the office.

I shook my head. The man was insatiable, a trait I found I really appreciated. Dashing off one more text, I hit send before descending into the station.

BELLE: I promise later there will be satisfaction.

As I swiped my Oyster card, I realized I'd lost my connection and shoved the phone back into my purse. There was something soothing about taking the Tube, and I settled into my seat, studying the other passengers. Mums trying to keep their toddlers from toppling over when the car banked hard. Tourists trying to decipher an Underground map before they missed their stop. Teens listening to music, completely oblivious to the world around them. And a couple shamelessly making out in the corner.

That was something I couldn't imagine doing with Smith. Considering how far he'd already taken me, I hadn't thought there was a limit. Still, just seeing the pair go at it made me smile.

Bollocks. Edward was right. I was falling for Smith. That or I'd swallowed a load of butterflies. It seemed that overnight I'd become one of those girls walking around with her thoughts in the clouds and a goofy smile pinned to her face—and I couldn't care less. The lights overhead flickered momentarily as we shot through a tunnel, casting a shadow over my happiness.

There were things I didn't know about Smith. We hadn't spoken of our pasts, although I guessed he knew a lot more about me given how carefully he had screened my application. I shouldn't be so easily consumed by him. Not until he started opening up, but considering how he made me feel, did it even matter?

I was still pondering this question two connections later when the overhead speaker called my stop. As soon as I was out, I checked my phone.

SMITH: Let's spend the night together.

Apparently, the Stones had a song appropriate for every occasion. All of my doubts evaporated at the thought of his hands on my body. I had a million questions for him, but I couldn't expect them all to be answered at once. Maybe his newly discovered playfulness was the first step in letting me get closer to him.

But I couldn't help toying with him now.

BELLE: You can't always get what you want.

That would get him riled up. In fact, I'd never met a man who so easily got what he wanted, especially from me.

Another message appeared on my phone, not from Smith. An address. Apparently someone had their numbers mixed up. I slid away the notification as another text arrived from him. I could almost hear his voice as I read it.

SMITH: Gimme shelter.

The song immediately began to play in all its raw, brutal power. That he'd chosen that one sucked the air from me. It was the crux of the problem. A wall separated us still, and I wanted nothing more than to tear it down brick by brick. I knew then that I would give him shelter. I would give him anything he asked. I only wanted to know what a man like him needed protection from.

I couldn't continue the game. No response felt appropriate. The only thing I could offer him was myself. I had to hope that would be enough.

It felt good to be home. My flat had been my safe space for the last few months, protecting me from the threats of the real world outside. Jane had opened her door when I needed it most, and even now with life starting to finally look up, returning here felt like the solace I needed from the changes taking hold over me.

I threw my keys down next to a stack of yesterday's mail and called out for my aunt. The voice that answered made me shudder.

"We're in here."

My mother's voice.

Steeling myself, I forced a smile and walked into the living area. Some children look like their mothers, but once again I was struck by how different we were. I looked much more like my father, which was perhaps the reason my mother's lips pursed as I came into view. I was an unwelcome reminder of the life that she had lost.

Her eyes were as dark as the raven hair pinned elegantly up on her head. It had begun to gray at the temples since the last time I saw her, but I kept this thought to myself. As always, she was impeccably dressed in a rose dress suit and pearls. We both liked expensive clothing. That was as similar as we got.

Mother scanned me, not bothering to hide her disapproval of my dress and its revealing neckline, but she didn't say anything.

Our relationship was built on what we left unsaid.

"I didn't know you were coming to town," I said, leaning in for the obligatory cheek kiss. She accepted it without returning it.

"You wouldn't commit to a meeting time," she reminded me, "or tell me anything about this new job. My aunt hasn't been forthcoming either."

Jane smiled pleasantly at her and poured hot water into a chipped teacup. She held it out to her.

Mum took it, grimacing as she spotted its imperfection, and turned the irregular side away from her. I hated her for that.

"I've been very busy." I dropped into an overstuffed armchair and crossed my legs, knowing that it drove her crazy.

Ladies cross their ankles. I heard her voice correcting me in my mind. Most of my memories of my childhood included useful tidbits such as that. If she had any idea how unladylike I'd become, she would probably faint.

"What is on your neck?" she asked, leaning forward to zero in on whatever she had spotted.

My hand flew to my throat, but it was too late. I hadn't actually checked myself for marks. Now I had no idea what she was referring to. Bite mark? Bruise? Hickey? They all seemed pretty likely.

Jane swooped to my rescue. "It looks like her seat belt must have rubbed her the wrong way."

"Seat belt?" Curiosity colored my mother's words. "I didn't know they used seat belts on the Tube."

"Belle has her own car now," Jane said.

I glared at her. So much for saving me. Jane shrugged, as if to say 'let's put our cards on the table.'

"Your own car?" my mother repeated in a strangled voice.

It didn't matter that the family estate's garage housed a dozen luxury automobiles that we couldn't afford. All she heard was that I had betrayed her.

"It's not mine," I fibbed. "It's for work. I only use it to run errands."

I'd already decided if I ever left my job, I wouldn't keep the car, which made it a perk of my position and nothing more. I left out that it was a Mercedes.

"What is this job anyway?" she snapped. "And before you get smart with me, I didn't appreciate your off-color remarks the first time."

"I'm not a stripper," I reassured her. Well, not really. I

didn't know if there was a term for a woman who shagged her boss. "I work for a lawyer as his personal assistant."

"At least it's nothing important." She leaned over and placed her teacup on the table in front of her. She might have just thrown it at me for all intents and purposes.

It amazed me that after all this time she could still hurt me with her words. Of course, I'd never developed a thick skin so much as I had a smart mouth. My sarcasm bothered her more anyway.

"Belle is quite happy with her new position." Jane rose to my defense, glowering at her. There was nothing like seeing my aunt's feathers ruffled.

"Unless it pays the mortgage then it's not important," Mum explained. She looked to me as if I would volunteer to write her a check.

My salary could pay many of the estate's expenses, but it would leave me with very little to get back on my feet. Since I'd left for school, the ties that bound me to my childhood had frayed. In the last year, they'd broken entirely. Still, guilt tugged at me.

"Just enough for rent," I lied.

Jane bit back a smile across from me, barely hiding it before my mother turned on her. "It's disgraceful that you would charge your own niece rent."

"London is very expensive." Jane blinked as if this was reason enough. Neither of us were about to tell her that I hadn't written Jane a check since I'd moved into her spare room.

"I came with good news." Despite this announcement,

my mother sounded anything but happy. She twisted the strand of pearls around her neck.

"Please share," Jane finally prompted when it was clear she was waiting for us to show a respectful amount of interest.

"We've been approached to rent the estate to the BBC for that period drama the Americans like so well."

"Wexford Hall?" I offered, frowning.

"Yes, they were unable to reach a deal with the Abernathys. Apparently, Philip was quite demanding in his negotiations and suggested they contact me about using our home for future filming." Mother's pointed look could pierce flesh.

"He wasn't doing us a favor." I got right to the heart of the matter.

"Don't kid yourself, Belle." She dismissed my response with a wave of the hand. "It was clearly a peace offering. Philip wants to make amends with you."

"Philip is engaged to the woman he cheated on me with." Only my mother would walk into my own home and suggest I take back the asshole.

"He's very unhappy. He feels he made a mistake."

I froze for a moment as I processed what she was telling me. Clutching the arms of the chair so I wouldn't fly out, I leveled my gaze with hers. "Please tell me you've become a psychic."

"He came to see me earlier this week. I gave him my blessing to approach you." It was clear from her tone that she saw no issue with this.

"He's engaged!" Maybe if I said it louder, she'd finally hear me.

"Men make mistakes. Lord knows your father made plenty."

"Father didn't sleep with other women. He was loyal." The rage simmering inside me began to boil over.

"Yes, but he made mistakes. However, the estate was always his top priority. How would he feel to hear you were shunning a chance to protect it from ruin?"

That was my mother. It was up to me. It always had been. Staff needn't be trimmed. Cars couldn't be sold. Considering the BBC offer was the first concession she'd ever made regarding her lifestyle. "His loyalty to that estate —to you—killed him."

"He killed himself," she said coldly.

My hand clapped over my mouth as an unwanted mirror swam into my head.

Dangling, lifeless feet. Daddy was being silly and he wouldn't stop. I got on a chair and tugged his leg, but he still wouldn't come down.

Screams. Screams from her mouth.

And then I hit the floor hard. I curled into a ball. Mummy didn't even care that she'd knocked me off.

She just kept screaming.

Screaming and pulling on him.

Tears filled my eyes as I covered my ears.

Jane's arm wrapped around my shoulders as I tried to claw my way back to the present. When I found myself back in my flat, the tears belonged to me and not the five year-old girl in my memory.

"Get out," Jane said, pointing toward the door.

"We have business to discuss," my mother said, ignoring her. "Thanks to your father's poor business acumen, all decisions regarding the financial state of the estate must be approved by my daughter."

"You don't have a daughter," I croaked past the rawness creeping up my throat.

"How I wished that was the truth. A son would have been useful. He would care about his family. Instead I was stuck with you," she snarled.

The barb didn't stick. I'd known she felt this way my whole life. "Do whatever you want with it. Because if you leave it to me, I'll burn the fucking place down."

"Language!" she reprimanded me.

"You obviously didn't hear me," Jane roared. "Get out of my house, Ann!"

She stood, tugging down her tailored jacket and cast a hateful glare at me. "I'll send the BBC contract for you to peruse. Either sign it or take Philip back, but standing by and ruining what I've rebuilt is not an option."

Her final words were still ringing in my ears when the door slammed closed behind her. It was a joke really. In the last nineteen years, she'd rebuilt nothing.

Certainly not me.

CHAPTER TWENTY-TWO

The contracts were in my inbox when I arrived at the office three hours ago, and I was still staring at them. One stroke of the pen would sever a tie that had bound me far too long to past mistakes—mistakes not of my making. But it would also introduce scrutiny. The decision to withdraw my inherited stakes in my father's nightclub shouldn't raise any eyebrows, but it would. I'd set the wheels in motion months ago, hoping to dissolve my interest quietly. There had been nothing to risk then.

Now that had changed.

My extended family could offer Belle protection. That was never a question. The question was what it would cost me—and her. And that protection was absolute until my partners deemed either of us a threat. Whether or not I chose to sign the papers decided the man I'd become. For a fleeting moment, I considered if my father had faced a similar dilemma.

The door to my office creaked open, and Belle poked her head through the gap.

"Am I disturbing important lawyering?" she asked, but her cheerful smile didn't reach her eyes.

I pushed back my chair and patted my knee. "You are always welcome to disturb me, beautiful."

She hurried over to me and settled onto my lap. She was as stunning as when I'd dropped her off this morning, polished and radiant, except for the red rims around her eyes. Tipping her chin so she faced me, I studied her anxiously. "What happened?"

"Nothing. I'm tired." It was a lie, but a well-meaning one. It wasn't the dishonesty of someone ashamed of wrongdoing. I'd spent enough time around guilty people and criminals to know. This was the lie of someone guarding herself. She had been hurt. I stiffened in my seat, attempting to remain calm. It would wound her more to force the issue, even though doing nothing to the offender left me feeling murderous. Then it occurred to me that I might be the assailant. Perhaps I'd pushed her too far yesterday evening.

"Maybe we should take it easy tonight," I suggested. "Grab takeaway and watch a movie on the sofa."

"You have a sofa and a television?" she said in mock surprise.

Her mood was shifting, and I pulled her into me, determined to lighten it entirely. "I'll admit I don't often use them."

"Too busy bedding women?" she guessed, nuzzling under my chin.

"Do I detect some jealousy?" I had, and I liked it. "Usually I'm stuck at work at night. Lately, I've had a reason to go home though."

"A quiet night sounds nice," she finally said, "as long as it ends with a good shag." She shifted, straddling her legs over my lap and bunching her skirt in the process.

My fingers dug into her hips, holding her there. "That I can promise you, beautiful."

"I took my knickers off before I came in, so I'd be bare and ready for you," she whispered, grinding her pussy against my trousers. The raw eroticism was at odds with the sweet flutter of her lashes. She was chaos, charming one moment and wanton the next. Knowing her was the most exquisite turmoil I'd ever experienced.

A knock at the door startled us apart. Belle shot me a questioning look. I couldn't blame her. It was a Saturday afternoon. We should be the only ones here. There were only four people who had keys to the front door. I didn't have to guess who was visiting.

"Hammond," I informed her. "We had some business to discuss."

Another lie so close to the truth that the edges of it blurred. He would be here to talk business, but I wasn't expecting him. His presence indicated news had moved more swiftly through the grapevine than I had predicted. I'd hoped to confront this next week. Now Belle would be here to witness the fallout.

"Come in," I called out, bracing myself for the fast approaching storm.

"I should go," she murmured, and I did my best not to look relieved. There were things she would learn about me in time, but it was too soon to unveil the ugly underbelly of my life. Not while she could still run.

Belle smoothed down her dress swiftly, regaining her composure before Hammond strode through the door.

"The lovely Miss Stuart." Hammond spread his hands in greeting. "Can I pour you a drink? Smith keeps the good stuff socked away for me."

Picking up her purse, she fluttered her lashes sweetly at him. "I was just on my way out. Next time."

Next time. My hands balled into fists at the thought. Every time she was in the room with him, I swore there would never be a next time.

"I'll see you at your place?" Belle spoke to me, but her eyes were glued on Hammond as though he was a snake that might strike at any moment.

I'd always liked smart women.

"It may be a few hours." I glanced to Hammond, who confirmed this with a wink. I wanted to kiss her but not in front of him. It would only be ammunition, and frankly, I didn't want to share her even for a moment with him. God knows even the most innocent action could be perverted to suit Hammond's twisted desires. Belle disappeared out the office door with a faint farewell, but despite her graceful exit, I sensed her need to flee.

Hammond lit a cigar as the office door clicked closed.

Thick puffs of spicy smoke wafted through the room, and my mind flashed to my father sitting in this office. Both the memory and my current visitor were unwelcome.

"I'm told you're pulling out of Velvet." He didn't waste time. No, time was money to a man like him, and he'd never let you borrow one red second of it.

I dropped onto the sofa and slung an arm over its low back, releasing a heavy sigh but none of the exhaustion that had brought it on. "Where did you hear that?"

"Does it matter?" He took the chair opposite of me and assumed the same position. He'd always loved the imitation game. Although he seemed to have forgotten that he'd taught it to me. Mimic your opponent. If they act casual, be casual. If they lie, lie as well. When they ask questions, ask another.

"I suppose not. It's not a secret." I crossed my leg and watched as he did the same.

"Then why not come to me?" What he was really asking was whether or not everything was on the up and up.

"Honestly, I didn't think you'd care. It was my father's hobby, not mine." Hobby was a kind word for it. Obsession would have been more appropriate. Aberration still more correct.

Hammond stroked his jaw, his eyes and thoughts distant. Mentioning my father always had that effect on him. The memory of the man was enough to send us both spiraling back through time. "You can't cut your father's legacy from your life, Smith."

"I can try," I said through clenched teeth.

"You might as well slit your own throat then and drain his blood from your veins. It would be just as practical." Hammond's words took on the stern, fatherly tone that I loathed. I'd found it soothing once. That had been my first mistake.

"I'm a silent partner. Georgia can handle Velvet without me. I haven't even stepped foot—"

"That's not what matters. Velvet is an important thread linking you to this family."

He called them threads, but they were chains. We each wore them, some more willingly than others. Hammond's extended family was linked through his many entrepreneurial endeavors. By the time one realized the true nature of the business, they were bound too tight to escape. Velvet was a chain I needed to break.

"I have more than enough threads connecting me. Need I remind you that my name is on every contract you sign." This wasn't a hand I wanted to play. Not with Hammond who rarely saw past sentiment and instinct. Facts never interested him. It was an important thing to keep in mind.

"And you have the protection of your profession. One that I gave you."

"That's funny," I said lightly. "I seem to recall the Law Society granting me that profession after a few years of school."

"This isn't a lark." Hammond jumped to his feet and I rose, reversing his imitation game back on him. "You will maintain your ownership share in Velvet, and if I continue to hear more disquieting rumors—"

"And who are you hearing these rumors from? I know you've never had a taste for legality, but I'm partial to having access to all the evidence." There was a rat amongst my inner circle. The news didn't shake me. I paid my people well enough, but I never expected their loyalty. I learned a long time ago that loyalty was a whimsical notion that had disappeared along with chivalry. Occasionally I got glimpses of both but never long enough to believe they existed. But I couldn't allow the betrayal to go unrecognized. It would only feed Hammond's paranoid nature.

"You think I don't own your people? Doris. Garrison. Mrs. Andrews. Everyone can be bought for a price. They just can't be bought by a Price. Your father made the mistake of learning that lesson the expensive way." Hammond blew smoke in my direction and glanced toward the door Belle had exited through. "Someday, I'll own her, too. Sooner or later, everyone needs something from me. And the delicious part is that you won't even know when I buy her off. She'll come home and suck your dick and play house just like—"

His rant was prematurely cut off by the hands around his throat.

My hands.

"All I have to do is squeeze," I warned him.

"Then you're both dead, but it won't be quick and clean this time," he wheezed, his cheeks reddening. His cigar dropped to the floor. "My heirs will see to that. You'll be there to see it, too. All that bright red blood on her pretty pale skin. She'll be alive. She'll be begging you. And there won't be a goddamn thing you can do."

"How do I know you won't order it as soon as you leave?" I demanded, wringing his wiry neck harder. Shoving my shoulder into his chest, I pinned him against the wall.

"You don't," he admitted with a gasp. "Guess you'll be a gambler after all."

I pictured it: his eyes bulging out of his head, his doughy flesh shifting from red to purple. And I could almost imagine the feeling of freedom that would accompany his final moment—a relief I'd never known.

But that freedom would be short-lived.

My hands dropped to my sides. Hammond inched away, rubbing his neck.

"I'm glad you came to your senses, boy."

"I'm not your boy," I snarled.

"Your father would be disappointed in how little respect you show your elders." Hammond crushed the smoldering tip of his cigar with the toe of his oxford, leaving a black hole in the Oriental rug.

"I think he'd be more disappointed that he was dead before he could destroy every last person he claimed to love." I turned my back on Hammond. I couldn't afford to let him see any more. Not while I was so raw. Now while I was so out of control. I would slip again and there would be consequences.

"Your mother lived a perfectly lovely life after his

death." Hammond fastened the button of his blazer, shaking his head in disgust.

She'd been a shell of a person since that day, and we both knew why.

"Yeah, thankfully, someone took care of her." I pulled the stopper on the Macallan I kept for clients and poured myself a drink.

"Drinking this early?"

I wanted to tell him to shove his fatherly tone up his ass. He hadn't earned it. No one in my life earned the right to call themselves a father. I gulped it down and poured another. "I'm in business for myself. I'm calling it an early day"

"That's where you're wrong, son." Hammond placed a heavy hand on my shoulder. "You're in business for me."

I bit back a laugh. If only he knew the truth, but then again, he'd refuse to believe it.

Hammond paused in the doorway, his hand on the knob. "I'm going to forget this ever happened. For your father's sake. But don't ever pull that shit again."

I gave him a terse nod then swallowed my second Scotch. As soon as he was gone, I grabbed the bottle.

I'd had a plan. One that required patience. But more importantly: no attachments. Now all that had gone to hell. Because of her.

There were two ways to keep her out of Hammond's sights: never let her out of mine or make her a nonissue. One was more foolproof than the other. It was also the one I wasn't certain I could live with.

I'd have to drink until I could. What did they say about the road to hell? Who fucking cared. I was already on it.

My FATHER WAS BURIED in a graveyard next to eighteenth century poets. Hammond had pulled one final string, obtaining the plot for him—a nod to my father's love of books. On the few occasions that I'd ventured here, I'd wandered through the ivy-clad tombstones wondering if it assuaged his guilt. Tonight I knew it couldn't.

A statue of justice with her blindfolded eyes and scales stood guard over his grave. Considering his love of literature, my father would certainly appreciate the irony. I stared at her unseeing eyes. She had been a popular image in university law classes. Most of my classmates had believed she actually existed. I might have once, too, but I didn't remember being that naive.

Humphrey Price. Beloved Father and Husband. Protector of God's Justice.

I laughed, filling the quiet cemetery with the hollow sound. It echoed across the stones. Drawing the nearly empty bottle of Scotch from my coat pocket, I dropped to the grass in front of his marker. I raised it to him.

"I suppose we finally have something to talk about. Where should we start?" I paused as if he might respond. "No ideas? Well, there's woman troubles. You had your share of those. Although based on your marriage, you might not be qualified to offer me guidance there. We could discuss the law. Judging from the rather ostentatious display erected in your honor, you might have more insight into that topic, especially given the clientele we share."

I took a swig out of the bottle. "Oh, hell."

I chugged the rest and tossed the empty bottle on his plot.

"You would have loved that, but then again you loved anything with a higher proof content than your legal cases, right? I have to ask you. Did Hammond spin you gold in exchange for my soul? Is that how the story goes?" Hatred churned through my blood, slowly raising it toward the boiling point.

"I guess I'll be seeing you soon. For now, allow me to leave you with a token of appreciation for everything you did for me in life." Pushing myself to my feet, I stared down. He was down there, rotting, his flesh food for worms. He didn't belong here next to men of talent and character. His place was in hell. I could only hope he burned there now. Unzipping my fly, I whipped out my dick and pissed on his name. It was the closest thing to solace that I would ever offer him.

CHAPTER TWENTY-THREE

I'd meant to go straight to Smith's house, but Hammond's appearance sent me in another direction. Before I'd fully comprehended what I was doing, I'd found myself in Chelsea. The address that had been sent to my mobile wasn't visible from the street. If it had been anywhere else, I might have reconsidered exploring, but this was Chelsea. Still when I found the purple door tucked carefully off a quiet side street, I paused.

I had no idea who had sent me the text message. Or why. Not that I had enemies to speak of. I sincerely doubted Pepper Lockwood would go to this much trouble to return a broken nose. No, I hadn't come this far to turn back now. I tried the handle but it was locked. Searching for a knocker or doorbell, I came up short. I was about to give up when the door buzzed and clicked open. No one met me at the entrance. The hallway was dimly lit, but the walls had a lustrous sheen that drew my hands to them.

Velvet.

In the distance, a faint rhythm pounded. It was a bit early for a nightclub to get going, even for a Saturday, but instinct told me this was no ordinary club. I pushed myself forward, trailing my fingers along the plush wall coverings. The simple wrap dress I'd thrown on in my rush to get ready this morning wasn't really dance floor material. Hopefully, the early bar crowd wouldn't notice. When I rounded the corner, I knew that they would.

I clamped my mouth shut, sucking back the gasp that tried to get out, but I couldn't keep my cheeks from heating.

The fuchsia-haired bartender scanned me up and down from across the room while I tried not to look directly at her rubber waist cincher or the pierced nipples it boosted into display. I flashed her a smile, wondering whether I should turn tail and run or play it cool. Clearly the text had been sent to the wrong mobile number. I gripped my purse tightly, preparing to make as dignified an exit as possible when a couple in the corner caught my eye. The woman was wearing a collar tethered to a leash. Memories of last night poured into my head. I had been that girl yesterday. I hoped to be her again tonight.

Maybe I wasn't as out of place as I'd feared.

Gathering my courage and ignoring my nerves, I walked up to the bar. "Gin and tonic."

The bartender's eyes narrowed, but she grabbed a bottle of Nolet's and poured the drink. Apparently this place catered to the kinky and the wealthy. I took a sip of my cocktail, my eyes glued to the couple on the couch. The woman knelt at his feet while he spoke to another man seated across from them. Both men were fully clothed, but the only thing she wore was the collar. Would I do that if it were Smith holding my leash? The question aroused me, and I considered shooting him the address in a text, but then I would have to explain how I had wound up here. And I didn't have a good answer.

As I watched, the other man stood and approached the couple. The woman's head fell forward to hide her tears, and her lover brushed a hand over her cheek. I touched my own, knowing exactly what that caress felt like. Then he handed the other man her leash. Her head stayed down as she crawled away with him. The two headed down a corridor, and my stomach turned over.

He had given her to someone else, and she had gone willingly, despite her sadness.

Throwing down my credit card, I called for my tab.

"It's on the house," the bartender said, pushing it back to me.

"I'll pay." I practically spat the words. I didn't want to owe this place anything. Not when it was clear what was expected of women like me.

Like me.

Oh God, what had I gotten myself into?

But Smith would never.

She shrugged and started pouring another drink. "That's expensive shit. I'd rather you paid, too, particularly if you're going to waste it. But it's not up to me."

"Who is it up to?" I pressed, looking around me. I'd been sent here, admitted in, and now someone was paying for my drink. It was clear this was no longer a coincidence.

"It's up to me," a woman's voice informed me.

I spun on my stool, shocked, even after recognizing her voice.

Georgia Kincaid stood there, lips pressed tightly together. She closed her eyes for a moment before motioning that I should follow her.

"You aren't supposed to be here," she hissed as we headed down the dark corridor the man had taken the woman down.

"Whatever." I halted in my tracks, refusing to follow her any farther. "You're telling me that you didn't send me this text?" I waved my mobile at her.

"That's exactly what I'm telling you," she said in a cold voice. Her bony fingers closed over my upper arm, and she yanked me through a blue door. "What are you doing here?"

"I already told you. I got a text." I was beginning to lose my patience with Georgia. I hadn't had much to begin with. "What is this place?"

"Even you aren't that dense." Georgia shut the door and pressed herself against it. It was easier to see her in the better lighting, and my jaw dropped. She was wearing a black lace bustier and not much else. Leather straps corseted her trim waist and matched the cuffs she wore on her wrists.

I didn't know if she was going to kill me or flog me.

"A sex club. Lovely. I knew I was overdressed." I spun around in the room, hoping to see a sign marked 'this way out.'

"Don't get all prudish on me now. You can't be too uptight if you're fucking Smith." Georgia sauntered past me and dropped onto a red velvet divan.

I ignored her and focused on what I really needed to be concerned about. "Why would someone send me here?"

"Maybe they want to spank your bony ass," Georgia said dryly. Her arm curled under her head as she leaned back, exposing the tops of her nipples over the frilly strapless top of her corset.

"I'm going to need you to try to not be a twat for one minute," I snapped. Few things made me uncomfortable in my skin, now I was in a place that made it crawl, with a person I despised. I wanted answers and then I wanted out. Immediately.

"And I need to think." She glowered at me as she stood up and started pacing the room. "Let me see your mobile."

"No way in hell." I wasn't about to give her access to the private line Smith had given me.

"Chill, princess. Show me the text." She moved beside me, looking over my shoulder at the screen. Her breast brushed my upper arm and I jumped away. "Please calm down. I'm not trying to have my way with you."

"I'm sorry. This place is a bit overwhelming." An apology was in order, even if I loathed her. I had no reason to suspect she wasn't trying to help me, and it was pretty obvious that she hadn't been the one to send me here.

"Velvet," she said, tapping the mobile to pull up the message's detailed report.

"What?" I asked in confusion.

"This place is called Velvet," she said matter-of-factly, then switched focus to the task at hand. "There's nothing here to say who sent this to you. Do you always blindly go to places at the request of anonymous callers?"

I could tell exactly what she thought about that. "This is a private line. Only one person has the number."

"Smith?" she guessed, and I nodded. "But that message wasn't from him."

"How was I supposed to know?" I'd meant to ask him at the office until we were interrupted by Hammond's appearance. Then I'd forgotten.

"Because Smith would never send you here." Georgia paused to let this sink in. She planted her hands on her hips. "You'll have to tell him you came."

"Why would he never send me here?" I asked in a small voice, completely bypassing her advice. Up until this moment, I'd been ready to leave here and never speak of it again. Now I was being told that I couldn't.

"That's for him to tell you," she said, tacking on, "when he's ready. But tell him yourself that you came."

"And if I don't?"

"He's going to find out," she warned me. "It's up to you whom he hears it from. I suggest it comes from your lips. Since you're fucking him, I'm certain he's shown you a taste of his preferences. You're not ready for real punishment yet."

I tilted my chin up and stared her in the eye. "How do you know?"

"Because you were sitting down," she said in measured syllables.

My knees buckled, and I fought to stay on my feet. I had to look away from her. My gaze zeroed in on an innocuous abstract painting on the wall behind her. I focused on the strokes of black and white until I regained control over myself. "I'll tell him," I said finally. "But answer one question for me."

Georgia crossed her arms over her chest. "I can't promise you I will."

"Has he been here?" I barely got the question past my dry tongue.

"Yes." She held up her hand as my mouth opened again. "That's all I'll tell you, and I only told you because you already knew. It's up to Smith what else he chooses to share with you. But remember this, you don't know what secrets he keeps behind closed doors. Now I'm escorting you out of here."

I didn't put up a fight as she led me back to the side door. Georgia stepped onto the street beside me, despite her daring ensemble.

"Get rid of that phone," she said quickly. "Tell Smith, and in the future, don't be so fucking stupid."

"I went to a club," I retorted, feeling braver outside Velvet's walls.

A grim smile twisted across her lips. "No, you didn't. You walked into the lions' den."

CHAPTER TWENTY-FOUR

The gates to Clarence House were always open for me. Except for when they weren't. As dismal rain drizzled from the autumn sky, I explained for the tenth time who I was to the guard, who was obviously new.

"It will be on your computer," I explained.

"Miss, you might be correct, but the royal family has been quite clear that they don't wish to be disturbed." He backed up a step as he informed me of this.

My eyes narrowed. He should be afraid of me. I had half a mind to climb the gate. By the time he figured out the phone system to call reinforcements, I would be long gone. Of course after the day I'd had, I would probably be arrested. Edward would love getting the call to bail me out.

Edward.

"I assume Edward is allowed in?" I asked him.

His eyebrows knit in confusion under his beret. "Prince Edward?"

"No, that vampire from the movies," I snapped. "Of course, Prince Edward."

"Well, yes-s-s," he stammered. A bead of sweat appeared on his forehead, but I knew he couldn't wipe it off in front of me.

"Can you call him?" I asked sweetly, attempting to ratchet down my bitchiness.

"I could, but—"

"Either call him or find Norris, but do not make me call Clara's mobile and wake up the baby!" Apparently remaining calm was a futile endeavor.

"Yes, Miss. I mean, Ma'am. I mean, Sir."

I shook my head. "You're heading in the wrong direction there, soldier."

"I'm not a soldier, I'm a—"

I held up a hand, incapable of listening to his correction. "Just call him."

I watched through the guard stand's window as he fumbled with the phone and eventually got someone on the line. A minute later, he came back and handed me my I.D. "I'm sorry for the confusion, Miss Stuart. We've tightened security."

"And you just started?" I guessed.

The confused look I'd come to expect crossed his face. There was no point trying to help him through it. The kid was a lost cause. I waltzed up to the front entrance, marveling at the grandeur of Alexander and Clara's temporary home. Soon they would be forced to make a move to one even larger, but for reasons known only to them and a few others, they'd stubbornly chosen to remain here for the time being.

The guard at the door opened it for me and I stepped inside. Despite its spacious interior and the priceless antiques and art that filled each room, it had a cozy, casual feel. At least relative to most palaces. That was why they had wanted to bring their baby home to this place. Here they could focus on building their family instead of ruling a monarchy.

Alexander met me at the top of the stairs. "Edward texted me. I'm sorry for the trouble."

"I figured you might not want mobiles going off with a newborn." I brushed beads of rain from my hair.

"That was thoughtful." He sounded grateful for my caution. I supposed half of the world wanted to get a glimpse of Elizabeth or a statement from the new parents.

The thoughtful Belle had disappeared when she crossed the threshold. "Of course. Now I need to see my best friend, and I don't care if she's resting. I really am sorry, but this is an emergency."

"And if I refuse?" he teased.

"I'll remind you that not only did I know her first, but I convinced her to sleep with you."

"You learn something new every day," he said with amusement. "I suppose I owe you one."

"You owe me several," I informed him as he guided me down the hall. "How is she?"

"Breathtaking." His voice was filled with the same awe

that always accompanied his thoughts on his wife. "She's never looked lovelier."

When I walked into the nursery, Clara glanced up and gave me a small smile. Elizabeth was in her arms, sleeping peacefully. Clara's dark hair cascaded over her shoulder, and her skin glowed against the creamy backdrop of the nursery walls. The whole image reminded me of a portrait of the Madonna with child.

"I can wait," I whispered, realizing how insignificant my own needs were right now.

"No, you're fine," she said softly. "I should put her down, but I can't help wanting to hold her. Come here. She looks like an angel."

I tiptoed over, not wanting to wake her, and peered over Clara's shoulder. The baby's cheeks were rosy, and as I watched, she let out a tiny sigh and smiled in her sleep.

"She's perfect," I murmured.

"I have to agree with you," Alexander said from the doorway. His powerful form filled the doorframe as he guarded his wife and daughter. He crossed over to us and leaned down to take the sleeping bundle from her arms. "I've got her. You two go talk."

I nodded my appreciation to him. Clara struggled to her feet, and I reached out to help her up.

"This is going to be a long recovery," she said with a sigh as we headed across the corridor to her bedroom. A fire had been lit, and we hunkered down into the two cozy chairs stationed beside it.

Pulling my knees into my chest, I searched for where to begin.

"Male trouble?" Clara guessed, flipping on a lamp next to her.

"Is it that obvious?" Earlier today I'd been so certain my relationship with Smith was heading in a positive direction. Now I wasn't.

"I recognize the face you're making. I believe I made it several times over the last year." She screwed up her face into a cross between a frown and a grimace.

"I hope I don't actually look like that," I said in a flat voice, but I couldn't help but laugh.

"You look much prettier when you pout," she promised me. "I'm still all swollen from last week's blessed event."

"I think motherhood suits you. Alexander told me you'd never looked lovelier, and he was right."

Clara's expression shifted, a smile lighting across her face at the mere mention of her husband.

"Watching you fall in love with Alexander showed me how messy love can be, but also that it's worth fighting for," I told her. It had been messy with me and Smith from the start. After today things were bound to get worse. "What I don't know is why you chose to fight at all?"

She exhaled deeply, and I could tell she was choosing her response carefully. "This isn't going to sound very helpful, but I don't think I ever really had a choice. Being with him was inevitable. I actually tried to fight loving him and I couldn't. That was exhausting. When I decided I wanted to be with him, it wasn't any less difficult. It was simply easier to fight for us than against us."

"I think I understand." I did understand. Since I'd met Smith, I had tried to keep him at a distance. Even after I'd given myself to him, I had pushed him away. And still we kept returning to one another. "Does it feel a bit like addiction?"

"This is serious," Clara said, shifting forward. She winced and grabbed her stomach.

I dropped to the floor in front of her. "Are you okay?"

"Yes." She waved off my concern and leaned back again. "I'm still recovering, remember? Now stop trying to change the subject."

I stuck my tongue out at her and scrambled back into my seat. "Believe me, I want to talk about this. I can't seem to sort it out on my own. It's like my head is a jumble."

"You're falling in love," she said in a gentle voice, "and that is scary for you, especially after Philip."

"I never loved Philip," I admitted to her.

"I suspected that, but that doesn't mean your relationship with him didn't affect your life. You may not have loved him, but you trusted him and you gave your loyalty to him."

"And then he royally screwed me," I finished for her, tacking on a sheepish, "No offense, Your Majesty."

"You are never allowed to call me that," she informed me. Her eyes went distant for a moment as a wry grin spread over her face. "Look how much has changed for us since we left Oxford. I'm married and you're shagging your boss."

"Plus you becoming the Queen of England," I added dryly. Neither of us had seen any of this coming, which is why it made the rocky terrain more treacherous to navigate, especially since we were increasingly doing it alone. Or rather, with someone else at our sides. It felt good to be here with her now. It was as close to normal as either of us were getting. "You know I always have your back, right?"

"I count on it," she said. "Back to this whole falling in love business."

I groaned. So much for our moment. "I don't know if I'm in love with him."

"That's the thing about the fall. You don't really feel it until you hit the ground."

"And up until then?" I asked. Since admitting I hadn't loved Philip, I realized I'd never been in love before. All of this was new to me, and it was a change that wasn't entirely welcome given today's revelations.

"You feel exhilarated—like you're flying. There's moments of panic, of course, but then you let go again."

"And when you hit bottom?" I asked.

"Just hope he's already waiting to catch you." Her words were bittersweet, almost wistful.

"Like Alexander caught you?"

She shook her head, pursing her lips ruefully. "I'm pretty sure I caught him."

"Only you would be strong enough to," I told her. I

moved to the arm of her chair and sank down beside her, hugging her close to me.

"It's worth it," she continued.

"What is?" I murmured.

"The fall. The hard landing. If you know it's the right person."

There was a time when I would have asked her how I knew I was choosing correctly. I didn't need to tonight.

CHAPTER TWENTY-FIVE

*N*ight had fallen, but I hadn't moved. I belonged here among the moss and ghosts—a shadow of a man adrift in the space between life and death.

The soft crunch of footsteps on grass came near, and I startled out of my malaise. Knocking over the empty bottle, I hurried to my feet to face the intruder. At this time of night, it was either a sentimental tourist wanting to commune with the dead artists buried all around me or someone who knew where to look for me. In either case, I wasn't interested in company.

"God, I can smell you from here." Georgia came into view, waving a hand over her nose. She was dressed in leather pants so tight that I imagined she'd had them sewn on and a matching motorcycle jacket. She'd obviously come here from the club. "How much did you drink?"

"Not enough," I said, kicking the bottle at my feet. "I'd offer you some, but Dad and I drank all of it."

"You are drunk if you think your dad is here. News-flash: he's worm food." She dropped to the grass, folding her legs beneath her. Apparently she thought she was invited to my private party.

"You're comforting as always." I sat back down beside her. I could ask her to leave, but expecting a favor out of Georgia was like believing in life after death. Utterly pointless.

"I had no idea you still came here." She gazed past me at the tombstone and let out a long sigh.

"I haven't been here in years."

"Why tonight?" she asked, fixing me with a penetrating stare that would leave lesser men fumbling for words.

She'd never had that effect on me. "The better question is why are you here? Or rather, how did you know I would be?"

No part of me believed Georgia had simply stumbled into the graveyard and happened upon me. She was seeking me out, which was never a good sign, particularly since we'd chosen to limit our contact with one another.

"You're not nearly as mysterious as you think you are. Hammond mentioned he visited you at the office."

"Did he mention I nearly choked him?" I asked her, wishing I hadn't finished the bottle of Scotch so quickly.

"It might have come up," she said wryly. "And since my father reminds you of yours, I played a hunch."

"You're good at that." Too damn good. It was unnerving how easily she got into other people's heads, especially when it was my head. It was what made her good at her job and better at her hobby. Not that there was much difference between the two. Either way, she was screwing somebody.

"I didn't come here to discuss dear old dad."

"I didn't think you had." At least she had found somewhere relatively safe to talk. The only witnesses to our meeting had lost the ability to tell tales long ago.

"Your charming new plaything showed up at Velvet today."

The boozy haze enveloping me evaporated instantly, and I was back on my feet, looking for something to hit besides marble grave markers. "How the fuck did that happen?"

"A third party sent her the address—on your private mobile."

Goddammit, Hammond hadn't been lying when he'd told me he'd gotten to my people. "I'll have to fire my staff."

"Including your assistant?" Georgia pressed.

"I doubt she sent the message to herself," I said coolly as I mentally calculated severance pay.

"You know it's the right move. She needs to be cut loose, Smith." The cattiness she'd exhibited toward Belle was absent from this proclamation. Georgia was being rational and undeniably smart. I couldn't feign security concerns with Hammond if I kept her on.

"It's more complicated than that."

"Don't tell me that you didn't see this coming. Or were you too blinded by your erection to think straight?"

"Fuck you, Georgia," I growled.

"We swore no attachments. Not even with each other. I believe your words were 'we have to be calculating.'" Her tone dared me to challenge this fact, but I couldn't.

"We're not the type to get attached." Which is why I hadn't seen Belle coming.

"She was chosen to fulfill an objective," she continued. "Now that's been blown to hell. There are other avenues for us to pursue."

"We can pursue them without me abandoning her. If anything, her continued presence is a smoke screen. Her connections haven't escaped Hammond's notice. If he suspects—"

"Jesus, do you hear yourself?" she interjected, shaking her head and sending dark locks blowing in the breeze. "She'll be a target. Is that what you want?"

"It's a smart plan," I hedged.

"You'd risk her life? She must be nothing more than one sweet piece of ass. That's cold, even for you."

"I learned from the best." I couldn't look at her. The truth was that I had learned ruthlessness from someone else. Georgia had merely honed my capacity for it.

"Destroy her then." Georgia shrugged and pushed up to her feet. Brushing off the back of her pants, she continued, "It's no skin off my back, but we both know you can't handle more blood on your hands."

"I thought I was cold."

"You are, but you're also not a murderer. It's the one sin you've avoided."

It didn't feel that way though. I'd never stolen someone's final breath or stopped a heart, but I'd been stupid. People had died. Although technically, she was correct, and I hated her more for it. "Unlike some."

"I was born for sin. It's in my DNA," she said with a scoff, unwounded by my barb. "So take my advice. Let her go."

"Why should I?" I demanded. It wasn't like Georgia to get sentimental. Getting in her way simply meant getting knocked down.

"Because you care about her," she said in a soft voice, "and if you're still capable of that, maybe there's still hope."

For the rest of us. She left it unsaid but it was there, hanging in the air between us.

"Don't hope for absolution," I warned her. "God abandoned us long ago."

CHAPTER TWENTY-SIX

I took the lift down to the lowest level, stripping off my dress in the corridor and kicking off my heels. I needed to think, clear my head. Today's revelations had settled over my chest, leaving me gasping for air. I pushed open the door and walked to the edge of the pool. Without thinking, I dove in, instantly freeing myself of my own weight. I stroked across the bottom, only emerging to suck in a breath and disappear once more below the glassy surface.

Smith's past didn't belong to me. I couldn't hold him accountable for the life he'd lived before we met. But I no longer understood how I fit into it. Our relationship had evolved rapidly into a compulsion. The mere fact that I was here now was proof of that, and it forced me to ask what I actually needed from this.

I knew what I wanted. His body. His soul.

Him.

Every part of me craved more. He'd consumed me, but what happened on the other side of this affair? If I walked away now, it would destroy me. How much worse would it be in a week or a month? Or a year? I could only dream of holding onto him that long. I floated to the top, keeping my face under water until my lungs burned from the effort. I was searching for proof that I was alive outside of his existence. My arms drifted to my sides and I let it all slip away. The fear. The anger. Until all that remained was desire. It had to be enough.

I was dimly aware of a surge of water. The sound of a splash. I lifted my head, sputtering and sucking in air as two arms coiled around me, drawing me higher out of the water.

"Belle!" Smith shouted, slapping the side of my face. There was no playfulness. Only a thwap that stung across my cheekbone.

Thrashing in his arms, I broke free and dove away, swimming as fast as I could, but he was on me. This time when he caught me, he hauled me around and crushed me to his chest. I blinked against the burn of the chlorine and gathered my strength to fight him off again. My palm collided with his chest, catching on wet fabric. Startled, I looked down to discover he was fully clothed. My eyes flashed to the edge of the pool where only his shoes rested.

"What the hell are you doing?" I screamed.

"Oh God." He grasped the nape of my neck and forced me to him. My body reacted immediately, ceasing to struggle against his hold on me. I dissolved into his arms, tears mixing with water until I no longer knew if I was crying or drowning.

It was how I always felt around him.

"I saw you in the water," he choked out. "I thought…"

I saw it through his eyes then. My body floating on the surface, weightless and still. The image flashed to my father's feet.

And then I knew. No matter what I did. No matter how far I pushed it. He had brought me to life, breathing essence into my being with his kiss—with his touch.

"You promised me things," I accused, losing what precious little control I had over my emotions in a torrent of sorrow and betrayal. "You promised to protect me, but you never told me why I needed protection."

"I know." He brushed water from my cheeks, hushing me with gentle sounds until I'd calmed. "I heard what happened today—where you went. I'm sorry you had to see that."

"Because it was your dirty little secret or because it's what you have planned for me?" I bit out, smacking his hard chest until my hands ached.

"You don't belong there. I never wanted you to see that place."

It wasn't enough. I wasn't certain whatever could be. "But those are the things you want to do to me. The things you've already done! Which is it? Which piece of your life is the lie: me or the club?"

"Some choices we don't make for ourselves. That place, my life—my profession—was my birthright from the day I was born. I didn't ask for any of it. I didn't want it. I can't expect you to understand. I don't ask you to."

But I did understand. I'd spent my own life torn between the reality of my family's name and what I wanted for myself. I'd never been able to see either without the other. It had directed me, perverting my fate long before I understood the nature of my inheritance. My mother had taught me to value luxury and material goods because that was how she filled the void inside her. It was how I'd filled my own until Smith came into my life.

I couldn't shake the feeling that I was trading one vice for another.

"I do know. I understand, but that doesn't solve anything," I whispered, afraid of what I was really saying.

"No, it doesn't," he agreed. "I'm not certain I'm capable of being normal. I've been fucked up too long to know. But you make me want to search for it, and when I saw you in the pool, that feeling slipped away. I'm not losing it again." He grabbed my face roughly. "I'm not losing you."

"What if you don't have a choice?" The question tore through me.

"When I pulled you out of the water, I knew I had a choice. That we always have a choice. There's no assurance that they're easy ones, but we do have them. All those people that told me I didn't and forced my hand—all those people that did the same to you—they were lying to us, beautiful. We can choose the direction we travel. The only thing left to decide is if we do it together."

I wanted to believe it was that easy, but I knew it

wasn't. "What about choosing to be honest with each other?"

"That's something we can do—in time. There are things I can't tell you about my life. Ugly things. You've seen my darkness. You've let it touch you. But I don't want that for you. I don't want you to spend your life looking over your shoulder," he said in a low voice. "But I also can't bear the idea of turning you away."

"Then don't," I pleaded, burying my face against his neck. "Let me in here."

I placed my hand on his chest, measuring the hard, steady beat of his heart.

"You're already there, beautiful. Isn't that enough?"

It was tempting to believe it could be. "No. You claimed me, Smith. Chose to protect me. I want the same. I need to claim you as much as I need to protect you."

"No one can protect me." The words were hollow, so unlike the confidence that usually oozed off of him.

But despite his rejection of the idea, I saw the truth. He'd opened himself to me. He was vulnerable. Exposed. Could the rest come with time?

"The reality is that you don't need my protection. You're strong. You choose to face the storm when others fly away from it." He kissed the tears from my cheeks and smiled sadly.

"So have you," I informed him, choking on the raw ache in my throat.

"Birds of a feather," he whispered. "Stay with me. I

know you have no reason to wait for answers. I'm asking you to take a chance. Fly into the storm with me."

He urged my legs around him and pressed his forehead to mine, never breaking eye contact.

"I'll shelter you," he promised.

My answer was there, hiding in his tumultuous gaze. He never guarded the secrets there. Not from me. I didn't know their names or crimes. I could only accept that with time I would.

So I corrected him. "We'll shelter each other."

CHAPTER TWENTY-SEVEN

I stood in the hallway, staring at the crack of light under the door. A wail shattered the air around me, freezing me to the spot. I forced my hand to reach for the knob, but no matter how much I stretched, I couldn't reach it. With each scream coming from the other side, my panic rose. I lunged forward and fell.

Fell.

Fell.

I jerked awake, still panting as I sat up in the bed. Smith lay beside me, sprawled on his stomach with the sheet tangled between his legs. I considered shaking him awake, but before I could, my dream returned to me. I'd seen that door before.

You have no idea what he keeps behind closed doors.

Georgia's words at the club.

I didn't think as I slid silently from the bed. Grabbing a blanket from the end of the bed, I wrapped myself in it and padded into the hallway. The lift dinged as it arrived, and I tensed as the insignificant sound echoed in the silent house. Inside I pushed the button for the third floor. I hadn't ever made it back there after Smith had shown me the room he'd set aside for me. Perhaps if I had, my curiosity would have gotten the better of me before now. The doors slid open, revealing a dark hall, but as I stepped into the corridor, a series of automatic lights illuminated. One by one they blinked on. The final light switched on between the two doors at the end of the hallway.

My footsteps fell heavily as I slowly walked forward. I had no idea what I would find. Most of me screamed to turn back and flee to the safety of Smith's bed, but I continued, propelled by an unseen force. It seemed to drive me. I paused when I reached my destination, my eyes flashing between the open door that had been given to me and the one that remained closed directly across from it. When my hand reached toward it, my fingers closed over the knob. It turned effortlessly.

The door had been closed, but not locked.

A slant of moonlight fell in a streak across the room, but it wasn't enough to see by. Sweeping my hand across the wall, I found the switch. Only one bulb flipped on but it was enough.

Everything about the space was eerily similar to the room Smith had shown me. The one I was permitted to be in. But as my eyes adjusted to the light, it came into clearer focus. Heavy dust coated the furniture and cobwebs hung from the ceiling. The bed was unmade, sheets wadded into a ball at the foot and the comforter hanging half off the mattress. A half dozen pillows were scattered across it as though someone had simply gotten up for the day and left it.

Smith had a housekeeper. A woman I'd never met. But I knew from the pristine condition of the rest of his house that she was diligent, which meant this room had been left in this state purposefully. I wandered to the desk where mail waited in a neat stack. Dust billowed around me as I picked up a letter and blew it off to read the address. It wasn't a surprise that it was posted to this house, but my heart skipped when I saw it was addressed to a woman. Margot Pleasant.

If this had been her room, why would she leave it like this?

I searched through the pile of unopened envelopes, hoping for a clue. Nothing was out of the ordinary except their condition.

Turning away, I continued my search, stumbling over a heel on my way. I leaned down and picked it up. It was about my size. Tossing it into the corner to avoid tripping over it again, I stopped at a vanity. Bottles of perfumes and tubes of lipstick littered its top, covered in so much dust that I couldn't read their names or brands. I looked up and froze. My face stared back at me. Not once, but a hundred times. Small slivers of my mouth and eyes and nose reflected in the shattered glass.

I yanked open the drawer of the vanity, discovering more cosmetics and nothing else.

I spun around, zeroing in on my next target. A large cedar chest under the window.

Who was this woman? Nothing in this macabre museum of her life gave me any answers. I would have to keep digging.

Opening the lid carefully, I peered inside the trunk. A thin, reedy cane rested at the bottom next to a pair of handcuffs and rope. The rest of the items were harder to make sense of. There were clamps and tubes attached to chains and hoses. Rummaging through it, my hand closed over a dildo. I dropped it immediately. One woman's treasure…

My throat constricted as I backed away from the chest. Smith hadn't wanted me in here for a reason, one that was becoming increasingly more obvious. The tightness found my stomach. I should leave, but I couldn't stop looking. Not until I was certain.

God, I hoped I was wrong.

The closet door loomed in the far wall, beckoning me toward it. Steeling myself, I headed straight for it and pushed the open door. When I switched on the overhead light, a row of dresses greeted me. Beautiful gowns and simple shifts. Shoes and more shoes. And next to all of it, a selection of suits, tailored to a specific man.

Tears swam into my eyes as I caught a familiar wool sleeve in my hand. They were all black. It was the only difference from the ones he wore now.

This wasn't her room. It was their room.

"She kept her name," Smith said behind me.

Whipping around, I found him standing in the room behind me, holding the letter I'd cleaned off. His hair was tousled, and he wore a fresh layer of stubble, but nothing else. The brutal masculinity of his naked body stirred a familiar ravenousness in my core. I closed my eyes and tried to shake the feeling from my body, but his presence was too powerful. When I reopened them, he'd moved closer to me, making his magnetic pull even harder to resist.

"It was a blow to the ego at first, but after time it made sense," he continued. His voice was distant, caught in the past.

"Margot." Saying her name out loud made her feel more real. I wanted to take it back, wishing I'd never spoken it in the first place. "Did you love her?"

It was the most important question, and the one that should matter least.

"I loved her more than she loved me," he admitted, his eyes returning to me. "We were young and stupid and filthy rich. I'd had the world handed to me without asking for the bill. I never imagined the price would be so high."

I swiped at the liquid threatening to spill down my cheeks, embarrassed to be jealous even though it seemed certain I had a right to be.

"Where is she?" I asked although I dreaded his answer.

"Dead." The word was flat. Emotionless. A statement of fact and nothing more.

"I need to go." I shoved past him, but he caught me by the arm.

"You need to understand!"

"Understand what?" I exploded. "That you keep a shrine to your dead wife? Who, by the way, you've never mentioned. Or maybe understand that she's dead? Tell me what you want me to understand."

It was clear he didn't have an answer to that.

"What do you expect me to do? Hold you? Drop to my knees and suck you off so that you'll feel better?" I yanked away from him and sat down on the edge of the bed. "Maybe you could fuck me and pretend I'm her."

Rage blazed in his eyes as he hauled me off the bed, throwing me over his shoulder. "I don't want you to be her."

"Put me down!" I demanded.

"No. Not until you calm down."

"My apologies," I hissed. "Please put me down, Sir."

"Don't do that," he warned me as he carried me kicking and screaming toward the lift. "Do not sully our relationship."

"Oh, it's fucking sullied." I whacked his shoulder blade with my palm, only managing to hurt my own hand.

We got off on the second floor. I'd stopped trying to fight him. Now my plan was to run the moment he released me. He couldn't keep a hold on me forever.

"I'm going to set you down," he explained when we entered his bedroom. "And you're going to want to run. Swear you won't."

"Or what?" I dared him.

"I'll tie you up and fuck you until you don't have enough strength to leave."

"You wouldn't." But deep down, I knew he would, and even worse, I knew I would enjoy it.

I wasn't about to give him that satisfaction.

"Fine. I swear."

As he lowered me to the floor, he whispered. "Remember that I'm not only stronger, I'm faster, beautiful."

"Don't call me that." I crossed my arms over my chest. He could try to talk his way out of this all he wanted, but there was no backpedaling. He'd crossed a line.

"The day she died," he began, "I shut that door. Then I went to the cabinet and got my father's gun."

Despite my attempt to remain remote, my mouth fell open. An overwhelming longing to take his hand flooded through me, but I held my ground, even if I was listening.

"Things were a mess between us. I suspected she was seeing someone else. She was as hotheaded as I am. It made for interesting fights."

Another grotesque similarity between the two of us. I gulped, attempting to swallow this revelation.

"It was rainy. A car hit her. She and the other driver died on impact."

"I've heard this story before," I said softly, "but it had a different ending."

"An accident. Nothing more. At least, that was how I saw it. I blamed myself. She had gone away to cool down after a fight."

"An accident is hardly your fault." I couldn't believe I was comforting him.

"No one ever bothered to tell me that. By then, my father was gone. My mother had checked out on me a few years later. I had this house and an important job, catering to my late father's clientele. I wanted one person in my life to be real, I closed the door and accepted the lies." He paused and looked me directly in the eye until I turned my face away. "Do you know why I don't go into the pool? My father drowned there."

"An accident." The word slipped off my tongue, but this time it left a bitter taste in my mouth.

"Hammond told me I was born under an unlucky star." His jaw twitched, and before I could stop myself, I ran my hand along it. Smith caught it and held it to his face.

"Am I just a replacement?" I whispered the question.

Smith's eyes closed. "No. You're the original."

"I saw the toys. I've been inside Velvet." I shook my head. "I'm not sure I belong in your world."

"You're wrong, beautiful. That isn't my world."

"But why do you..." I trailed away, unable to ask the question.

"I was introduced to kink at a young age. Hammond makes certain of that. He started screwing Georgia when she was fourteen. Most of his business centers around sex, and she is the shining jewel of his empire. He molded her to a very exacting standard. You see, everyone has to have vice. I had too many. The only one that stuck was dominance. I'd love to blame him for that, but it's on me. I'm built that way."

"Me, too," I admitted, my voice trembling. "You tamed me."

"No, beautiful. I just was lucky enough to see you wanted a leash."

I forced myself to ignore the hunger gnawing at my core. Giving in to it wouldn't solve anything. "Why hide it from me?"

"If no one can see your scars, why show them?"

The answer splintered across my heart. It was easier to pretend—to project the semblance of a normal life. "I've gone through the motions since I was child. Always following the path chosen for me. I don't want to do that anymore."

"Birds of a feather," he repeated his earlier sentiment. "Neither do I."

"Then why continue representing him? He's a pedophile."

"I can't explain that to you."

Two steps forward. One step back. "Like hell you can't!"

"You have to trust me." He laced his fingers through mine and brought my hand to his lips. "I never intended for this to happen between us, and now I have to think for both of us."

My eyes narrowed into slits. "I can think for myself."

"I want you to think about yourself," he corrected me gently. "On Monday, I'm firing everyone that works for me, including you."

"And I thought we were getting somewhere." I tried to pull away from him, but he tightened his grip.

"You're going to work on Bless. I've already funded your business account."

"No!" I shrieked. "I didn't ask you to do that."

"It's not a hand-out. I've drawn up paperwork fully vesting an anonymous party in the company. Me. I recently sold my interest in Velvet, and I need to invest that money somewhere."

"It sounds like a hand-out," I grumbled.

"I need you to stay busy, especially since we'll be spending less time together." The note of apology in his voice did nothing to soothe the misery that accompanied this revelation.

"Because you'll be focused on hiring another staff," I said flatly.

"Amongst other things. I don't want you to know any more than that."

"Why?"

"It wasn't a coincidence that I hired you. You were handpicked for the position for me. I didn't know why until later," he admitted, "by then it was too late."

I stared at him, completely flabbergasted. "To fire me?"

"To let you go." He dragged me roughly into his arms. "You should have walked out of that office that day. I should have thrown you out. Now it's too late for both of us."

As his words sank in, I knew he was right. I'd come

back to him again and again, ignoring the warning signs, and I would continue to.

"Will I see you?" I murmured into his chest.

"Yes." I heard the smile in his voice. "You can't keep me away. We just have to be careful."

"Until when?"

He pressed his lips into my hair and remained motionless for a long time before answering. "I wish I knew."

I didn't say anything. I'd gone numb, unable to process all the information.

"However," he said, his words strained, "if you choose to leave tonight. Or in the morning. I will understand. I won't promise not to come after you, but I'll try to respect your wishes. Regardless, the business account will be waiting for you."

"I don't want your money. I want you."

"You have me, beautiful." His head angled down and he kissed me. "All of me, even my bank account. Deal with it."

"I can be defiant," I reminded him, smiling grudgingly despite the ache building inside me.

"Channel that into Bless, and no one will be able to stop you."

"And until Monday?"

By picking me up, he answered my question, and he carried me back to bed. Dropping me onto it, he eyed me as a knowing smirk twisted across his lips. "Until then I'm going to make you come until you can't remember your own name—or any of this. Just you and me."

I crawled forward and beckoned him closer with my

finger. When he was within reach, I ran my tongue over the ridges of his abs. "I bet I can make you forget your name first."

"As long as you don't forget it, beautiful." He grabbed my shoulders and threw me back on the mattress. Pouncing on top of me, he pinned me to the spot and lowered his mouth to my belly.

I wouldn't. That was my choice—to stand in the wind and withstand the rain even as the first ominous clouds appeared on our horizon. Smith's hand shot out and grabbed mine as he moved between my thighs. We would face the coming storm together.

ACKNOWLEDGMENTS

Thank you to super agent Mollie Glick for supporting what I want to write, and to Joy Fowlkes who keeps things running smoothly. My foreign agent, Jessica Regal, is a goddess. I can't wait to see all my dirty words in other languages.

Lindsey, you keep my life functioning, and you were doing that long before you became my assistant. Let's continue to conquer the world together.

A huge thanks to Sharon, who is the best publicist I've ever had! You're a genius and not just because we think alike! And all my love and thanks to the Sassy Savvy Fabulous team—Linda, Jesey, and Melissa. You rock my publicity and marketing world!

Thank you to Bethany and Josh for impeccable editorial services. Somehow you always know what I mean to say, even when I don't. And thanks to Cait Greer for putting up with all my formatting needs.

I get by with a little help from my friends and significant amounts of booze. Thanks for the sage advice and deep, boring business chats, Laurelin. Sierra, your comments always make me laugh.

Lauren Blakely, it's hard to believe you weren't a cheerleader in high school, because you're so good at it! Thank you for being a bright spot.

To the FYW girls, you continue to amaze me! I'm humbled to count myself among you.

Thank you to my Royal Court! Your pics and posts (but especially your pics) make my day. I love how many of you I've gotten to meet this year, and I can't wait to meet the rest of you!

I owe a special debt of gratitude to many bloggers. No one would read my books without the amazing ladies out there pimping them. Milasy, I think you're starting to get your answers. Trish, you'll always be schmexy to me! All of my gratitude to: Cocktails and Books, the Book Bellas, Short and Sassy, A Literary Gossip, The Laundry Room. I know I'm forgetting some of you. Remind me to buy you a drink the next I see you.

Stay dirty, my friends!

A significant amount of this book was written at The Historic Elms Resort, which provided the perfect place to zero in and focus. Many thanks to the friendly staff for their hospitality, enthusiasm, and club sandwiches.

I wouldn't be doing this if not for the support of my family. Thanks, kids, for cheering on my books even if I won't let you read them yet, and to my husband, who lets me spend time with the men in my head without getting (too) jealous. Love you.

ABOUT THE AUTHOR

Geneva Lee is the *New York Times, USA Today*, and internationally bestselling author of over a dozen novels. Her bestselling Royals Saga has sold over one million copies worldwide. She is the co-owner of Away With Words, a destination bookstore in Poulsbo, Washington. When she isn't traveling, she can usually be found writing, reading, or buying another pair of shoes.

Learn more about Geneva Lee at:
www.GenevaLee.com

CPSIA information can be obtained
at www.ICGtesting.com
Printed in the USA
BVHW031035280220
573637BV00001B/254

9 781635 765335